Not Your Father's Eldadorian Empire

Book Two of the Fovean Chronicles Intermission

by Robert W. Brady, Jr.

Those who believe it better to rule in Hell than to serve in Heaven are vastly undereducated about the seriousness of Hell!

The Fovean Chronicles Intermission
Book One: Not Your Father's Eldadorian Empire
© 2011 by Robert W. Brady, Jr.

ISBN: 978-0-9793679-5-3

This book is a work of fiction. Names, characters, places and incidents are products of the author's imagination or are used factiously. Any resemblance to actual events, locales or persons, living or dead, is entirely coincidental.

Cover art: by Adrijus Guscia

Back Cover: None

10   9   8   7   6   5   4   3   2   1

Dedication:

This book is dedicated to my good friend, Anthony Edwards.

You gave a lot of your time into giving a group of teen-agers a lot of good memories. In large part, this series is a thank-you that you deserved much earlier.

Map of Known Fovea

Prologue:

Glennen lay on his bed, sodden and freezing in a grand room with gigantic bay windows paned with real glass. The floor was hard wood and polished to a shine except where the steel-shod boots of the King's visitors had marred it. He lay in a four-posted bed with a canopy, piled high with quilts. The Heir, Duke Rancor Mordetur of Thera, sat at the table by the door. The King's Shem Hannen, his advisors, sat in the couches by the window. A gigantic mirror hung across from the bed on the far wall.

Glennen hadn't shaved in several days, but he had been drinking regularly. His son, Tartan, stood by the king's side as two royal healers tended him. He could hear Mordetur talking to the Shem Hannen.

"How long has this been going on?" the Heir asked.

"Since All Gods' Day," one of the Shem Hannen, Datreve, said. He was first among them. All three had a similar look to them – four males, three with long, white hair, all wearing long, white robes, balding crowns and wrinkled skin, all of the race of Men.

"He began drinking early, he drank all day and into the night. Then he started to break things until he passed out. Two days later he started again."

"This is what he does now," another, Devarre, said. "He drinks, he attacks, he tells us things that are on his mind."

"Sometimes they are terrible things," the third, Guerrin said.

"He cannot cope with the loss of his Queen," Devarre said. "And of course, we can hardly hold him responsible for his actions."

"Except that we must," the fourth oligarch, Haldarch said. Of the four, only he kept his hair close-cropped, the rest keeping their white hair cut down past the middle of their backs.

That at least was true. Glennen had begun to develop what Tartan knew as 'the yellow sickness,' the addiction to alcohol that killed so many, especially warriors in their later years. He wouldn't stop if he didn't have to, and he didn't have to unless the kingdom revolted or someone assassinated him.

Tartan often wondered which was the Heir's plan.

"There is no way to get Tartan to take over in his place?" Mordetur asked, as if he'd suddenly needed to refute what was in the Prince's mind. Tartan, hearing his name, looked up from his father. "Even just as reagent or something, for the duration of his treatment?"

All four Shem Hannen shook their heads as one. "Eldadorian law in unique, in that the monarch has all power to rule. Glennen always feared that somehow his Dukes would rise up against him."

"Can he proclaim a new law?" Mordetur asked

They nodded. "You are wise, your Grace," Guerrin said. "When he is sober, or just a little drunk, we must get him to proclaim that the Heir can assume power in a crisis of health."

"I will commence the document," Devarre said.

"No, I'm the Heir," the Duke said. "It should be Tartan – "

"Tartan has no standing to rule," Haldarch said. "If he were to suddenly take power, it would look like a coupe."

"And it will look exactly like that if I take over," Mordetur pressed him. "And do you really want *me* to be in control of Eldador right now?"

"Your recent attack on Outpost IX," the Datreve said.

"You fear that it will be a direct affront to the Trenboni," Devarre added, his wise eyes twinkling.

"I fear that they could use it as justification to retaliate against anything Eldadorian that they want, and call it my just desserts," Mordetur said.

The healer placed a thin, blue-veined hand on Tartan's shoulder, and whispered in his ear that his father would rest now, that the worst was behind him. Tartan had to wonder if that could possibly be true of anyone with the yellow sickness, even as he led the healer to the table where the Heir consulted with the Shem Hannen.

"He will live," the healer said. "You were wise to bind his head – his neck was snapped. We have repaired it."

"I owe you another debt, your Grace," Tartan said.

"I am at your service," Mordetur said, inclining his head to Tartan, "and to your family's service, your Highness."

"Actually, you are 'Highness,' your Grace," Tartan said. He hated this man. Rancor Mordetur's greed and avarice, his need to crush all enemies, real or imagined, had cost Tartan's mother her life. "If I am correct on the rules of etiquette, then Highness falls below Majesty, and you are the Heir."

"Correct as ever, Prince Tartan," Guerrin said. "You are my brightest pupil."

He nodded.

Mordetur squared off on Tartan, looking him directly in the eye. "We need to get your father well," the Duke said to him. "Do you agree?"

Tartan couldn't return the look. He couldn't make promises to the Man who'd done the things that the Duke had done. He turned to his father instead, then to the Shem Hannen lined up behind him, then finally to the Duke, but focused on his face, not his eyes. "I do."

"And if we can get him to give you the power to rule in his place, until he is well, would you work with us, and be guided by us?" Mordetur asked

Tartan looked into Mordetur's blue, blue eyes for a moment, and then looked away. "Would I do as you say, and would I give power back to my father when he was well?" he asked.

Mordetur nodded.

Tartan thought about it.

In that single moment, Tartan lost everything for his family. Mordetur might be many things, but a fool had never been one of them, and although a risk-taker, not when it came to the power that he'd already decided that he had. Rancor Mordetur, also known as Lupus the Conqueror, took all power in the Eldadorian Kingdom, and brought on the wrath of all other nations. Thousands died trying to prevent a backwater nation from becoming the focal point of all things on Fovea.

They failed and finally, in his avarice, Mordetur took his war to those other nations, at the cost of his family, his allies, and the allegiance of his Dukes.

When that happened, it was Tartan Stowe, as a Duke not a Prince, who ascended the stone steps to the marble throne of Eldador, now an Empire, to rule in regency until the Conqueror's return. It fell to Tartan Stowe to succeed where his father had failed and to hold a nation together.

This is his story.

Chapter One:

Alone on a Throne

Tartan Stowe had lost count of the courtiers who'd tried to tell him that he belonged on the throne in Galnesh Eldador. Now that his behind warmed its cold stone seat, he couldn't imagine that they were happy about the circumstances.

In his father's day, Eldador had been a backwater nation, a collection of free cities paying limited homage to its capitol, Galnesh Eldador – literally Eldador the Port in the Uman language – fighting among themselves and occasionally sending representatives to the Fovean High Council, a collection of emissaries from the nine Fovean nations surrounding Tren Bay.

Lupus the Conqueror, of the race of Men, had appeared sixteen years ago to change all of that. A mercenary general of the Daff Kanaar, the most feared army-for-hire on Fovea, he had befriended the Eldadorian King, becoming an Earl, then a Duke, and then the Heir to the Eldadorian throne.

The Heir – chosen over Tartan Stowe, Glennen's own son. Glennen hadn't believed that a man's birth made him a King. When Glennen's wife fell to assassins, and Glennen right after to depression and strong drink, Lupus had stepped up to the mantle of the second Eldadorian King, his wife Shela at his side, an Andaron and the most accomplished sorceress of her time.

Eldador had become an Empire and Lupus its Emperor, taking on the name Rancor Mordetur. Lupus spent the next fourteen years building Eldador into an economic and a military juggernaut through a system of reduced taxes and frantic expansion. Lupus had united the Fovean cities where Glennen had failed, built its economy on trade and free land for peasants, and its military on his reputation, earned from his time with the Daff Kanaar.

Finally Eldadorian soil wasn't enough for the Emperor's avarice, and he collected his warriors to march on the rest of Fovea. He'd prepared the most massive army in history, over 100,000 strong, for the invasion of his nearest neighbor, Andoron, his wife's homeland.

War raged. Before Lupus could get his first attack wave out of Eldador, sixty thousand Confluni had landed on Eldador's Andurin peninsula and driven deep into Eldador's center. Keeping away from major cities, they'd destroyed crops and ravaged herds until Tartan himself had met them in the Battle of the Vice with the Emperor's son, Vulpe. The two had stopped the Confluni and the Daff Kanaar had driven them into the Forbidden Sea, but the damage had been done, and Eldador left wounded to begin a conquest.

Lupus' answer had been to switch from Andoron to Volkhydro; the Fovean High Council's had been to meet him there with a combined army of fifty-thousand warriors. The two armies clashed in Medya.

However while his warriors died on the field, Angron Aurelias and his Casters abandoned that combined army and struck the Eldadorian capitol itself. The only Mordetur left at the capitol to meet them had been Princess Lee Mordetur, the Emperor's daughter, a fledgling Sorceress, alongside the Duke Hectar, his son Hectaro and Tartan, who'd come as an advisor just days before. Angron Aurelias disabled a magical conduit called 'Central Communications' that the country depended heavily on and used it in an effort to capture Lee. The attack and subsequent loss of Lee left the Eldadorian people demoralized, and the government crippled by the death of one of its most influential Dukes, Hectar, as well as the capture of his only son, Hectaro, trying to defend the Princess.

After the attack the Uman-Chi King and his warriors had escaped the city. In the week since there had been no communication between Galnesh Eldador and the Emperor. The magical residue of Central Communications blanketed Galnesh Eldador and most of the Eldadorian nation in some sort of interference that kept spell casters from communicating to each other, and reduced the government to using fast messengers and carrier birds. With Hectar cold in his grave and his son Hectaro gone with the Princess, Tartan had stepped up to the throne to rule both the Kingdom and the Duchy of Eldador in regency until either the Emperor or another of his family could return. His first act had been to order the replacement of the palace Wolf Soldier guard with his Angadorian Knights, now that the Wolf Soldier guard could be considered compromised with the treason of the Princess' personal guard.

That order had proven easier to give than to enforce, and even now 100 Wolf Soldiers stood watch in their usual stations in the throne room. Sitting that throne, Tartan Stowe had never felt more his mother's son and less his father's. Alekennen, his mother and the first queen of Eldador, had been remarkable for her fragile beauty, and Tartan favored her brown eyes and hair, her high cheekbones and long, fine fingers, her delicate limbs and elegant neck. Glennen, the first King, had been a bull of a man who'd made himself a king from a travelling swordsman and wanderer, had lent Tartan his deep-set eyes and firm jaw, but they didn't serve the Duke as they had the King.

"Supreme Commander, you are summoned here to explain your actions, and the actions of your Wolf Soldier command," the leader of the Shem Hannen informed the Uman J'her, standing before Tartan and the throne. The race of Uman, a species apart from Men, tended to be slight and wild, canny in their intelligence and fair in their skin, remarkable with pointed, lobeless ears and tilted eyes. J'her was more like a Man, his expression stern and his jaw set, muscle standing out on his forearms from swinging a sword for a living.

Tartan knew that the Supreme Commander stood down the Emperor when he had to. He commanded the most feared troops in the world. He might actually be interested in proving himself against the Angadorian Knights.

"Your Grace," J'her began, but Tartan interrupted him.

"You will address me as 'Highness,'" Tartan informed him.

Dressed in the gray and black uniform of a Wolf Soldier and the steel sleeves of an officer in the guard, J'her allowed himself a wolfish smile. "I think not," he said.

Tartan straightened. The three Shem Hannen advisors to his right, white-haired old Men in white robes who had served Eldador since its onset, did so as well. J'her had, until now, simply been ignoring orders – this was outright defiance.

"You address the throne, your Excellence, and you will hold it on high," Tartan tried for the middle road. The Emperor had told him once, "When you can't win one way, go another and call it a win after the fact. Most people will believe you, if you've ever won before."

"I hold the throne high," J'her informed him, "but I am not an Eldadorian Regular, I am a Wolf Soldier, and I serve Lupus the Conqueror directly, not Eldador."

So much for that. Tartan would have thought that J'her would take the compromise, if only to respect form. He'd known J'her for years as a student of the Emperor after his father died. He'd considered this Uman a friend.

Uman lived almost twice as long as Men. They existed closer to nature and thought wilder thoughts. In Eldador, most nobles were Men, because Glennen came from the race of Men, however most Uman didn't aspire to such positions anyway. Those that did, like J'her, were formidable for their sharpened senses and longer years.

"J'her," Tartan said, and now the Supreme Commander straightened, "you have been ordered to stand down the Wolf Soldier guard in the palace, to my Angadorian Knights."

"I heard you, your Grace," J'her said. "However, I don't recognize your orders. I don't serve Eldador. My orders come from Lupus."

"If the Emperor knew that your corps were compromised –" Tartan began.

To his shock, J'her's hand went right to his sword.

"You were *there*," J'her informed him, through gritted teeth, "when Lupus thought that the Pack had been compromised. You know what happened.

"We take care of our own."

"Highness," one of the Shem Hannen intervened, "perhaps it would be wisest to send to Thera, to Duke Two Spears. Surely the Empress' brother –"

"The Empress' brother is occupied with holding one of Eldador's most important cities," Tartan informed the old Man, "and *I* am here now. Supreme Commander, I have given you an order."

J'her barked a laugh.

"Try and enforce it," he growled.

Tartan had let his temper get the better of him, and pushed too soon. On a field of battle, he might consider taking his thousand Angadorian Knights against three times their number in Wolf Soldiers. In the confines of a city or the palace – well, it's hard to get a charger ten times the weight of a man up a flight of stairs.

"You are dismissed, Supreme Commander," Tartan informed J'her with a wave of his hand. J'her turned on his heel with no salute and no salutation, and marched himself down the imperial throne room.

Tartan wondered to himself if it wouldn't be a miracle, if he lived to see the dawn.

***

J'her marched himself back to the Wolf Soldier common barracks, still fuming from his meeting with the presumptive Heir, Duke Tartan Stowe.

The Uman had liked that kid until he'd stepped up to the throne and decided, as the Emperor loved to say, to 'start throwing his weight around.'

J'her had thrown it right back at him. It would be a dark day in history when some upstart protégé of Lupus the Conqueror would order the Wolf Soldier guard to step down. J'her felt tempted to send the head of a few of these so-called 'Angadorian Knights' back to the Duke as an example.

"I know that look," he heard from behind him.

J'her spun around in the narrow corridor with his sword half-drawn, when he recognized M'den Grek. He'd walked right past the Wolf Soldier Major and not realized it. J'her felt a half-smile crawl across his thin Uman lips as he slipped his sword back into the sheath.

"Am I so bad?" he asked.

M'den, another Uman, caught up to J'her in three steps and extended his hand. They took each others' wrists and M'den looked J'her right in the eye.

M'den wasn't as large or as strong as J'her, but everyone knew him to be smarter. Brown hair, brown eyes, pale skin and an earring in the top of one lobeless ear, M'den's features were unusually graceful and soft for a male. Where most feared the weapon on J'her's hip, even more were wary of the weapon in M'den's head, every bit as deadly.

"I think we both know that no one was going to catch D'leer," he said, referring to the Wolf Soldier sergeant, an Uman woman, who'd led the squad that betrayed the Princess. "The woman played her role perfectly. Who knows how much information she passed to Angron Aurelias?"

J'her released M'den and shook his head. He turned back down the corridor and started marching again, M'den beside him, waiting for him to speak.

"You weren't here," he said, "when Lupus first came to the capitol and replaced the royal Eldadorian guard with us. Lupus just gave the order, but I'm the one who had to carry it out – I and a few like me, who are all dead now. The Eldadorians didn't like stepping down, either, but they were terrified of the Killer of Conflu, and the Man who'd sacked Outpost IX. Still, I had to murder more than a dozen of their officers, and then hide it so that Lupus didn't look like an usurper."

"Did Tartan know you had to do this?" M'den asked. J'her smiled again – always to the heart with him. J'her would have led up to the question, where M'den went right to the throat of it.

"I happen to know that he did," J'her informed him, his eyes fixed forward. They were coming up to the inside door to the outer barracks – wooden beams wrapped in steel, one of the hard points in the palace. From this corridor, the Wolf Soldier guard could get to almost anywhere inside, and yet the barracks seemed to be a separate building, disconnected from the main palace. Glennen, it seemed, did not wholly trust his own palace guard.

Maybe now Lupus couldn't, either. No wizard could find the Princess, nor Hectaro. He would have expected that Angron Aurelias would be crowing from the spires of his city if he had the girl. It seemed to all of them that the two had been lost – the Duke's heir, like a good Wolf Soldier, deciding it was better to die than to be taken prisoner.

D'leer had taken the confidence from the Pack, and that more than this upstart Duke had J'her's hackles up.

"But we were as many as the Royal Eldadorian Guard," J'her continued. "They couldn't beat us one-to-one, and they knew it. These Angadorian Knights know that, too."

"So until he sends for more of them –" M'den began.

J'her stopped before the door and turned to face M'den. He put a hand on the other Uman's shoulder and looked into his eyes.

"If that should happen," J'her said, "then Tartan Stowe has given up the defense of the south for his ambitions here. If *that* should happen, then we will send to Thera for Duke Two Spears ourselves."

"And if Two Spears says that *he* wants that spot on the throne?" M'den asked him.

J'her looked away and then looked back again. He dropped his hand to his side and let it rest on the hilt of his sword.

"If that happens, we have full-fledged civil war," he said, "and you and I better hope that the Conqueror comes back to us to fight it."

***

Growing up in the palace in Galnesh Eldador, after his father had become a drunk and Lupus' Wolf Soldiers replaced the Eldadorian Regulars in every significant security role, life had become a day-to-day struggle to avoid the scrutiny both of the Heir and of the nobles who wanted Tartan to become the Heir.

More often than not he'd found a sanctuary in the royal stables, among the groomsmen and the horses, day-dreaming in a pile of hay or sharing his woes with his brother Terran or his sister, Alekennen.

Now that he'd all-but *become* the Heir, wielding if not the title then certainly the power of the Eldadorian second-in-command, he found that peace again here when finally the court was ended for the day, and all that was left to Tartan Stowe was letter-writing or meeting with those same nobles, most of whom either still wanted him to become the Heir, or wanted to make their fortunes against him.

In his worn, black leather pants and a white homespun shirt, worn black riding boots and his sword-belt over his shoulder, he wandered the expanded stalls, walked through the new sections, seeing Shela's influence now with more and better horses and a whole side-stable for nothing but Blizzard's colts and fillies.

Blizzard, the Emperor's white stallion, wouldn't be here now. Blizzard came from 'The Herd that Cannot be Tamed,' sacred to the goddess Life, far to the north. Sixteen years ago Lupus had distinguished himself as the only living person ever to tame one of those horses. Since becoming a King and then an Emperor, he and his wife had made a serious effort to breed that horse, with only limited success.

He passed a mirror that the Empress had installed here and gave himself a sideways glance, catching himself in mid stride and looking for all-the-world like a scaled down version of the Emperor himself, dressing like him without even having realized it.

His pants were black, the Emperor preferred brown. The white homespun shirt was embroidered, not plain as the Emperor preferred, and the sword hung shorter. He didn't wear the square-toed boots that the Emperor loved, and he didn't have a steel chain across each instep, but standing still, looking at the man who now regarded him with short brown hair and tired, brown eyes, it was impossible to miss the influence that the Emperor had imposed on him.

"He's like a sickness, isn't he?" a woman's voice said from behind him.

He didn't turn – he didn't know why not, except that he

recognized that voice the moment that he heard it, and somewhere in the back of his mind, he knew that she'd turn up here eventually. He kept staring at himself in the mirror, almost waiting for the image to change, for the transformation to complete itself and for Tartan Stowe to actually *become* the Emperor of Eldador.

"You touch him," the woman continued, closer now, "and you're affected. Infected, whether you want to be or not."

"You sound like you know that first hand," he said, finally.

She stepped up behind him, just as remembered her. Her green eyes, a dusting of freckles across the bridge of her nose against fair skin and flaming red hair, streaked with gray, found his in the mirror. She wore the tight black leather of a fighting woman, a bandolier of daggers across her ample breasts, black, flat-heeled boots laced up her shins. She almost flowed more than she moved, stepping on the balls of her feet as if she expected the ground to cave in below her. She didn't touch him, but she made it clear that she could if she wanted to, that in one of those fluid motions she could have her arms around him or one of those daggers in his back.

"I thought you fell during the Battle of the Vice," he informed her, turning from the mirror finally. He still didn't turn toward her. He wanted to take a look at the horses that Blizzard had sired. Her presence didn't change that.

She laughed. "I've fought unscathed through worse fights than that," she said. "You hired me to scout for you, and I scouted. That job ended with the battle."

Tartan nodded. She walked a step behind him and to the left, where she could have a knife in him before he turned, if he'd gone for his sword. He wound his way through the stalls, waiting for her to tell him why she'd come here.

As if he didn't know.

"That was a hell of a brawl," she said finally, still feeling him out.

"That it was," he agreed. It isn't every Duke who out-foxes Uman-Chi Casters, hundreds of years his senior. At twenty-eight, Tartan Stowe had done more with his four thousand than the Prince and his mother had done with ten.

Tartan had gone home to Angador afterward and, when he'd gotten there, he'd learned that the Emperor had described the battle as the victory won by his two sons – Vulpe Mordetur, the Prince whom he campaigned with now, and Tartan Stowe, the Duke he'd left behind.

Those few words, that simple opinion, had meant more to Tartan than the battle ever could.

Before then, he hadn't believed that the Emperor even liked him.

"I left for the West after that," she informed him, as Tartan neared the paddocks he'd been looking for.

"And ended up north?"

Tartan could see the stallion, Bastard, almost the size of the Emperor's horse, Blizzard. Bastard belonged to Hectaro Gelgelden. One of the advantages of living in Galnesh Eldador over a frontier duchy like Angador was access to things like the Emperor's stallion. Hectaro had gotten Blizzard to seed his mare, and the Emperor had let him keep it. Other than this gray, and the black stallion Little Storm, one gray mare bred to the Long Manes tribe in Andoron and one other chestnut mare here, Blizzard's progeny had proven too wild to ride.

In an effort to take a member of the Imperial family prisoner, King Angron Aurelias had taken a communications portal that the Empress had created and turned it into a portal that living beings could pass through. Rather than be captured, Lee Mordetur had used her limited skills as a Sorceress to twist the King's magic and turn the passage into a screaming void. When Uman warriors under the King's command and traitorous Wolf Soldiers seemed ready to overwhelm Tartan Stowe, J'her and Duke Hectar Gelgelden, Tartan had seen Hectaro pick up Princess Lee and leap with her into that chasm. Even the Uman-Chi hadn't tried to use it after. In fact, it still existed as a gaping hole atop a tower in the palace – past the strength of their strongest wizards to close. Its existence blocked all communications magic moving into or out of Galnesh Eldador.

Tartan didn't hold out a lot of hope for Hectaro Gelgelden returning to collect his stallion.

"I'd heard you were here now," she said, "and I wanted to find out if you still required my services."

That got him to turn around finally. He didn't have a lot of friends in the palace, not anymore. His old friends were the children of Dukes and Earls, and most of them actually *were* Dukes and Earls now, the rest in the military, on the Emperor's campaign, making names for themselves out of his victories. Mostly he had suitors and acquaintances here – persons who wanted to further their ambitions through him or against him.

Her name was Jean. He'd hired her as a scout when he found

the Confluni in Eldador. He'd never seen one better. She'd moved in and out of their lines like a hawker at a bazaar. He didn't need another friend here, especially not one who would leave without warning and turn up a few months later.

But Jean wasn't here to offer her services as a friend.

Tartan turned back to the paddocks, specifically the one where Bastard waited. This horse had been cooped up too long, he knew. He needed to be turned out, to run, however even that was dangerous. Turn all of the stallions out with the mares and they would kill each other trying to take the herd. Turn them out together and they would work out a hierarchy, however every time a new one was introduced, the fight began again. Ideally the horse's owner or handler would work him every day, however both of these were Hectaro.

All of his life, Tartan had loved horses. His wife, Yeral, had studied them under the Empress, and was the founder of the new Angadorian breed. Long winded, medium-legged with small heads and huge flanks, the Angadorian steed had been bred for lancers who made long, sweeping charges, their horses and their riders in armor. He recognized many of them here.

Bastard pawed the ground and snorted in his paddock, looking for his owner, no doubt. Blizzard and all of his scions were provided stalls with high ceilings, and paddocks with steel bars, rather than wooden, because Blizzard's issue were powerful enough to kick their way through a common wooden fence, and most had. Tartan picked out a carrot from a sack the grooms kept here, and held it out for the stallion. As far as he knew, only Hectaro had ever mounted Bastard, and only because he'd spent as much as half of every day with the animal since its birth.

"That horse looks familiar," Jean commented, placing her instep on the lowest of the paddock's steel bars. "Is he by Blizzard?"

The horse craned his neck but didn't move from his spot. He wanted the carrot, but he didn't want to approach the Man.

"Out of an Andaron mare," Tartan said, as softly as he could. He didn't move. Waving the carrot would just prolong the horse's anxiety. He stood still as a stone, waiting for the 17 hand gray to assure himself that this was safe.

"Seems that those are the mares he does best with," Jean said. "Same as his owner."

Tartan let himself smile at that. It hadn't occurred to him, but in fact that seemed true.

The horse took a step forward, then retreated back, craning its neck again. Its eyes were a whitish blue, a rare color that only existed in grays. He saw the intelligence there – this was a very good horse. He had to suppress a pang of jealousy for not having him or one like him.

"There's another gray like him, isn't there?" she continued. "And a black?"

"And a chestnut," Tartan said. The horse took the step again, and another. He extended his lips until they almost brushed the end of the carrot, then pulled his head back.

Tartan couldn't keep the smile off of his face.

"Where's the chestnut?"

"Turned out with the herd," he said. The gray reached once again, then took another step. He nipped off the pointy end of the carrot, then pulled back his head to chew.

"There he goes," Tartan whispered to the stallion. Bastard regarded him with one eye.

"She's safe with the herd?" Jean asked him.

He sighed. "She leads it," Tartan said, watching the stallion, trying to avoid looking him in the eye. The stallion would take that as a challenge and then he'd be another week regaining the ground he'd lose.

"Some people think the stallion leads the herd," he continued, more lecturing from rote as he paid attention to the stallion. "That's not true, though – there's always a lead female, and the stallion really just guards the herd, usually from the back."

"I didn't know that," Jean said. He could see her smiling from the corner of his eye.

"So to all the world, it looks like the male is the leader, when in fact it is a female?"

The stallion took the step again, and this time took half the carrot in his mouth, trying to pull it from Tartan's hand. The Duke held on tight, though, and pulled the horse's head closer. With his other hand, he reached out very slowly and rubbed the stallion on the forehead, between its eyes, under its forelock.

The horse snapped the end off of the carrot and chewed, sniffing for the rest of the carrot but not pulling away from Tartan.

"You got him," Jean commented.

Tartan kept rubbing. "I always get him," he said. "I got him every day for the last week. He still doesn't know about me, though. I don't plan to throw a blanket on his back until he comes over and gives me a good sniff, and I don't think we'll see that happen during the War months."

The War months, the late spring to the fall running from the month named after the god War to the month named for the god Order, were when nations traditionally campaigned against each other. This was the 3rd of Chaos, leaving Water and Law before Order.

"Am I going to have to wait that long for your answer?" Jean prodded him.

Tartan held his hand out flat, the carrot stub in it, and the horse took it, rubbing the palm with his teeth but not biting him. For a stallion that was a warning – I'll take your food, but don't forget who you are. Tartan lowered his hand and rubbed the great, soft nose until the stallion pulled away.

With any luck, he'd be replaced by the Emperor by the month of Life or early Power, and he'd leave on this horse.

Until then, he had to survive here.

"I'll need someone to keep an eye on things," he said, "but I can't look like I need her."

She nodded, saying nothing.

"I think that I might have trouble with the Wolf Soldiers. They don't plan to stand down and I don't plan to ask their permission every time I want to make a change here. Either I have to get them out of here, or I have to get them on my side, and right now I don't know which is better."

"I'm not enlisting in the Wolf Soldier guard," she warned him.

"I wouldn't ask you to," he said. The stallion stepped away to the far side of the paddock, to watch him. Tartan turned and leaned his shoulder on the iron bars, keeping the stallion in the corner of his eye in case he decided to send a kick to the bars, but without being in a position to end up staring the stallion down.

It was all a game, he reminded himself. The stallion, his duchy, this war, the throne – there were games, and games within games, and some shared rules, and some did not.

When he was a younger man, he'd thought he had to win them all. He'd torn himself apart inside because he couldn't be the one on top of every single game, and because he couldn't even play in some of them, but as he'd grown older he'd realized that being a duke in Lupus' empire wasn't about that.

Anyone could be the winner of the games – that was his father's mistake. He'd won all the games, but the games never ended, so he was always playing, until he just couldn't play anymore.

"I'll need you to make contact with Wolf Soldier commanders and some of the Court Barons," he said. "I don't need you sewing any seeds or starting any conflicts, I just need to know who's thinking what and who's talking to whom."

She nodded. "I can do that."

"As for your payment," he began.

She raised her hand. "I have a son," she said. She looked into his eyes, searching them. It wasn't the sort of thing that he would do, but it was something he'd expect from Jean.

"He's like you," she said. "I see him in some of the things you do. He's dark, a loner. He loves animals like you seem to – he wants to know horses, but I don't know how to teach him."

Tartan nodded. Easy enough to explain that he would be fostering the son of some unnamed noble or wealthy common. He'd be surprised if Jean hadn't already developed his cover story.

"Done," he said. He extended his forearm for her to take.

Instead she took his hand and kissed the back of it, then dropped it. Without another word, she turned her back on him and walked out of the stable. He let himself watch her behind as she moved.

In this new Eldadorian Empire, victory was being the *object* of the games, either centrally or indirectly. Let someone else do all of the work, and then congratulate them on their victory or console them in defeat. Not playing in the games would elevate him to a higher status than the winner, just as not challenging the stallion would elevate him over the horse that he could never hope to break into submission. In his due time, it would all come to him.

Chapter Two:

Dark Child

"His Excellence," the squire announced, to the court in Galnesh Eldador, "Lurien Elt, of the Eldadorian House Elt, son of Krevain of Lupha."

Tartan could barely suppress a smile. Since the invasion of Volkhydro, Lupus had renamed the former capitol of 'Volkha' to 'Lupha,' and the port city of 'Hydro' to 'Hydrus,' declaring both for the Eldadorian nation and all citizens Eldadorians. An alarming number of Volkhydrans had embraced their new status after their army's poor performance on the battlefield.

It would be expected that some of them, especially the more wealthy and ambitious, would send their sons for fostering. Jean had presented herself with her son, as his nurse maid, or in fact Tartan wouldn't have known better.

The boy waited at the doors to the throne room at the end of the red carpet that led from there to the throne. He stood about four feet tall, with long black hair down past his shoulders and wide, staring eyes almost black themselves. His hands were too large for his body, the nails left long and several pointed. When he began to walk, he dragged a clubbed foot behind him, thump-thump-thumping down the carpet.

He dressed in a black doublet and hose, a short black cape over one shoulder, a wide black belt on his waist and a dagger in the belt, its hilt encrusted not with jewels, but seemingly with bits and strands of things that didn't belong on a handle.

Jean's eyes shown on the boy, is if a light emanated from him and only she could see it. Lurien himself stared straight ahead at the Duke, a cat-like stare that Tartan found unnerving. He waited for the two of them to travel the distance down the throne room, then leaned forward in the throne to address the boy.

"What is your age, lad?" he asked.

The boy looked him right in the eye – a good sign. "Soon to be fifteen, Highness," he said. Tartan would have guessed ten. "Born in Life's month."

Tartan nodded. "And you seek to be fostered at the court?"

"Or wherever you will be," Lurien said. "My people are unaccustomed to Eldadorian ways, and you are of its oldest house."

Oldest house of two generations, Tartan thought to himself. The boy allowed himself a smile that Tartan found contagious. It was a wry jest worthy of any noble.

"And you, woman?" Tartan demanded of Jean, as he would of any servant.

She curtsied properly, dressed now not in her leathers but in a proper blue dress, cut high on her neck and low on her heel, the bodice properly laced and tiny, dark-blue bows on her voluminous skirt. She'd tied her red hair up in a bun behind her head, accentuating the gray over the red.

"Jean, your Highness," she said, her eyes properly lowered. "I've tended the young master his whole life."

"I've no time for a boy who can't exist without a wet nurse, you understand that, son?" he asked Lurien.

"Perfectly, your Highness," Lurien said, without a glance at Jean.

Tartan nodded. "Your woman can report to the kitchen – I'm sure they'll keep her busy. You can take a room in the guests' tower for now, until we see how your fosterage works itself out."

Lurien nodded, Jean curtsied again. "Take a seat in the gallery, Lurien, and see how things work in an Eldadorian court."

Lurien bowed at the waist, a hand before and behind him, a style that Tartan didn't recognize. He thumped over to the gallery where a few of the dignitaries in the first row opened up a seat for him on the end. Jean retreated down the red carpet for the kitchens.

The palace revolved around the kitchen staff. It was the perfect place to station a spy. The only place as good would be the stables, and

Tartan already had that covered.

The next bit of business was in the form of a squad of Wolf Soldiers. If he'd known that they were here, Tartan would have had them come up first.

"Colonel Gartheld Daggonin of the Eldadorian Regular Corps," the squire announced, "with retinue."

The Colonel marched himself down the aisle, the Wolf Soldiers with him. Tartan knew the Colonel in passing – one of many who'd moved from the Wolf Soldiers to the Eldadorian Regulars. His own advisor, J'lek, had done so. It was rumored that J'lek was J'her's son, but neither spoke of it.

"Your Grace," Daggonin greeted him, inclining his head. That was ominous. The Colonel came right from the front lines – he'd been appointed the military regent for Lupha. If anyone were here to remove Tartan from the throne by force, it would be such a one.

"I sit the throne, Colonel," Tartan reminded him, more to see where this was going.

"Hrumm – hrm! So you do," Daggonin said, clearing his throat. He dressed in Eldadorian greens with steel sleeves and leggings, a sword over his back. His white hair circled the bald spot on the top of his head, his full moustaches drooped two inches past the corners of his mouth. He had full lips and a ruddy nose, and his brown eyes seemed to be searching Tartan's face for weakness.

"My pardon," he said, when Tartan didn't flinch, and bowed. "Your Highness. Hrrrm! I've come to collect status for the Emperor. We've been – hrrumm, hrmmm! - unable to make use of Central Communications, either into the capitol or to any of the – hrrm! - major Eldadorian cities."

"I've sent messages to the Emperor of the attack by Trenbon on Galnesh Eldador," Tartan said, trying not to seem defensive. "I see where you might have passed by these –"

"Hmm - ha," Daggonin interrupted him. "Yes, nasty business, heard of it. Your Highness, the Emperor dispatched me before he heard of any of this and – hrumm – I think we both know what his reaction's going to be when he finds out about his – ha, hrrm - daughter."

Tartan nodded. He would have liked to have this conversation in private, not in open court, however he had no way of dismissing the Emperor's personal emissary. He could only hope that common sense would dictate to the Man that he needed to excuse himself.

"And so – huhumm," Daggonin continued, "while Outpost IX is still not a smoldering ruin, I think perhaps its best that you update me – hmm, Ha! – and then get someone onto a fast ship for Hydrus."

Tartan nodded again. Here was his chance. "Shall we resume after court, then, Colonel? I have advisors, such as J'her, whom I would like to include."

"J'her? Hrrrmm, yes, of course, your Highness," the Colonel's eyes swept the gallery for him. "Yes, let me find the Supreme Commander, and await your – hrrm! - orders, sir."

Tartan waved him off, wincing internally. Of course the one military man would want to talk in private to the other, and of course J'her would poison him against the Duke trying to put his own warriors in place in the palace. As a former Wolf Soldier, Daggonin was accustomed to taking J'her's orders and knew very little about Tartan.

He couldn't remember if Daggonin had been one of the Wolf Soldiers involved in his first raid on Andoron. It had been the invasion where the Emperor, then a King, had established the Wolf Rider tribe on Andaron soil, at the lake where the Great Mid River met the Safe River. That hadn't been one of Tartan's more shining moments – in fact, he'd made his first kill then, and puked all over himself and his horse.

Wolf Soldiers *still* joked about that.

The Colonel turned smartly on his heel and left, the Wolf Soldiers saluting the throne as a squad and following after the colonel. Daggonin should have saluted, as well, but he was clearly distracted and had forgotten. At least, that's what Tartan hoped for.

Court dragged on after that. When Lee had sat the throne, there'd been a parade of lesser nobles trying to get loans from the Eldadorian state, to be used to raise levies. They only did that when they planned to raid each other, which had been common enough when King Glennen had reined. Lupus didn't permit it, but of course Lupus wasn't here, and it was the invasion by Conflu that made them desperate enough to want to try again.

Tartan remembered his father explaining to him why the Earls and Barons fighting was such a great thing. "First," he'd said, "they kill off the excess peasants, meaning fewer mouths to feed. Second, the ones that survive are all blooded veterans, meaning that we're stronger against invaders." Even then, the idea had seemed awfully ruthless to Tartan. Glennen believed that the strong had a right to prey on the weak, and the weak best served the rest by dying.

The Emperor valued peasants' lives, however it was more because he wanted the revenues that each could generate. His daughter had denied the money to the lesser nobility and had instead sent out an army of court barons, unlanded nobles who hung about the court, as 'advisors to the throne.' What they could advise on was anyone's guess, however it so involved the lesser nobles with their own intrigue that most forgot about making war on each other.

Now that the Princess wasn't a threat to them, most wanted to send back the court barons. Notorious lechers and lay-abouts, Earls and Barons strapped for cash preferred to see them as a burden on Galnesh Eldador.

Tartan found himself acting as if he were eager for their reports, creating a whole new round of intrigue. How deep did this go? What was the Emperor planning? In his first year as Heir, he'd actually deposed the Duke of Uman City, the father of Tartan's own wife, and replaced him with a court baron. Tartan had been in the palace then, so of course he would know about it.

If the intrigue bought him another month, he'd consider himself lucky. Like Lee, Tartan knew better than to loan them gold for their levies.

After court, Tartan dismissed the courtiers and waited for them all to leave. Only Lurien waited for him, sitting in the gallery, one hand on the dagger in his belt.

Tartan stood and summoned the boy. A cripple or not, a Duke didn't walk to the side of a common to address him. Lurien stood and thumped his way to the Duke, never moving his hand from the dagger's hilt.

"I've never seen a blade like that," the Duke offered, as the boy drew closer.

The boy immediately pulled it and offered it to Tartan, hilt first, his head down. Tartan didn't know what he expected from Jean's son, but whatever else, he had been schooled in some etiquette.

Tartan took the proffered weapon. The blade was dark, almost black, and cast no reflection. The crossbar appeared to be carved into two forearms, clasping each other at the wrist, rounded at the ends where the elbows should be. The hilt, rather than being covered in debris as he'd first suspected, in fact seemed to be interwoven of bits of leather, wire, string and even tiny pieces of wood. The dagger should have been heavier in his hand for its size, but instead was light as a butter knife, and almost seemed to couch itself in his palm.

"This is a unique weapon," he said, handing it back to the boy, handle first.

Lurien took it in an over-large hand, one of his sharpened nails actually touching the Duke's skin. The contact sent a chill through Tartan for some reason. "My mother found it on a battle field," he said. "The Battle of the Vice, I believe."

Tartan smiled. "I was there," he said. "I met your mother right before then."

"She informed me, your Highness," Lurien said.

Tartan turned on his heel, heading for the secret exit from the throne room – actually not much of a secret. A mural on the wall in the image of his mother, Alekanna, to the right of the throne, opened into a passage through the palace. Lupus had made such frequent use of it that it was better described as a side exit. The boy stumped after him, not seeming much impressed when the image of the former queen swung open.

"My mother," Tartan informed him, entering the passage.

"Excuse me?"

"The woman – the entrance to this passage," Tartan said. "The image of the first Queen of Eldador, my mother."

"Ah," Lurien stopped in the entrance and regarded her with his big, dark eyes. "Whoever painted this must have loved her very much."

Tartan smiled. "Everyone loved her," he said. The memory was still painful for him. "She died at the hands of Sentalan and Dorkan assassins, under the employ of Uman-Chi, working with Volkhydrans."

"So, in fact," the boy said, "not everyone loved her at all."

Tartan stopped dead in his tracks. He couldn't believe that the boy who'd just met him would *dare* to make a comment like that. His own fury actually surprised him as he turned to face the boy again.

Lurien looked up at him with his same cat-like expression. Tartan had expected some sort of sneer, or look of shame, or something indicating that he realized the grievous insult he'd just delivered.

Instead – nothing. Lurien looked up at him like a cat might watch a bouncing ball of string. As much as he'd wanted to strike the boy just moments before, the anger drained right out of him, into those dark, curious eyes.

"That isn't the sort of comment you should make, Lurien," he said, finally.

"Why?"

"Why?" Tartan repeated. "To comment on a man's dead mother – Lurien, how would *you* feel, were it Jean?"

Lurien shrugged. "My mother is a scout," he said. "She could have died in your service – she tells me that you thought she did."

War's whiskers, that he had, Tartan thought. No wonder he could make such a comment – the boy lived with the likely death of his mother every day.

Lupus had told him once that the difference between commons and the nobility is that nobles sought tragedy in plays and novels, and rejected it in real life. Commons sought real lives that resembled plays and novels, and by force accepted tragedies. The Emperor had told him this when they'd campaigned together during the Second Invasion of Thera, sitting their horses after the battle, near an Uman couple kneeling weeping by a dead child. Tartan had just commented on what a tremendous victory this had been, one to keep the troubadours busy for years to come.

He realized right then that the Uman couple wouldn't be throwing their pennies to the troubadour who sang them *that* song.

Without comment to Lurien, he turned back on his heel and down the passage to the stables, the image of the Uman couple haunting the back of his mind. The boy said nothing, content to follow him to the stables with no more sound than the thumping of his own clubbed foot.

Tartan had hoped for some private time at the stable, however he arrived just in time for the grooms and handlers bringing in the herd. In his southern Duchy of Angador, he kept the mares and stallions separate in their own herds, fillies keeping with the mares and colts between. In Andaron tradition most colts were gelded until a new stallion was needed, with never more than the main stallion and two spares for the herd. Galnesh Eldador's herd kept more geldings and fewer stallions than Tartan would have liked, but many more than an Andaron tribe, and then turned them out at night.

Tartan stepped into the aisle between twelve pair of stalls and into the path of three Eldadorian mares bound for their nightly feeding.

"Whoa!" Tartan shouted as a warning to Lurien. "Back, boy."

Lurien stood stock still as Tartan retreated past him. The boy seemed fascinated by the running horses, even as one bore down directly upon him.

Tartan realized too late that Lurien wasn't going to leap out of the way. These were war horses and, by their nature, they'd run down anyone in their path. The groomsmen and the handlers knew better then to send them wild through the stable, however when bringing the entire herd in, it was as easy to have more than one slip through the gate as it was to become complacent and just let them in, knowing that they preferred their own stalls anyway.

A mare nearly ten times the weight of a grown man bore down on the hapless boy, who stood his ground with that same cat expression. Tartan winced at what he was sure would be the boy's death.

Instead the mare came skidding to a halt, her nose barely bumping the front of Lurien's doublet. The boy, keeping one hand on his dagger, reached up with the other and stroked the side of her nose, looking into her eyes the entire time. Tartan knew from his experience that, even if the mare had stopped for some reason, she should have taken the direct eye contact as a challenge and reacted. Instead she lowered her proud head, and met Lurien forehead to forehead.

A handler ran up behind the mare, turning the corner to this part of the stable. His mouth dropped open to see the Duke and his charge with the freed mare. An Uman in the stable livery – brown canvas pants, brown vest and a white homespun shirt - he knew the consequences of what he had let happen.

Tartan straightened. "I hope you weren't too fond of this job," he growled. "I want the stable master and every member of his staff before me. *Now!*"

***

Leaning on the iron bars to Bastard's paddock, Tartan watched Lurien hand-feeding a carrot to the gray stallion. So long as he didn't get to close to the boy, the horse would go so far as to nuzzle his hand and bump him in the forehead for more attention.

What remained of the stable's staff watched from a safe distance. Tartan had culled their number by a third in retaliation for their irresponsibility. The Shela Mordetur whom he knew would have done far worse, and Tartan could help thinking that every last one of them knew it.

Tartan had never seen anything like this boy. It wasn't just the mare – any horse, every horse, seemed to love him, to see some sort of friend in him. Tartan had heard of this with crippled children and the very young, handlers who sighted that the horses seemed to 'know' that these were vulnerable and needed special care. Like a mother with a sick child, it brought out an instinct in the horse for being gentle.

"You say it's always been this way for you?" Tartan asked him.

The boy didn't look away from the stallion. "Always," he said. "Almost all animals, anything with fur, anyway."

"And you've never ridden?"

"Mother won't let me."

"And your father?"

That got the boy's attention. The stallion having finished his carrot and now licking his hand for the salt, Lurien turned his attention to the Duke on his left and said, "I never met my father."

Again, those curious cat eyes – as if he were fascinated with how Tartan would handle that statement.

Well, his mother wasn't the first after all. "You know what that horse's name is, don't you?" Tartan asked.

"No."

"Bastard," he said. Now Tartan measured the boy's reaction.

Lurien looked back into the horse's eyes. Bastard should have reacted, but didn't. The boy reached up and rubbed the side of the horses nose, and said, "Yes, I see that now."

Comments like that just didn't bother him, it seemed. He'd grown up having to be honest with whom his mother is. Jean had to be more than a common scout or spy, then. He'd have to speak discreetly with the Shem Hannen.

"Would you like to ride him?" Tartan asked.

Lurien considered. "I think that I should wait a while," he said, finally. "This horse feels like he's missing someone. Maybe one of the other horses, while we wait for him to come around."

Tartan nodded. He'd already picked one out in his mind – a gentle palfrey, nearly fifteen. The boy would need a special stirrup for that clubbed foot – fortunately it was the right, so that he could mount properly. He'd see how well the boy handled walking and a slow trot before he tried him out on something more spirited and fun.

"Let me show you what I was thinking of," he said, pushing away from the bars. "And then to the leather worker to get a saddle for you."

Lurien nodded. He cupped the stallion under the chin and, lifting his head up, planted a kiss on his nose. Tartan kept himself from lunging forward – any other stallion might have taken a good portion of the boy's nose and upper lip off right there, especially one of Blizzard's line. Bastard simply blinked his eyes, then turned around and took himself to the far part of his paddock, watching both of them warily.

Tartan shook his head. He couldn't help thinking of what he could accomplish with a fraction of the young man's appeal to horses.

Jean had brought him here to learn more about horses. That would be the least of what he'd be receiving.

Chapter Three:

The Secrets Within

Gartheld Daggonin, as it turned out, had been the military mind most responsible for the fall of Volkha to Vulpe Mordetur. In scouting the city with 1,000 regulars, he'd been surprised by the gate guard and surrounded by ten times his number in Volkhydran warriors, any help more than half an hour away.

The one responsible for this, a Daff Kanaar named Karel of Stone, had fled on his pony, leaving the one Millennium, as the Emperor called his legions of one thousand, to its fate. Daggonin had thought to take the gate itself, to form a circle of his warriors on either side of it, and hope that the Volkhydrans wouldn't be able to pour burning oil over his head before the Prince could come and rescue him.

Lupus had developed another new fighting style – lining up his warriors in columns with their shields and their short swords, creating a front line and then many rows behind them, and letting each man fight for only fifteen minutes (or until beaten) before rotating him or her back and replacing him or her with a fresh warrior from behind. One of the great disadvantages of fighting great battles was that the front lines were almost always doomed to die – and in fact the warriors behind them couldn't fight until they did so. This strategy allowed Lupus to fight with all of his warriors without killing them. Two hours into the battle when arms were sore and blades dull, it wasn't uncommon for half of his Eldadorian warriors to be unblooded and almost all of them fresh.

Outnumbered ten to one, Daggonin should have fallen in under half an hour. In fact he lost less than 200 warriors and was still fighting when relief arrived. If Daggonin had still been a Wolf Soldier, he'd have received the Mark of the Conqueror, a scar on his left cheek from the eye to the jowl. Instead, he'd received an estate in Britt, a region on the Eldadorian Peninsula, and been earmarked for general.

This was a Man worth listening to. Tartan tracked him down to Galnesh Eldador's War Room, sharing the story with J'her over a few cups of ale. Tartan had to guess that he was a man whose opinion was worth poisoning, as well. He stood and regarded the Duke formally, casting a sideways glance to the Supreme Commander.

Tartan took his forearm in greeting, feeling the dagger that the colonel concealed there. Daggonin felt the steel rod that Tartan concealed, as well. They looked in each others' eyes for a moment, then Tartan said, "I hope you've been accommodated."

"Hr-r-r-m! Better than a battlefield, worse than a parade, your Grace," the colonel said. Tartan didn't miss that he wasn't 'highness' any more.

He cocked an eyebrow. "Should you want one, you've earned it," he said.

Daggonin smiled. All three warriors sat, an Uman servant standing in one corner coming forward to pour ale for Tartan. "Perhaps when the – ah - Emperor can see it," Daggonin said.

"Any idea when that will be?" Tartan asked.

Daggonin shrugged. "I wish I did," he said. "Hmph! The Emperor rolled up the shores of Volkhydro faster than I would have thought possible. We've still got plenty of War months left for more – hrumph! - invasions."

J'her narrowed his eyes. "Surely Volkhydro is enough for one season," he said. "Gharf Bendenson isn't going to sit in Vol forever with his army."

"Bendenson is in Trenbon begging the Fovean High Council for united action against Eldador," Tartan informed them. He'd received the report this very day. "However, he wants them in Volkhydro, and they want to come here."

"To face you instead of the Emperor," Daggonin informed him.

Tartan nodded – no point in denying that. He was surprised when J'her offered, "They must not have heard of the Battle of the

Vice, then."

A peace offering? Tartan wondered. Daggonin must have told J'her something that he didn't want to hear.

"No, but I did," Daggonin said. "Lupus had a laugh at all of our expenses when he heard that tale. Ha!"

Tartan raised an eyebrow and drank.

"The Emperor was advised that the best thing that he could do with you," J'her said, "was to take you with him and teach you better how to fight. He told the rest of us that the best thing we could do is to learn from you – that if any man came against Tartan Stowe, they'd better bring a shovel for his own grave. It only made the story better that his own son had the West while you drove the Confluni from the East."

"At the time, I was more worried about the Uman-Chi Caster and his Lava Rain," Tartan said, then took a drink as he felt his voice about to crack. He wasn't used to this sort of praise in his life.

Daggonin nodded. "Now I've come to find out what happened to Lee Mordetur and, more importantly, what we need to – hrrrumph! - do about it."

Lee had been trying to contact her mother through the mystic orb in one palace tower they called 'Central Communications.' The orb was the focal point of a conduit that allowed all of the cities in the Empire, and certain gifted Wizards and Sorceresses, to speak to each other. Instead of finding her mother, Angron Aurelias himself, the thousand-year-old King of Trenbon, had stepped through the orb like a portal with two other Uman-Chi Casters and twenty armed Uman guards.

Tartan explained that to Daggonin. "When the Princess' Wolf Soldier guard also turned on us, it was up to Duke Hectar, his son Hectaro and I to defend the Princess, and suffice to say, against those odds, we couldn't do it. Hectaro saw this, threw Lee over his shoulder and leapt into the portal."

"So most likely they're back in Trenbon," Daggonin said.

J'her shook his head. "We have no reason to believe that," he said. "If they were, we'd have heard from Angron by now. Aurelias wouldn't even use the portal himself a second time."

"H-r-r-r-mph! Why not?"

"After the Trenboni came through," Tartan informed them, "I think that Lee was able to do something to change either the portal or Central Communications itself. Suddenly Aurelias was a lot more worried about the room than the Princess. I couldn't be sure, but I don't think that she went back to Trenbon."

"Where, then," Daggonin insisted. "Because, rest assured, the Empress will ask me, and I – hrrmph, ha! - won't be the one telling her that no one knows."

"In fact, however, no one does," J'her said. Tartan couldn't help noticing that the Supreme Commander was being amazingly accommodating.

"Our best Wizards are baffled," J'her informed the colonel. "They claim that Central Communications now makes so much magical 'noise' that it's difficult for them to be sure of anything."

"Hrrrmph, ha! In that case, I've been instructed to summon the Druid called 'The Green One' from Hydrus, and to ask him to intervene."

"Not the Empress?" Tartan had expected her to appear back in her rooms any moment, in fact. She knew no calling stronger than her children.

"If you can attest that Chawnee is safe here, - hrrrmph - and I believe that you can, then the Empress will stay with her Emperor."

That was surprisingly rational coming from her. "I have no fewer than two wizards and 100 Wolf Soldier guards on the girl at any time," J'her informed the colonel.

"Pull them," Daggonin said. J'her straightened. "On orders from the Emperor, hrrrm, Wolf Soldiers will maintain the palace, but he wants Angadorian Knights protecting Chawnee."

He took the time to meet both them eye to eye, before he finished, "And he told me that before he knew that Tartan had already come to Galnesh Eldador."

All three drank. Tartan couldn't have imagined a better outcome for the meeting, and that put him right on his guard.

***

Tartan Stowe had come to Galnesh Eldador with one thousand of his Angadorian Knights and without his wife, Yerel. He knew perfectly well that she took Uman lovers in his absence. A common practice among the Eldadorian nobility – in all of recorded history only one child had ever been born of the coupling of Man and Uman. Uman spoke their own language, kept their own council and themselves did not believe as much in fidelity as the race of Men.

In ancient times, when the Cheyak had walked the face of Earth, it was said that they had lain down with Uman and birthed Uman-Chi. Uman-Chi held themselves superior to all other races for that reason. They lived for centuries on their Silent Island – the nation of Trenbon in the center of Tren Bay.

Tartan had never bedded any other than Yerel – he'd seen his drunken father, after his mother's murder, chasing women, abusing them, having to be contained through the efforts of then-Heir Lupus and his Wolf Soldiers. He'd also seen Lupus, so dedicated to his Shela, who could have had one hundred other women if he wanted, and who remained faithful. In his mind somewhere, he associated the two things and then didn't cheat on his wife, regardless of her behavior.

When he summoned Jean to his bed chambers, then, many eyebrows were raised among the house staff. It couldn't be helped, and in fact made her more interesting to the people whom he wanted her to spy on. If she appeared to have his ear through sleeping with him, then others would want to know what she might have learned.

"Your Highness," Jean said, entering with a curtsy.

He'd chosen the Heir's apartments – the ones where Lupus and Shela had once slept. The rooms included a bed, couches, a table with chairs, an armor stand and armoire, thick pile carpets – all chosen by the Empress. He rarely came here except to sleep and cared very little about any of it.

"Close the door behind you, Jean," Tartan instructed her.

Jean cocked an eyebrow and did as she was told. Turning her back to him, she dragged the double doors closed and slid the bolt that locked them.

"Shall I be earning my keep, then, Highness?" she asked him, facing the door.

Tartan sighed. "I'm a married man," he informed her.

She turned and put her back to the door. Her green eyes had a look to them that was almost Uman in its wildness. She reached up and pulled one of the pins from her hair, letting it cascade down around her shoulders.

"A noble man, among the nobility, no less?" she asked him. "I wouldn't have known there could *be* such a thing."

Tartan allowed himself a smile. "I answer for myself, not the peerage."

She started toward him, her hands on her hips, looking down, seeming to put one foot directly in front of the other, although it was difficult to tell under her skirts. "So, all of this, out of the goodness of your heart, then?"

"You're earning your keep, or you best be," Tartan said to her, not moving from where he leaned against the foot of the bed. "If you can't learn the things I want from you in the palace kitchen – "

She waved his question off with a disgusted look. "I've already been approached by three court barons, a visiting Earl and a lieutenant from your Angadorian Knights," she informed him. "If the rest of my time here is like today you'll need to grow more ears to hear me."

Tartan chuckled. He knew the lieutenant from his Knights – the man was notorious. "Then I've won your services cheaply," he said. "Your son is more gifted with horses than any I've seen."

That stopped her. "In fact?" she pressed him, looking him in the eye.

"Surely you've noticed how he is with animals," he said.

"How could I not?" she asked him. "Since he first walked he's been a beacon for every stray beast for fifty daheeri. I don't ride, but I've seen him with both domestic and wild horses, which is why I brought him to you."

"Is that what you were doing that day when I met you?" he asked. "Looking for me?"

She laughed and took a few steps closer. He could touch her now if he wanted. He smelled the bread and herbs on her from the kitchen. "I had other business then," she informed him. "You'd be surprised to learn of it. No, I thought of you once I saw you with your Knights. You're one of few Men who care more for his horses than his ambitions."

Tartan couldn't argue, having thought the same thing himself. He also didn't like where this conversation was going. "So, what did you learn from the barons and the Earl?" he asked.

Jean smiled and looked him in the eye again. She clearly liked the suggestive banter. "From the barons – lechery, as expected. I'm warned by every female and young boy in the kitchens to keep my distance from them, and not to be caught alone in a room with any. I'm sure you know their reputation."

Tartan frowned. The women he could have guessed at, especially the Uman, however the boys came as a surprise. He'd have to pursue his own investigations.

"As for the Earl – he comes from a village called Lee's Hope," she continued. "He tried his fortunes here with Lee Mordetur, thinking that the name of his village would get him what he wanted from her.

When that didn't happen, he returned to have you remove the court baron that she sent to assist him."

Tartan nodded – he remembered the man. His name was Steffen, as he recalled.

"Well, he's decided that he needs to try for more children, but his wife isn't interested. I suppose that I look fertile, dressed like this."

Tartan barked a short laugh and shook his head. He'd spent his life with women raised to impress him with their proper manners and prim ways. It was oddly refreshing to speak to one with Jean's outlook.

Jean warmed to his humor. "You should have heard your man's proposal," she told him. "He is quite impressed with his lance – and I'm not sure he meant the one he keeps with his horse."

"Sounds like him," Tartan said. "If you're wise you'll stay clear of him."

"Fighting with a dagger, thinking it's a sword?" she asked him. He didn't get it right away, then blushed crimson.

"I wouldn't know," he said. "But as much as he fights, I'd have to assume the point is dull."

He surprised himself with the comment.

She turned on him and moved to the couch against the far wall, next to the doors. She squatted down, reaching under it, and emerged with a clear crystal decanter, stoppered with a crystal plug, and two plain glasses. He raised an eyebrow as she popped the stopper onto the couch cushions with her thumb.

"You just sensed that there?" he asked her.

Holding the two glasses in her left hand, she poured from her right, two fingers to each. "I *planted* them there," she informed him. "A good spy keeps her tools in more than one place."

She offered him one glass. "This is a tool of your trade?" he asked her, taking it. He waved the glass under his nose. Uman-Chi brandy.

"The best," she informed him. "Men will say anything to get under a woman's skirts. They only tell the truth with this."

He chuckled and sipped. The liquid warmed his tongue and throat, smooth as cream but with a kick like a stallion. She matched him – he'd also rarely seen women that could drink like that. Perhaps the Empress, though usually she stayed sober.

They made small talk into the night. He was surprised by how long he let her stay, and how sorry he was to see her go. In the end, he helped her loosen her bodice and she tousled up her hair. The best excuses were the most obvious ones, after all, and he wouldn't be telling the palace staff anything worse than what they would invent, anyway.

Dousing the room's two lanterns, he shucked his clothes into a pile on the floor and then slid into his bed, thinking for the first time how very large that bed had become.

***

His father had held court almost every day, but for only a few hours, as Tartan remembered it. Lupus didn't like to work on what he called, 'weekends,' meaning the first and last day of every week. He'd made a standard of that, which others followed throughout the Empire. Where many Dukes and Earls had fretted that this would mean that their new-found, super-productive economy would lag behind all others, in fact a little time off made farmers and city workers more productive for the other five, and a whole new economy arose from accommodating all of that free time.

So on the seventh day of Chaos, when servants only did their minimums to keep the palace going and throughout the city people roved the streets in droves, shopping and dining and seeing plays, Tartan Stowe collected young Lurien from his rooms in the guest tower for what promised to be the boy's first ride.

His mother had made an excuse to be at the stables, not that she needed one. Many of the kitchen staff came there on weekends, some to feed and pet the horses, a few to ride the retired ones, mostly to socialize or because they had relationships with the staff there. The servants in the palace were often called 'the story within Eldador,' and having grown up there, Tartan was no stranger to it.

Lurien had his hair tied back and wore a black beret to keep it. He'd gotten himself black boots more like the Emperors than Tartan's, with square toes but no chain across the instep. He'd dropped his black doublet for a gray homespun shirt, and his black hose for black leather pants. He kept the same belt with the same knife.

In his boots, the clubbed foot was far less pronounced. Tartan had already had a saddle altered for him. They walked together with only a slight thumping into the stables.

"Right, he just walked off, then," one Uman was thundering at someone else, from the Emperor's private paddocks.

"Well, I didn't turn him out."

"Are you sure he didn't just get himself out?" a third voice demanded. Tartan couldn't imagine a good reason for this conversation and sprinted for the paddocks, leaving Lurien to keep up as best he could.

Five of them, three Uman and two Wolf Soldiers of the race of Men, stood outside of Bastard's empty paddock.

Tartan stopped dead in his tracks. Dread washed over the three Uman faces.

"War's Whiskers!" he swore.

"Your Highness," one said, but the senior Wolf Soldier put a hand on the Uman's breast and turned to face Tartan.

"Your Highness," he said, "Bastard is missing and cannot be found. We see no evidence of his paddock being tampered with, however they aren't locked –"

"Of course they aren't locked," one of the Uman spat at him. Tartan recognized his new stable master, Heleen, in the brown stable livery. "You can't lock them in – what if there's a fire, or one's down with colic?"

"Or you want to steal one, let's not forget about that!" the other Wolf Soldier added, a hand on his sword.

"Silence, all of you," Tartan ordered them. Lurien came thumping up behind him, winded. His mother was on the other side of the five at the paddock. Tartan caught her eye for a moment and she shrugged.

"Who found him missing?"

"I did," Heleen said. "I feed him myself – he wasn't here. Must have been thirty minutes ago. I summoned the guard."

"Gate closed?"

"And latched," she said, and put a hand on the steel paddock bars. "And he didn't jump out, because a stallion that big would have left a divot big as a dog on both sides if he tried."

Tartan nodded. He'd have told her to account for the staff, but he'd just fired so many of them that there *had* to be both new ones and disgruntled former ones.

He should have suspected this, except that no one could handle that stallion.

Well, he thought, turning to Lurien, almost no one.

"Lad?" he said.

Lurien looked up him with those huge, curious cat eyes. Tartan absolutely couldn't read him. The boy didn't have a look of guilt, or anger, or defiance, but then he didn't seem quite innocent, either.

"Your Highness?" he said back.

"Do you know anything of this?"

"How could I?" he asked. "I only come here with you."

"He's true, there," Heleen testified for him. "I can't say as there's been any wandering the stables. In fact I've been trying to get him out here to fit that new saddle, and he's not come."

That in itself was suspicious, Tartan thought. Why should he be avoiding the stables, unless he knew what was going on and didn't want to involve himself.

What if his mother had the same gifts that he had?

Too many questions. "Get the 'sayers in here," he said finally to the Wolf Soldier guard. "Question everyone. If that doesn't get you anywhere, then hunt down the ones we've let go, and question them."

"Permission to send out riders, just in case?" the Wolf Soldier asked him.

"I'll take care of that," he said. This job was better suited to his Knights. They'd been complaining of their boredom lately.

"Horses can't fly," he informed them all. "And one that big is going to be noticed, even in the middle of the night. Let it be known, the penalty for turning him back is going to be a lot easier to bear than the penalty for taking him."

He turned on his heel and left, Lurien following him. Let the boy come along, Tartan thought. Lurien bore watching now, and if they *did* find the stallion, he might be useful in getting him back. Bastard was still ten times the weight of a Man and not friendly.

Tartan allowed himself a little smile despite himself. So much for the Emperor's plans for not working on weekends.

Chapter Four:

A Horse is a Horse

Tartan knew that a horse as large and as dangerous as Bastard couldn't disappear into the shadows, however this one had. Nine hundred Angadorian Knights had travelled out ten daheeri from the capitol and back in every direction and found nothing. Tartan himself had inspected the mare herd, and the Wolf Soldier guard had searched the city proper. No ship had left with him, and no truthsayer found anything even remotely like a lie or innuendo from the palace staff.

"Everyone's talking about it," Jean informed him, in the Heir's chambers, "but they're all asking the right questions."

"And the guard on Central Communications?" he asked her, sitting on one of the couches. Jean had come to serve him his afternoon meal: a delicacy brought to Fovea by the Emperor, called a 'sammich.' Cut bread, roast beef, a tart cheese with lettuce and tomato. Jean prepared it with a tangy dressing that Tartan had never had before, and served it to him with a chilled white wine.

He took a plate from her, noting that she'd made another for herself. Any servant who thought to dine with him would normally find herself mucking stalls for a year if she were lucky. Somehow it wasn't the same with Jean.

"Nothing," she said. "I carried a tray to them just yesterday.

One of those Wolf Soldiers actually had the initiative to check the orb – it isn't changed."

Tartan nodded and took a bite of the sammich. Lupus encouraged his Wolf Soldiers to be creative and independent – he'd emulated that with his Knights.

"Wow, this is really good," he commented on the sammich.

She nodded and said. "It's in the dressing, made from a kind of radish that grows in Conflu. I can tell the kitchen to stock it if you want."

"I do," he said, and took another bite.

She watched him eat, moving to sit on the arm of the divan under the room's one open window. "My son believes you blamed him for the horse's theft," she said, finally.

He watched her for a moment, then washed out his mouth with a sip of wine. After the sammich, the white wine seemed to explode in his mouth with flavor. This woman might be a good spy, he thought, but she'd missed her calling as a chef.

"I did," he said, finally. "He was the only one I knew who could handle that stallion, and your arrival was quite a coincidence."

She snickered. "I wouldn't have moved so fast," she said as she took a bite from her sammich, not denying that she'd steal from him, just letting him know that she'd be better at it.

"That's the conclusion I came to myself," Tartan said. "You'd have figured out a way for someone to give it to you, or you'd have had it out of here and us believing that it was in its paddock for at least a few days."

She smiled, and took a sip of wine. "Wow," she said, through a mouth full, "that *is* good."

"I know."

"So when does my son start learning to ride," she asked of him.

He almost choked. "We have this horse to find –," he began, but she shook her head.

"Bastard is gone, you lost him," she said. "It's been three days. That horse isn't even in Eldador anymore. I'm doing a job for you, and I'm not doing it for free."

He nodded. He wished he could have argued with her, but he saw no way. He'd made a deal and he needed to honor it.

"Send him to me," he said. "I have to meet with J'her and Colonel Daggonin – a fosterling would need to witness a meeting like that. Then I'll take him out on a gelding I picked for him."

She nodded, and took another bite.

He finished his sammich and took another sip of wine. He was tempted to have her make him another one. "How are the rumors about you and I?" he asked her.

She smiled, and finished her wine to clear her mouth. "I'm the envy of the palace," she said, "which made me more popular with everyone but your Angadorian lieutenant. That colonel that you mentioned has been sniffing around me."

A married man, Tartan knew. "I'd like very much to know what he's been thinking," Tartan informed her.

She nodded. "Consider it done – how long do I have with him?"

"Not too long."

She poured herself another glass of wine. "You know you're going to have to bed me pretty soon, if you want to keep up our game," she said.

He watched her sip the clear wine, meeting his eyes over the rim of the glass. He'd thought about this himself – it was clear from the condition that he'd left his sheets in, if from nothing else, that they two of them weren't intimate. That would start rumors, as well, however they wouldn't be useful.

Too many questions surrounding them would have people standing back to watch, not participating, and that would neutralize Jean.

"Plan to spend the night here, tonight, then," he informed her.

She nodded. "So dies your noble nobility," she commented.

He frowned. He didn't want to make a statement like, "I do this for the Empire," and find her gone by the afternoon, however he couldn't sustain a comment like that on his honor, either. "My nobility isn't something that I put in other hands to measure," he informed her, finally. "If you find me quite unbearable, Jean, find an opportunity to hide bed clothes here and feel free to make yourself comfortable on one of the couches."

She smirked and set her glass down. Reaching out her right hand to his cheek, she didn't stroke his skin as much as feel it.

"I gave myself to another man once," she said, "for reasons of my own. I paid a heavy price for that, and still do. In the end, I didn't find him unworthy of my affections, he found another more worthy than I. Let me assure you, I found that slight more painful than the sharpest dagger in my side.

"You may find it hard to give your body and not your love, your Highness," she warned him, "and only one of those is truly able to heal the scars that another might lay upon it."

With that she took his plate from him, and put it with his glass and hers on a tray. She picked that up and departed the chambers without another word, leaving Tartan watching her and wondering how something that seemed to come about so simply had become so quickly complicated.

***

Tartan didn't have to summon Lurien to him – the boy appeared in his same riding outfit from the weekend before, at the door to the chamber, just as Tartan had finished changing into his own.

"Your mother?" he asked the boy.

"Is supposedly in Volkhydro," Lurien informed him with that same, curious cat expression. "But yes, Jean informed me that we'd ride today."

"I apologize for the delay," Tartan said, standing before the one polished steel mirror in the room and making sure that he looked proper. He wore a rapier at his hip – mostly because the boy walked around armed, and therefore he really should, too.

"You do?" Lurien asked him. "Why?"

Not what Tartan expected. He looked the boy in the eyes. He'd never seen a brown so close to black – it was almost as if the boy had a giant pupil and no color at all.

"I made a promise to you, boy," Tartan said, moving past him and out the door. Lurien turned on his clubbed foot and followed him. "I should have kept it, and I didn't."

"You had to find Bastard, though," Lurien reminded him.

Tartan shook his head – he'd never had this problem getting someone to receive an apology from him. "Regardless," he said, "we'll meet with two of the Emperor's most important soldiers, and then we'll ride."

They thumped through the palace and up into another tower where he'd told J'her to have Daggonin ready for him. Soldiers and servants alike stood aside for him and lowered their heads – a deference befitting him as Heir, were he actually to *become* the Heir. Normally the Emperor would have an armed escort – even as the Heir himself, he'd never had less than twenty Wolf Soldiers more than an arm's reach from him. Tartan couldn't stand that sort of protection – he'd had it his whole life as a Prince and it drove him crazy not to have any privacy. Within the palace walls, he walked alone or with one or two advisors.

A meeting room took up one whole floor half-way up the guest tower. With room for twenty people in comfort, an oblong table with padded chairs ran across its middle, sideways to a balcony by an open doorway through which sunshine and a strong breeze filled the room, and two windows on the other side for the same effect. It was one of Tartan's favorite rooms in the palace – one both the Emperor and his father had rarely used. As a child he and his brother and sisters had come here to play their games, practice their art and just talk. Coming here now gave him a nostalgic twinge, remembering it.

Rather than a brother or a sister, he found an Uman Supreme Commander and a Colonel of the race of Men. J'her had brought a squad of Wolf Soldiers with him, leaving them standing at ease by the balcony. On the table they'd spread several rolls of parchment and weighted their corners down with colored stones.

"Your Grace," Daggonin said, standing. Tartan sighed. He didn't want to fight the issue with such an influential officer – one who clearly had the Emperor's ear – however he couldn't just let that go, either.

"Is there a reason why you're resisting referring to the person running the Empire at home right now as 'Your Highness,' Colonel?" Tartan asked, pulling out a chair from the table across from him.

Lurien pulled out the chair next to him, saying nothing. Daggonin raised an eyebrow and looked to J'her for support. J'her kept his focus on Tartan.

"Is there a reason that you're pushing that?" the Supreme Commander of the Wolf Soldier guard asked, in turn.

As a boy, King Glennen had caught Tartan in a fight with a larger boy once. The reason escaped him – probably one of a million slights that growing boys level on each other as they forge each other into men. Tartan had expected a reprimand from his father, a comment on the behavior expected of a Prince. Instead Glennen had clapped him on the shoulder and praised him for not being afraid to fight, telling him, "So often, the fight goes not to the more powerful, but to the one who wants the victory more."

Lupus had told him the same thing. In the Second Invasion of Thera, Lupus had been cut off from his own troops and surrounded by Confluni. Where almost any commander would have put up his sword, or perhaps sacrificed his horse and run back through the armed warriors to where his own troops could save him, Lupus had pushed deeper into the ranks of the invaders until *they* gave way. That had opened up the path behind him, and *then* he had retreated.

"Don't be afraid to take on a larger enemy," he'd said, as Shela had fretted over the multiple wounds that he and his horse had taken. "Sometimes you'll beat them just by standing up to them. However, once you've won, don't stay when you're outmatched. Leave with your victory intact – because *that* is the defeat that they'll remember."

So many times, Lupus had quit the field victorious, with his enemy beaten but not vanquished. However, J'her would be a student of the Emperor, too.

Perhaps a twist on these two monarchs' teachings was needed?

"Yes," Tartan said, forcing himself to look J'her right in the eye and hold him. "One of two things is going to be decided right here, and right now, J'her. Either you're going to recognize and legitimize me as the regent of the Emperor, or I'm stepping down *right now*, in favor of you, and I'm going back to Angador."

That hadn't been what J'her expected. The Uman straightened, and Tartan knew that he'd called it right.

"You can't - *brhmm - mmm - mmm* - do that," the Colonel said.

"Watch me," he said, quoting an expression that he'd heard from the Emperor. "I'll take my horse and my Knights and I'll forget that Galnesh Eldador ever existed."

J'her and Daggonin looked into each other's faces.

They knew without saying anything. Every citizen in the Empire would be seething with, 'The Wolf Soldiers have taken over the capitol.' They wouldn't stand for it. There would be riots in the streets and demands for the Emperor to come home. His war would, essentially, be over, unless J'her was willing to implement marshal law.

If that happened then every Duke in the Empire, and every Earl and Baron with them, already stretched for gold after the damage done from the Confluni invasion, would withhold their taxes and demand for the Emperor as well. It would be even worse.

A noble had to run things in the capitol. They'd accepted Lee and they'd tolerated Tartan, but the moment the Supreme Commander of the Wolf Soldiers pushed a noble out of that seat and sat there himself, then it was a military coup.

"We'll send to Thera for *brhm -ha!* Two Spears," Daggonin challenged him, but J'her raised his hand.

By the time the Emperor's brother-in-law could get there, if he even came, then it would be too late. In fact, it could even be made to look like Two Spears was *retaking* the capitol, and then there would be rumors of civil war.

"I'm not standing down the Wolf Soldier guard for the Angadorian Knights," J'her said, finally. "I'll call you regent in Chawnee's name, if I must, but this is Rancor Mordetur's nation, not yours, and if you think to rename for the Stowe's – "

"I have no intention to retake the throne in my father's name," Tartan said. "Believe me, I don't want it. It is the Emperor's order that my Knights guard the Princess, we'll keep that role. As well, the outlying guard to the city is more suited to my Knights than your Wolf Soldiers."

"But not the wharves," J'her argued.

"Nor the - *brmm-ha!* - Andurin Peninsula," Daggonin added.

J'her looked sideways at him, "His Knights already have the center of the country," he said. "What need has he for the Peninsula?"

"However, I agree, regardless," Tartan informed them. He hadn't considered that, but it was true. Were he to become an usurper, then he'd just divided the nation in two.

It occurred to him that this might have been what J'her had feared all along.

J'her and Daggonin straightened, and Tartan with them. Each warrior made a fist over his heart, saluting Tartan.

"Then rule well, in regency for the Princess, your Highness," J'her said, as senior officer.

He nodded – the Emperor didn't salute back so he didn't. They dropped their hands to their sides and turned their attention to the papers that they'd brought to the meeting.

"If we can agree on that," Daggonin said, indicating one of the parchments, a map of known Fovea, "then - *brm-brm-ha* - I think we are on a better path to decide what to do with these instructions that I bring from the Emperor."

***

Almost two hours later, a grim-faced Tartan almost marched himself from the meeting, Lurien thumping along behind him. The boy hadn't made a sound the entire time – he'd watched them with his curious cat eyes, fascinated by the things they did and said.

"What was your opinion of that, boy?" Tartan demanded of him.

Lurien considered. "Well," he said finally, as they approached the bottom of the stairs, "First thing – you got them to recognize your rule. You can have anything you want, now."

Tartan gave a little chuckle, turning to the right at the bottom of the stairs and heading down a long, stone passage to the Imperial stables. The passage was empty, but he heard voices none-the-less. Keeping the palace clean was an all-day, every day job, and someone was always cleaning something somewhere, so Tartan didn't worry about it.

"And what do I want?" he pressed the boy.

Again, the consideration. Tartan couldn't help admiring the job that Jean had done with Lurien. Most boys would blurt out the first thing that came into their heads – himself included at that age – but this one played with the problem like any feline, tested it and turned it upside down before he answered.

"You don't want to rule the Empire – you've had too many chances to have that," Lurien said. "You don't want to be left alone, either. You could have that, too."

"You seem to have done a good job figuring out what I don't want," Tartan said, turning a corner. The voices were closer here, but hushed. It had to be a unique acoustic of the stone passage that he could hear them at all.

He looked down into Lurien's curious cat eyes. "Mother taught me that, when solving a problem, eliminating unlikely answers can make the likely more clear," he informed Tartan.

Tartan nodded. He'd seen the Emperor do the same thing, and done it himself.

"I think you want to keep this part of the Empire safe, so that your own part to the south remains secure," Lurien said, finally. "You spoke of going back there and forgetting the capitol – you had to be ready for them to call you on that promise. You want to preserve Angador by preserving Eldador."

Tartan nodded. That was as much as he'd let himself admit, anyway. There was a deeper need – he wanted to show the Emperor himself that Glennen's son could run things, could be trusted by him; that Tartan Stowe had enough of his father in him to keep the Empire together.

Tartan stopped dead in the passage. He heard the murmuring clearly now, deep in a passageway running to the east of the palace. He heard both a male and a female voice, both with Uman accents, urgent in their tone, clearly arguing.

Lurien stopped next to him, the boy's eyes searching his face. Anyone else might have just kept walking, however Tartan had grown up in the palace, and he knew the way life went here.

Servants, warriors, courtiers and nobles – these are the people who populate the royal estate. Servants speak gaily when they think they're alone, and not at all among others. Warriors speak only when they have to, mostly listening for orders. Nobles seek to speak over each other, to draw attention to themselves. Most court barons couldn't whisper if they tried. Courtiers might speak in hushed tones, but wouldn't be meeting in the dark recesses of the palace, risking being overheard. In fact, most intrigue happened outside of the palace, on trails and in taverns or the market place.

Hushed, urgent conversation stopped the Prince-turned-Duke in his tracks because it had no business here, unless it spoke of imminent action.

"Are you any good with that dagger of yours, lad?" Tartan asked Lurien, sliding his own slim rapier from its sheath as slowly as he could.

"Mother taught me – " he began, then his head whipped around behind him.

Six Uman in plain leather vests and leggings charged down the corridor behind them, their faces masked with black bandanas, short stabbing swords already drawn. Tartan recognized the preferred weapon of the Wolf Soldier guard.

They ran two-by-two, the passage confining them. Tartan pushed the boy behind him with his left hand, taking the *en garde* with the sword in his right, pointing his left toe forward and turning his right foot sideways behind him. The passage would keep them from getting around him, meaning that, at least for the now, the boy was safe.

If they were smart, they would go for the child and then use him to get Tartan to put up his sword. Tartan wouldn't fall for that, and he didn't want to see the boy die.

"Pull it, then," Tartan informed him without looking away from the charging Uman, "because you may need it soon enough."

The front two Uman closed, the first swinging his sword in a downward chop, the second swinging low, right to left, going for a knee. Tartan instantly recognized that they'd worked together before. The second row would be stabbing, pushing past the first to needle him as he countered the more imminent threat. The third row would run right past him.

The light rapier caught the chop in mid-air, directing it harmlessly to the inside, even as Tartan's sword point described a figure-eight in mid-air and cut the second Uman across the bridge of his nose. A steel edge pinked his doublet even as the Uman whom he'd cut on the front row pulled back, the two warriors behind him crashing into him. The other Uman from the front recovered his weapon and pulled back for a thrust while the Uman behind him struck low for a knee.

Tartan wrapped the front Uman's sword up with his own, turning sideways, using both weapons to block the chop to his knee. The Uman stood side-to-side with him for a moment, looking into his eyes from over the bandana, then let out a loud moan and slipped back against the wall. Tartan felt more than saw Lurien at his hip, pulling his dagger from the doomed man's groin, spinning back behind the Duke.

The three on the right were back on their feet, one wiping the blood from his face. The two on the left pulled back together, the one in front aiming high, the one behind going low, knowing that they couldn't take him, but forcing him back so that all five could address him at once.

Tartan pulled his sword free from the dying man and pinned the closer Uman's sword to the wall with his own. His left hand took the other's right wrist, Tartan pulling the warrior past him and off balance where Lurien could finish him. The Uman whom he'd pinned punched him right between the eyes, making him step back, seeing stars.

He shook his head and, as if from nowhere, there was Jean leaping past him, dressed in her black leathers, a bandolier of daggers over her breast and one in each hand.

Tartan had never seen anyone or even any *thing* fight with a fury like that. The woman made a back-handed slash across one Uman's throat, driving the dagger in her left hand like a finger into the eye of the Uman behind him, still in mid-air. She landed on the ball of her left foot, spun and kicked the Uman next to Tartan under the chin, his head making a hollow sound as it collided with the stone wall, then she flipped the dagger in her right hand, catching the blooded blade by its point and hurling it at the third Uman on the right, catching him right in the breast. The warrior's eyes widened over the black bandana as he realized he'd been done in.

Tartan drove his fist deep into the stomach of the Uman next to him, then again, and again, as the last warrior threw his sword down, turned on his heel and retreated. Jean pulled another dagger from her bandolier and threw it, then the one in her other hand, after the fleeing man, bringing him down before he took ten steps. The Uman landed face down, tried to push himself up off of his face, then collapsed, bleeding out on the stones.

Tartan pulled the weapon from the hand of the Uman whom he'd struck and forced the warrior on his face, planting the instep of his boot on the back of the Uman's neck. He turned to his left to see that Lurien had, in fact, taken the second Uman in the stomach with his own blade, and stood over him now, the weapon dripping red, another dead warrior at his feet.

Seven, Tartan thought. He'd counted six, but they'd killed seven. Jean stood panting feet from him, her blood-spattered breasts heaving in her leathers, a look both of anger and exhilaration on her face. Here was a woman who sought the challenges of open, wanton combat, but who didn't mean to see them around her son.

She squatted down and pulled the black bandanas away from the faces of the Uman she and her son had killed. Tartan also realized that he hadn't taken even one himself. Yet, he was the only one wounded – a red stain growing on his doublet. He wiped his mouth with the back of his hand and looked for blood, but didn't see any.

"I don't suppose you know these, your Highness," Jean asked him, still panting, making the title a sarcastic point.

Tartan would have been more surprised if he had. Uman faces, easy enough to come by in Eldador, and Wolf Soldier swords were something that anyone could get anywhere. Of course J'her would confirm that these were not, neither had they ever *been* Wolf Soldiers, but then, that's what a suspicious regent would expect.

Tartan shook his head. "No," he said, "but someone went through a lot of effort to make sure that whoever replaced me thought that Wolf Soldiers did this, and I think I'd like to know who."

Chapter Five:

Deeper and Deeper

Tartan's father had informed him once that torture was the way a cowardly monarch held his nation, when he knew one day he'd lose it. Torture led to more torture, then to the type of desperate actions that those who wouldn't *be* tortured took, and finally the real enemy became the government that allowed it to happen.

The Emperor had told him something different – that is wasn't torture that made the monarch fail. If the monarch wouldn't do what he had to in order to defend his people and his reign then he'd lose both. The people expected that the monarch should be reasonable in what he did, whatever it was. Excesses were what separated a good ruler from a bad.

Everyone knew that Lupus the Conqueror would torture if he had to. When it came to his family there was practically no atrocity he was incapable of. Once, when the Bounty Hunter's guild had been focused on destroying him, they'd come after his daughter. The Emperor's wife had had caught the Bounty Hunter in the act and burned the man to ash. Lupus had thrown the ashes down the palace steps, warning that the next one would dream of this one's fate.

There hadn't been a next one, and though the Bounty Hunter's Guild howled over their comrade's fate, no one seemed to blame the

Emperor.

Tartan Stowe now had the one surviving warrior from the ambush on his person, hanging naked by his wrists in chains in a cell warded by protection spells both inward and out. A machine that made a gas from sheep droppings stood to one side; the Emperor had used this gas to interrogate prisoners. As a by-product it created a cleaning liquid that the palace staff swore by. Because of the latter, there was always plenty of the former, and Tartan was considering using it now.

"He breaths that, and of-a-sudden, his secrets aren't so important to him," J'her explained. He held a wooden cup with a copper tube connecting it to a long, steel vial. "We've used it successfully in the past."

"With no ill effects?" Tartan insisted.

Daggonin looked sideways at J'her, as did M'den, the Wolf Soldier Major whom most considered to be J'her's second in command. His own Angadorian Knight Lieutenant, Radmon Rukh, of the race of Men, stood behind him and to one side. Tartan didn't believe that these were Wolf Soldiers who had attacked him, however it was clearly time that he relied more heavily on his own people.

J'her smiled a little half-smile. "One time the copper tube broke," he said.

"The Empress told me a joke after that which I'd be embarrassed to tell in the barracks," M'den admitted. He was a slight Uman, with green hair much longer than J'her's, almost down to his shoulders. He wore Wolf Soldier grays and the steel sleeves of a commander, much like Daggonin.

Lurien kept looking at him for some reason, his wide-eyed cat-stare telling Tartan of his fascination with the warrior.

"Nothing more serious than that?" Tartan pressed them.

All of three of the Emperor's warriors shook their heads. "Lupus calls it 'laughing gas,'" J'her explained. "I've smelled of it – you simply become very content and at peace. It isn't that your secrets are forced from you, you simply don't care about them anymore."

Tartan nodded. Hardly torture then. He'd heard of a Dorkan Wizard whom Lupus had interrogated with the stuff; however stories twist like snakes over time in the palace.

"Proceed, then," he said. "We've a 'sayer available, regardless?"

J'her nodded. "On his way," he said. "Even those who resist the gas at first will eventually give up the truth if you bother them enough, and the 'sayer let's you know when that happens."

Truthsayers, which had been known as the 'barely gifted' before Lupus' reign, came from those who had the minor gifts of spell casting, without the abilities to use them for anything worthwhile. No master would train them, no court would have them, they usually ended up trying to teach themselves, and either destroyed themselves or fell to what other casters called 'the black mind,' essentially the power of their spells destroying their brains. Lupus had begun a program whereby these *barely gifted* learned vey minor magix, like truth saying, detecting cracks in stone foundations, verifying persons' identities, and other simple skills which made use of their talents without overtaxing their abilities.

Now 'sayers existed in every aspect of society, and flocked to Eldador by the hundreds. Lupus had a knack for finding value in life's simple gifts and trading on them.

J'her sent M'den into the cell with the cup and copper tube, and himself took control of the valve at the top of the vial. "He'll try to hold his breath," J'her warned, "so let me know when he's ready to breath – "

"I *have* done this before," M'den informed him, a grin on his face. J'her shook his head. The Uman in the cell kept his head down, his breathing calm and coming in low, even motions. Tartan recognized the Bounty Hunter training for preparing ones' self for torture. Already, he knew most of what he needed to about this one.

"Did you note that, Tartan?" Rukh whispered into his ear from behind him.

"I did," he said. "Been a long time since the Bounty Hunter's guild gave any problem to the Imperium."

"Except for trying to kidnap the Empress and her children," Rukh informed him, "although that was looked at as a rogue action, not their own."

"Who believes anything they say anymore?" Tartan asked him. "What we know is that they always hated the Emperor, they probably always will, and if they can cause him some trouble at home – "

"If they can be *paid* to cause trouble at his home, you mean," Rukh said, "then I agree with you, Tartan – they'd as like take their chances."

Both Men turned their heads back to the cell. The prisoner was already hanging limp in his chains, breathing of the Emperor's gas. J'her was looking at Tartan now for direction.

"Please, proceed," he said with a wave of his hand.

M'den took the cup away from the Uman's face. The Bounty Hunter, if he was one, looked upwards at him from his chains, a grin on his face.

"Hello," he said.

"Hello to you," M'den greeted him. "I'm afraid I've forgotten your name."

"Trill," the Uman said. "Trill of Sental."

"Trill the Bounty Hunter?" M'den asked. He'd recognized the training, too.

Trill shook his head. "No, no, no," he said. "Not that. Not that for a loong time."

Well, Tartan thought, *there was news*.

"But Bounty Hunters not of the Guild don't hunt," M'den said to him.

"Oh, we do ok," Trill informed him. His gaze wandered to the other people outside of his cell. "Are we going to have a party?"

"Yes," M'den informed him. "We are – we're celebrating."

"Oh, good," Trill said. "The Angadorian Duke must be dead."

Tartan stepped behind the much-larger Rukh.

"Oh, yes," M'den said, looking over his shoulder at the rest. "We've all wanted him dead for a long time."

"Ha!" Trill barked a laugh. "Don't tell anyone *that* - we charged a mountain because so many loved him."

Tartan allowed himself a little smile.

"Well, not *everyone*," M'den pressed him.

"Well, o' course not," Trill agreed.

He didn't say anything more, and started humming to himself. Tartan sighed.

"So, will you be paid now?" M'den asked him.

Tartan recognized what he was trying to do – he didn't want to just say, 'Who hired you?' for risk of tipping the Uman off, so he was searching for a way to get the Uman to tell him on his own.

"Been paid," he said.

"In advance?" M'den asked. "They must be very wealthy."

"Who?" Trill asked. "The Duke?"

"No," M'den said, "the people who paid you."

"I dunno," he said, and then he straightened. "And, y'know whut? I don' care. Yanno why I left the Guild for the Roo – um, yanno why I left the Guild?"

"Tell me."

Trill shook his head. "Because I got no love of nobles," he said, then spat on the ground at his feet. "Eveave's good justice to all of them – that's whut I say. I like Sental just fine because there ain't no nobles in 'er."

"But the person paying you was a noble," M'den pressed him.

Too soon, Tartan thought immediately.

He was right – the Uman took a squinted-eyed look at M'den, and shut right down. The Wolf Soldier grilled him for another hour, gave him more gas, but nothing could make him tell them more about the ones who'd hired him."

Finally, M'den came out of the cell, just as the 'sayer arrived.

"Well, that was useless," M'den complained. Tartan shook his head.

"We know that they were after me," he said, "not trying to put off the Emperor. We know that we have someone hiring retired or former Bounty Hunters, and we know they're nobles."

"We know that people love you, too," J'her said. "It does us a little good, but not much."

"We'll let him hang for a couple days, get the gas out of him," M'den said, "then take a more direct approach. I'll let you know when we've –"

"You will *not*," Tartan informed him.

"Your Highness," J'her said, and took a step closer to him, "if you fear the ramifications of torture, I can assure you the Emperor –"

"The Emperor," Tartan said, "is on his campaign, probably on a ship in Tren Bay. I am a son of Adriam, not War, and I am not going to have you touch hot pokers to this person's skin or yank off his fingernails."

"There's other things – " J'her began, but Tartan shook his head.

"If he resists the gas…" M'den argued.

"Then he resists it," Rukh spoke up. He stood up right next to Tartan, and added, "You may work for a Man who sees torture as acceptable. I don't. You don't beat your enemies by becoming them."

"Or worse than them," Tartan added.

J'her just shook his head. "Based on my experience, as Supreme Commander of the most effective force on Fovea, under the most powerful Man on Fovea, I can pretty much assure you that that is *exactly* what you do. When it comes to alive or dead, your Highness, second place is just not acceptable."

Tartan wouldn't hear it and he wouldn't justify it anymore. His father's words rang in his ears. "Find another way," he said. "Or leave him be – maybe his hunger will convince him."

M'den looked at J'her. "Won't work," he complained.

Tartan turned on his heel – sensing more than seeing Lurien and Rukh fall in behind him. It sickened him that anyone would put *that* much energy into arguing why he should torture someone else.

Before he could ascend the stairs up out of the dungeon, he heard Daggonin telling J'her, "The worst part is that now he's going – brrhhhrrrm – to have that boy thinking the same thing."

Tartan resisted the temptation to turn back around.

***

The gelding stood staring at them in his paddock, his ears back, his head down. When Lurien approached him, the horse turned his butt to face the boy – a warning of what it meant to do if pressed on the issue.

Tartan knew this horse, and it was as calm as he could want – perfect for the young man to learn on. Where war horses had deferred to the boy, this one wasn't having him.

Lurien sighed. "Are you sure we have to use this one, Tartan?" he asked.

Tartan crossed his arms over his chest. He'd spotted the boy's mother to one side of the stables, pretending to be talking with the staff. They'd enjoy the evening meal soon, so there was nothing for her to do.

He hadn't missed that the boy had spoken to him in the familiar. He caught the child's eye and held it.

"You'll refer to me as, 'your Grace,' if you please, young Lurien," he said, his voice an octave lower.

Lurien frowned. "Radmon Rukh called you, 'Tartan,'" he said, regarding him with that cat-like stare.

Tartan held Lurien's stare with his own. Yes, he thought, his Angadorian Knight Lieutenant had called him by his first name, just as Wolf Soldiers called the Emperor by his nick-name 'Lupus.' Tartan had learned at the Emperor's side, and had emulated him with his Knights.

He wasn't about to explain that to the boy. He'd given an order as a Duke and a mentor, and that was the end of it. Finally, Lurien looked away.

"When you're on a trail in the middle of Eldador and you've a choice between walking and riding him or one like him, what will you do?" Tartan asked him.

Again, like the Emperor, he'd made his point and then dropped it. Harping on a thing stole from its relevance – this lesson would stick better in the boy's mind if it ended oddly like this.

"You should be able to mount any horse, any time, and ride, once you're trained," Tartan continued. "If you leave it up to the horses, you'll walk."

"But he doesn't like me," Lurien argued.

"You know that already?"

"I can tell," Lurien said. "He doesn't – I don't know. He doesn't *feel* right."

"You haven't gotten close enough to feel him."

"No, in the head," Lurien insisted. He looked around him and saw another horse in another paddock – an uncut stallion barely broken to the saddle.

"What about him?"

Tartan laughed. "I wouldn't even ride him," he said. "Not without a healer present."

Lurien shook his head and stumped out of the paddock. 'Well enough,' Tartan thought. He wouldn't let the boy get on the horse, of course, but let him get bit and he might learn some discipline.

That's what Tartan had needed. He'd wanted to ride the wildest horse in the stables, until the day his father let him.

Lurien put his hand in the carrot pouch and pulled out a large one with the end still attached. Swinging it, he stumped over to the stallion's paddock, both the gelding and the new horse watching him.

"That will get a hand on him," Tartan warned, "but you can't bribe him every time you want to ride, or you'll ruin him."

"I know," Lurien informed him. He slipped the carrot under his belt, behind his back, and put his hands on the steel paddock rails.

The stallion gave the rails a resounding kick – what the Emperor called a 'mule kick,' standing on his fronts and kicking with both back feet. Tartan hadn't realized that the horse had been shod already – the paddock rail crumpled from the strength of a horse nearly 1,700 pounds heavy.

"Lurien!" Tartan warned him. "Back from there!"

But the boy, of course, didn't listen, and extended a hand to the angry animal. A stable hand came around the far corner of the paddock, ten stalls down, to see what the ruckus was, while Tartan leapt up off of the bench he'd been on to run to the boy's rescue.

His mother did nothing, watching.

The stallion kicked again, and again, the steel railing finally flying from the posts it had been attached to. Turning faster than should be possible for such a large beast, the stallion leapt over the wreckage into the same space as the boy.

Now they were all in real trouble – the stallion would be confused, his adrenalin pumping, and would instinctively lash out at whatever had irritated him. Lurien regarded him unmoving with that cat-stare, as if all of this were a play and he safely in the theater.

"Lurien!"

The stallion reared and, remarkably, Lurien came nearer to him. The stable hand called out the 'horse free' warning to the rest of the stable hands and came running – Tartan from the other side. Much as he wanted to sweep in and protect the boy, he forced himself to stop, to wait, knowing that if he added to the chaos, then all he'd do is ensure that both of them were trampled.

Better to let the handler who knew stallion take him, and hope that the goddess Life chose to smile on the boy.

Neither got the chance. The stallion came down on all fours, almost nose-to-nose with the boy and, as Tartan would have told him *never* to do, the boy looked him right in the eyes with that cat-stare.

The beast subsided, just as the mare before had. The stallion was an Eldadorian – he'd been bred for war – his nature was to run down unknown warriors without hesitation.

But he lowered his nose to Lurien, and Lurien stroked the side of it. Even a colt wouldn't have been so gentle. Lurien whispered something to the horse that Tartan couldn't hear, then turned his back on him and led him without touching him to the tack room, past three gape-mouthed Uman of the stable crew.

"Well," Tartan mumbled to himself, "isn't this just a day full of surprises?"

***

Lurien ran the horse ragged before they could put it up. They ended up riding through dinner, and until the darkening sky made riding too dangerous.

Afterwards Tartan dismissed the tired boy and called for dinner in his personal chambers. There appeared Jean again, a serving tray and wine in her hands and a look on her face that said that she'd be staying.

"Your meal, my lord," Jean informed him, closing the door behind her with her heel. She'd dressed in a demure palace gown, with a full skirt and bodice closed up to her neck. Nothing like the leather-clad warrior who'd saved him hours earlier.

She stood before the door, the tray at the level of her hips, and added, "Shall I be your appetizer, or your desert?"

Tartan smiled and shook his head, pointing to the caw-fee table by the room's couch. "Lay the tray there and serve us," he instructed her. "You can take off the dress if you like – I can't imagine that it's too comfortable."

"Your will, my lord," she said. She set the tray down, a pile of meats and vegetables fried in oils and herbs. The smell of it washed over him like a wave and Tartan's stomach growled. Riding took a lot more energy than most people realized, and instructing even more. His student had been eager.

"Your son must be famished," Tartan commented, as Jean stepped back and reached behind her for the clasps of her palace dress. "He'll be sore tomorrow."

"Sore or not, all he'll want to do is to ride," Jean commented. "I put food in front of him and it all disappeared before I left for here. He's probably dreaming of that stallion even now."

"I can't imagine how he does that," Tartan said, stabbing at the plate with a two-pronged fork.

The dress slipped down from around her shoulders, then she pushed it past her hips. Beneath, she wore her leathers, the bandolier around her middle. Tartan barked a laugh. "I wondered how you were so ready to take on those Uman," he said.

"Ever at your service, my lord," Jean said, smiling. She reached across the tray and popped open the wine bottle, an elegant red that Tartan recognized. As if to prove a point with him, rather than pour him a glass, she tilted the bottle back and took a mouth full.

Then she leaned across the caw-fee table, took him by the back of the head and pressed his lips to hers. Her tongue slid into his mouth and she exhaled the wine into him. He felt his eyes open wide, felt her kiss turn into a grin on his lips, just before she withdrew.

"Do you approve of the wine, my lord?" she asked him.

"Almost as much as the vessel."

Chapter Six:

A Close Shave

Tartan bedded Jean two nights in a row, then missed four for her 'female reasons.' She was a warrior as a woman and a warrior as a lover, taking what she wanted, pinning him down by his shoulders most of the time. She bit, she scratched, and in the end she left him panting, feeling more like conquered territory than a lover.

Where his own wife had simply lain for him, whispering in his ear and encouraging him, Jean had her demands and wasn't shy about them.

Waking alone, a week after he'd been attacked by the seven Uman pretending to be Wolf Soldiers, Tartan actually found himself missing her, until he realized that she was there.

"Hullo," he grumbled, pulling the quilts from the bed around him. Jean was dressed in her demure palace gown, billowing blue skirt and tight bodice up to her neck. The ruffles down the front seemed to contrast her large breasts to her flat stomach.

"I've brought you breakfast, m'lord," she informed him, indicating a tray with eggs, bacon and thick crusts of buttered bread.

He raised an eyebrow and looked to the window. The sky shown red in the first inkling of the true dawn. Normally he'd sleep another hour.

"Rearranging my schedule for me, too, now?" he asked her.

She smiled and turned her back on him, reaching for a pitcher and a glass. She poured his milk for him as he slid from the warm bed to touch his feet to the cold stone floor beneath. The Emperor had been the last resident of this room, as Heir, and apparently he'd not cared for carpets by the bed. Of course, if the Emperor didn't do it, then he couldn't.

He wondered if Lupus had felt the same way about Tartan's father.

"Colonel Daggonin is for Uman City," Jean informed him. "Left this morning with one hundred Eldadorian Regulars as escort."

Tartan raised an eyebrow. The Colonel should have asked his leave, as the regent of the Empire and for Galnesh Eldador's only Duke. This wasn't good news.

"You saw him?" he asked, slipping into his night shirt.

She turned and reached his glass of milk to him. "I finally managed to bed him last night," she said. "The man's a pig, but he's a pig with a conscience. I suppose he decided that it didn't count if he is off to war."

Tartan took the milk. He suddenly didn't like the idea that this woman was warming other beds. Spying is what brought her here, of course, and he couldn't have her beating the information out of these people, however he couldn't help feeling like she was offering something that was his.

She looked into his eyes and smiled that knowing smile of hers. She reached out her hand and stroked the side of his face and said, "No need for dark looks, my lord. The man is older and didn't have a younger man's appetites."

"What does *that* mean?" Tartan asked her, drinking.

"Well," she said, and turned away from him to arrange his meal on the caw-fee table. "For one thing, he liked to have his –"

"Enough!" Tartan barked, almost dribbling his milk back into the glass. "For War's sake, woman – is there no question you won't answer?"

He heard her chuckle, then she turned and said, "A wise man once said, 'If you don't want to know the answer, don't ask the question.'"

Tartan skirted around the far end of the caw-fee table and said, "I heard the Emperor say that once."

"And so," she informed him.

Sitting, he took a two-pronged fork and started to work on the meal before him. She uncovered a piece of ham under his napkin, browned on the side he could see, still steaming. She must have come straight from the kitchens.

"Your loyal Colonel," she informed him, sitting on the arm of his couch, "has orders to march on Andaron – specifically Chatoos."

"Not Talen?" Tartan asked her. Chatoos had been built at the mouth of the Safe River, bordering Conflu. It had been heavily fortified against any attack, and the Andarons considered it their strongest city. Talen, on the other hand, lay close to Eldador, and just outside of the Aschire forest. The way the Aschire loved Lupus the Conqueror, it would be an easy victory and far less expensive to hold than Chatoos.

"I thought the same," Jean informed him. She shook her head and stood, crossing the room to Tartan's toilet stand, and returning with a comb and a straight razor.

"What do you plan to do with *that*?" he asked her through a mouth full of ham and eggs.

"Groom you, of course," she said. "You're like the Emperor – you don't care how you look. Half of the palace staff is talking about it."

He took another bite and she left again and came back with the basin and a cloth. He continued to feed himself as she wetted and then worked on his hair.

"Ugh, what a tangle – does your wife send you out like this?" she asked him.

Tartan smiled and reached for his milk. "Actually, she says the same things that you do," he admitted. "I have three Uman grooms at the palace in Angador, and I can assure you that I don't miss any of them."

"They must all be males," she informed him, off-handedly. She deftly dragged a comb through his thick hair and trimmed an inch off of the side, then commenced to pulling and trimming the rest.

"You know how to do this, too?" he asked her.

"I, my Lord, am a mother," she said, not taking her eyes off of his hair as she worked. "I've been doing my son's hair since he started growing it."

Tartan hadn't even considered that. Of course, the commons would have to do each others' hair cutting. Who among them had the money for personal groomers?

"Don't make me look like your son," he told her.

She stopped, took him by the chin, the razor held absently in her hand, and tilted his head up to look into her eyes. "What's wrong with my son's hair?"

"There's nothing wrong with his hair," he said, eyeing the razor. "But if you start making me look like him –"

"Enough speculation already," she said, and pushed his chin back to where it had been. "No need for someone to go to Volkhydro to investigate his heritage."

"Exactly."

She sighed, and continued trimming him. He finished his meal between her motions, eating very little of his own hair, then sat quietly for her to finish.

"He's taking twenty thousand," Jean commented, off-handedly.

"Hmm?"

"Daggonin," she said. "He's taking twenty thousand Eldadorian Regulars."

"Theran Lancers?" he asked. She shook her head.

"The Therans are in Volkhydro," she informed him. "They turned the Battle of the Foveans at Medya with the Emperor's Canine Corps. Supposedly, he has another thousand of *them* that he's bringing, too."

The Canine Corps were the Emperor's answer to enemy horsemen. He'd trained huge dogs, some even more than the weight of a man, to leap at horsemen, avoiding their lances if they had them, and to knock them from the saddle. The dogs were raised not to be aggressive but friendly, considering the whole thing a game, so that they wouldn't ravage the fallen warriors, but go on to the next. When they weren't knocking down riders, they herded the horses and held them.

Some of these had been trained with Tartan's Angadorian Knights, and he had to admit that the idea was a good one. A Knight knocked from his horse, if the fall didn't kill him, was pinned by the weight of his own armor. Where mounted warriors might be so well trained that they prevailed even three-to-one, the dogs could unhorse ten to their number in a fraction of the time. They were much less expensive to train and to maintain than mounted Knights.

"I didn't know he had so many," Tartan commented.

"I think he's bringing some down from Volkhydro," Jean said, pushing his head forward to scrape the back of his neck. "According to

Daggonin, Volkhydro fell surprisingly easily."

Vulpe Mordetur, the Emperor's son, had invaded Volkhydro with 35,000 foot, 1,000 Canine Corps, and taken Volkha, renaming it Lupha in his father's name. He'd then marched East and taken Medya with his father's help and 25,000 warriors, then Hydro at the mouth of the Llorando with his remaining 20,000, and 2,000 Theran Lancers, leaving 10,000 in Lupha and a mere 1,000 in Medya, rebuilding the city as a port with the help of the northern Dwarves. Now the Emperor maintained a huge army at the renamed city of Hydrus, perched on the border of Sental.

Everyone expected his next objective to be Sental. Sentalans had been flocking to Eldador for ten years to seek land and a better life. The Sentalan nation was one of farmers who, until the Emperor had come to Eldador, had fed the rest of Fovea and grown fantastically wealthy. The state owned the farms in Sental and all persons were employees of the state for their entire lives. An Eldadorian man owned his own land and did what he wanted with it, paying a straight fifteen percent tax for the protection and the glory of the Eldadorian Empire.

Sental, it was expected, would fall to Eldador without a fight, so of course the Emperor didn't choose it.

"When does he hope to land?" Tartan asked.

Jean raised Tartan's head up with a finger under his chin, then began wetting his face with the towel and water from his basin. If Tartan hated anything, it was to be shaved. He usually let himself go for as much as a week, until he felt the prickle of his beard against his pillow at night, between shavings.

"You have such baby-soft skin," Jean commented.

Tartan groaned inwardly. All his life he had been reminded that he'd inherited his mother's features – her soft looks, her kind eyes, her willowy frame. His father had been a brick of a Man, broad and strong and severe. No one every claimed that Tartan reminded them of his father.

No one.

"His landing?" Tartan pressed her.

"Hmmm?" Jean said, scraping his cheek with the razor. Where normally this was somewhat painful, Jean's delicate touch didn't seem to hurt at all.

"Daggonin," Tartan said, letting the exasperation come through in his voice. "When does he hope to land in Andoron?"

"Ah," Jean said, and turned his face by the chin to get at his other cheek. "A month, at most," she told him, not looking in his eyes. "The warriors are marshaled in Uman City."

That made no sense, Tartan thought, as Jean delicately scraped around his mouth. The Emperor had the ships to move 35,000 or more at a time. Again, he should have marched them through the Aschire forest and taken Talen, then Chatoos if he wanted it.

"You don't believe it either, do you?" she asked.

"Hmm?"

She turned his face right into hers, still holding onto his chin, and said, "The numbers, the time – they make no sense. Why isn't he rolling up Sental, especially if he's taken a Dorkan city? He could as like meet his Daff Kanaar allies in Sental Two with the troops he already has on the field, and before the end of the War months. Without Sental, Fovea starves."

"And with it," Tartan said, wincing as she did his neck, the blade finally becoming dull, "he has more grain than he can handle, and nothing to do with it."

Jean stopped and looked into Tartan's eyes again.

"How do you mean?" he asked.

Tartan had it, finally. He'd just needed to have the whole thing laid out for him before he saw. "Lupus' erk – nomics, this plan he has for making money."

"What of it?"

"He taught me once about supply and demand, and how delicate it is, and how you have to balance how much of a thing you make, with what you can get for it," Tartan informed her. "A farmer, for example, wants to grow as many crops as he can."

"So he'll be rich," Jean said to him, and started work on the other side of his neck.

"So he thinks," Tartan said, "but *every* farmer thinks that, and every farmer produces as much as he can. So what happens when everyone has as much as he or she can eat?"

"Hmmmm," Jean said. "Well, for one, they get fat."

Tartan chuckled – Jean pulling the blade away from his throat and giving him a warning look. He subsided and let her finish him, then took the cloth from her to wipe himself off with.

"When they have as much as they can eat," Tartan told her, "they stop spending their gold and silver on food, and start spending it on other things. So the farmer has all of these crops, and they aren't worth as much, or anything, because no one wants them."

"So the farmer doesn't get rich, unless he was the first one to market," Jean said.

"And so he is a very angry farmer," Tartan said, "who has to plow his crop back into the soil and hope to do better next year."

"Well, perhaps he lets his crop go to seed," Jean said, "and sells the seeds –"

"Some do that," Tartan said, "but then next year you have even *more* crops from those seeds…"

"And the problem gets worse," Jean said.

"So part of Lupus' plan is to pay what he calls 'speculators,' who travel Fovea for the government, and give free advice to his farmers and whoever else wants it, on what crops are being produced, by whom, and in what quantity. Not just in Eldador but in Sental as well."

"And you think that these speculators have told him that if he mixes the Sentalan crop with the Eldadorian crops –" Jean said.

"He must believe that, right now, taking Sental would put too many crops in the market, and cause unrest in new-conquered territory," Tartan said, and threw down the towel.

Jean shook her head. "But the Confluni army just ran through the center of Eldador," she said. "They destroyed crops and livestock – the speculators couldn't have predicted that."

Tartan considered. "The speculators usually predict for the next year, though," he said. "It's no good to know that the world needs wheat once you've planted barley. If the Emperor still has his speculators out, they're focused on next year's harvest, not this."

"And next year's harvest should be bad for Eldador," Jean said.

"Meaning that the Emperor may have planned to take Sental after all," Tartan said, "but instead is waiting for next year, because he needs their food now –"

"And will need it even more next year," Jean finished for him.

They looked into each other's eyes.

This whole way of thinking was new. Before the Emperor, each harvest had been a mystery. Famine came on the heels of a bounty – sometimes there was no beer because no one planted barley, and at others brewers dumped their kegs into the city streets because there was no money in selling it. Lupus had brought logic to what he called the 'eck – on – omee,' and he used that logic now as he planned to conquer the known world.

His father, Tartan knew, had no head for any of these things.

Like most rulers, he was baffled by what to plant, and didn't expand his nation because he always had a shortage of something. In fact, Lupus' Daff Kanaar mercenaries had made expansion more possible and more likely, because they provided needed soldiers to countries that couldn't support producing them.

"Imagine what the Emperor could accomplish, with thinking like that," Jean said, looking into his eyes, "if he wasn't so damn hungry to get his troops out onto the battlefield."

"Imagine what he'll accomplish," Tartan asked her, in turn, "and what he'll do when all of his battles are won."

***

Just as there was more to fighting wars than putting men into the fields, Tartan realized, there was more to ruling the Empire than giving orders and speculating on the Emperor's plans.

Tartan met with the Emperor's Shem Hannen daily. His father had commissioned four of them at the start of his reign to advise him and, as Tartan knew, to do most of the actual thinking for him. To his credit, Glennen didn't surround himself with people who just told him what he wanted to hear. Unfortunately, he didn't always listen to them, either.

Such meetings were conducted before every session of court. There was a favorite, windowless room to one side of the throne room, with a small, circular table and five chairs, a sconce set high in one wall for a torch with a mirror behind it. The room was ventilated well enough that they weren't gasping in the summer months but remained secure enough that they could be sure that no spy listened in on them. One door led here and a Wolf Soldier always guarded it.

When Lupus replaced Glennen, he'd kept three of the Shem Hannen and sent one, old Nevarre, with Tartan to Angador. Nevarre had been a wise and useful ally and would be advising Tartan's wife, Yeral, and his younger brother, Terran, now. The other three considered it their job to keep the Empire running, and grudgingly accepted Tartan's direction as regent, and only then because there was no one to tell them otherwise. J'her, he knew, spoke privately with them often, and Daggonin had, as well.

Little kingdoms within the kingdom – that's what Tartan's father had called these collections of power in the palace. Each could be counted on to be defended just as seriously as actual land would be, and by actual kings and dukes.

"Earldoms are screaming for forgiveness of their taxes,"

Datreve, the leader of the Shem Hannen, informed him. "You have ten waiting for you in court, now that you've recalled the court barons. Some of them actually arrived here before the barons that you recalled from their lands!"

Lee Mordetur had sent court barons – unlanded nobles with name and title but no property – into the Empire's earldoms as monetary advisors a month before she'd been abducted by the Uman-Chi. One of Tartan's first acts had been to recall them, thinking that they were an unnecessary burden on the Earls. Now he saw the Princess' logic. The court barons had kept the lesser nobility nattering about why they were here and what threat they might mean. Without that threat, the Earls were back to complaining of the cost of the war.

"Can we afford to cut their taxes?" Tartan asked them.

The Shem Hannen looked to each other, then back to Tartan. Clearly none of them had any grasp of the Emperor's erk-nomics, and expected him, as Lupus' most famous student, to guide them.

Lupus had spent countless hours trying to drill these ideas into Tartan's head, however the 'more from less' strategy was usually lost on him. In fact, it was the Emperor's wife, Shela, who usually did the best when it came to explaining how taking less tax from the Empire resulted in more revenue for its government.

"This is one of those things," Tartan said, finally, "where we're likely to do best by leaving what works alone."

"Then there are Earldoms that are simply not going to pay what they owe us," Haldarch, third among the Shem Hannen said.

All three Men, as well as Devarre, by some coincidence looked very much alike, and most people who didn't know them couldn't tell them apart. It was a joke throughout the palace that the Emperor called them '1,' '2,' '3,' and '4,' sometimes aloud without thinking of it, because he didn't know their actual names.

"I don't see why," Tartan argued. "If they make less, then we take less, don't we? I mean, they only pay on what they have."

The Shem Hannen looked between each other, then back at Tartan.

"We *have* informed them of this?"

"No, I think not, Lord Regent," Guerrin admitted. He was the fourth among the Shem Hannen, Devarre still being the second.

Tartan shook his head.

"Proclaim to all Earldoms that they may adjust their taxes to their lowered output, because of the invasion," he told them.

"However, inform them that we still employ the regional counters, and that if they take this measure as an opportunity to cheat, then the Emperor left His dungeons in good working order."

Datreve chuckled. "That he did," he said, "however I think we might go farther to remind them that he left his Wolf Soldier guard at home, as well, because no one doesn't know of old Yerel's fate for not paying his share."

That struck a chord with Tartan. While still the Heir, Lupus had hired himself, as a Daff Kanaar mercenary, to go to Uman City and to collect Duke Yerel's taxes. He'd deposed Yerel and later had him hanged. Tartan was married to Yeral, Yerel's commoner daughter.

Yes, as a Duke, he knew well what Yerel's fate had been.

"My apologies," Datreve caught himself. "I forgot myself – I didn't mean –"

Tartan waived it off. "Not a single thought otherwise, your Excellence," he said. "My father-in-law's example *should* serve as a warning to the Empire, especially in these trying times."

He was about to call an end to the meeting, and to begin the day at court, when an Uman messenger in the Emperor's green livery knocked on the small meeting room's door and begged to enter.

He handed a scroll with the royal seal to Datreve, who popped the seal open and read it. The Uman closed the door behind him while Tartan waited with the rest of the Shem Hannen.

"Hmph," Datreve said, finally, and cast the scroll onto the table. The other three leaned over it.

"What?" Tartan demanded.

"Dorkan has petitioned the Fovean High Council for aid against the unprovoked attack on Katarran, their most southern city," he said.

"We expected that," Guerrin said, still reading while he spoke.

"That, we expected," Datreve said. "What comes as a surprise is that the Emperor is sending his own man, the Green One of the Daff Kanaar, to sue for peace."

"What?" Tartan demanded. He snatched up the scroll, much to the chagrin of the two Shem Hannen who were trying to read it.

"Precisely," Datreve said. "In a month's time, it appears that Dilvesh, the Druid, will stand before the Fovean High Council and negotiate for an end to this war."

Chapter Seven:

Fosterlings

No one could possibly believe that the Emperor would sue for peace, especially in the wake of an abduction of his eldest daughter. Lupus the Conqueror had used the threat of action against Lee to inspire his warriors to sack Outpost IX. What vengeance would he be capable of now that they'd actually *taken action* against her?

Tartan had decided to release the news to the common people, and the palace buzzed with it. Some believed it was wonderful, other raged at the idea that they should stop with their victories so certain. Military people, both retired and current, argued the merits and the positions of stopping the invasion, especially with the Empire in so precarious a position.

Tartan met with J'her, M'den and his own Lieutenant Rukh in the same tower, at the same open room that he loved. He'd brought Lurien – this would be an important meeting for any fosterling to see. Already he was starting to think of the boy as his own responsibility, not quite as a son to him but as a cousin.

The two Uman were grinning wide – they probably knew exactly what was going on and reveled in the Emperor's brilliance. Tartan felt left in the dark and didn't know how to act, and that upset him.

"So I can assume that this is some ruse," he asked J'her.

J'her spread his hands, the smile still on his face. "I don't presume to instruct you, your Highness," he said. "The Emperor has sued for peace – I'm certain that he has his reasons."

"But you don't know what those are?" Tartan pressed him.

"As Lupus would say," M'den said, with a sideways look at J'her, "we don't need to know."

"It is good enough to believe in him," J'her added.

Tartan caught Rukh's profile out of the corner of his eye – the Man felt as frustrated as he. "You can't expect us to work in with the Emperor's plans if we don't know them."

"As far as you know," J'her said, "and as far as you need to know, the Emperor is doing exactly what he has to for the situation that he's in. You should act as you feel you should, and have faith that, if you need to act differently, then he will let you know it."

"Except that the Empire doesn't have Central Communications anymore," Rukh said, "and by the time we hear what the Emperor needs for us to change, then it could be too late."

"The Emperor is completely aware that he doesn't have Central Communications," M'den informed them. "He is doing what's he knows he has to do, and he's counting on you to do the same."

"Just run the Empire," J'her informed him. "Keep the gold flowing; keep the Earls and Dukes quiet. When you need to do something different, you'll either see it or you'll be told."

Tartan had been a student of the Emperor's for a decade – he knew the Man's arrogance and how impressed he felt with his own abilities. An all-out invasion of the rest of Fovea would, of course, be the ultimate proof to himself of his being the all-capable, all-powerful match for the combined minds of Fovea.

It would, of course, have levels within levels within levels, and tricks within traps within ambushes. He'd want to act it out to Fovea like a play to an amazed theater – he'd want a thundering applause in his own mind, to his own brilliance.

Tartan couldn't help thinking that it would blow up in his face like his Eldadorian fire. No one could watch all of the parameters alone. No one could out think the rest of Fovea, all at the same time.

Lupus might be brilliant, but that didn't make everyone who opposed him stupid.

Tartan stood, Lurien with him. "I shall take your good advice," he said, because there was nothing else *to* say. J'her would never help him, and Tartan had no way to force the issue.

He'd have to figure this out on his own.

***

Earls begging for more coin were relieved to hear that they still only had to pay a percent of what they produced, and if that amount was lower, then what they would pay was lower. They'd have to tighten their belts but they wouldn't starve, at least not entirely. Tartan sent messengers to his Dukes and asked for them to roll part of their taxes back into their earldoms, and to trade between the duchies in order to keep starvation to a minimum. He sent twenty ships, as well, to Sental, to buy futures on Sentalan grain and beef. He had to use his own money for that – the Eldadorian coffers were growing bare with the expense of more troops to pay and arm, and more ships to build, with earldoms and duchies paying less. Tartan had no problem with the expenditure, knowing the return he was likely to get.

Meanwhile, he kept up his lessons with Lurien, who demonstrated more ability each day, and maintained his relationship with Jean. The boy proved to him repeatedly that his gift with horse-kind was restricted to the most difficult and irascible of the herd. Horses which even the best handlers shunned immediately warmed to Lurien, while those more fit for a child his age would tend to shun him.

Meanwhile Jean spent her time trying to discover who wanted to convince the sitting Reagent that Wolf Soldiers had tried to kill him. J'her had proven himself to be ambivalent to the attack once he was sure that his own warriors hadn't perpetrated it. Tartan heard from Jean nightly for a week after Daggonin left, every time he bedded her.

"Nothing," she told him, again, her head pillowed on his chest, her hands on him. Lying naked with her, Tartan couldn't help thinking that he'd miss this when it came time to return to his wife.

His unfaithful wife.

"Well, being able to find nothing might tell us something, too," Tartan told her.

She turned her pretty green eyes up at him. Older than he, greyer, she still had moments when she could seem as young as a school girl, and that inquisitive stare of hers marked one of them.

So similar to her cat-like son.

"What do you mean?" she asked him. No more 'Your Grace,' or 'My Lord.' She'd become too familiar now.

"Common assassins wouldn't be able to cover their tracks so well," he said. "Even Bounty Hunters would have left something that our wizards could detect. These warriors were blanks, no past that magic could find, no one recognizing them at all. They fought like seasoned warriors, they fought together – this wasn't their first time."

"So, powerful magic," Jean said, looking away from him.

"Uman-Chi," Tartan said, and stroked her hair. "Even Dorkans aren't that good."

"Half of your Wizards *are* Dorkans," Jean agreed. "They'd recognize their countrymen's handiwork."

They discussed the assassins further, but there was little else to say. Someone wanted Tartan dead, and they wanted the death to disrupt the Empire and, if they hadn't been caught, then they'd try again.

But they'd be better at it next time.

***

Most of Blizzard's seed were unridable, the rest were particular to their owners. Bastard wouldn't allow anyone but the Hectaro on his back, and Little Storm wouldn't allow anyone but some traitor to the Empire called 'The Mountain.' That left a gray mare in the stables – one the grooms called 'Thunder Cloud.'

"She comes on you of a sudden," the Uman informed Tartan and Lurien. "Then she strikes you dead."

The groom had to have more than 100 years to him. His hair ran green-white past his shoulders. The end of his nose drooped a little, his lips ran pale and thin under brown eyes. The tops of his lobeless ears sagged back just enough to be noticeable. Dressed in groomsman's brown pants and vest with black leather boots and a white shirt, he moved on the balls of his feet, like he was trying to find stirrups to step into.

"She's killed?" Tartan felt his eyebrows knit in concern. Little Storm had killed, he knew. Blizzard had come close enough times where the Emperor groomed him himself.

The groom shook his head. "No," he said, "but she's thrown a Man as much as twenty-five feet."

Lurien, dressed in black leathers with a white shirt, had already moved to the mare's paddock. The mare was already moving toward him.

Jean held back with the house staff, watching. She probably wasn't aware that she had her apron twisted between her hands, but you could never be sure with Jean.

"What do you think, lad?" Tartan asked of him. He lined

himself up behind the boy, and sensed the groom behind him.

"She's angry," Lurien said. "Lonely."

"You sense that?" Tartan asked him.

Lurien shook his head. "I just... know it. She hates it here. She knows it's not where she belongs."

The groom snorted. "Perhaps she wants to be back up on the Wild Horse Plains," he said, "where her sire's from?"

Lurien shook his head. The mare was within a short jump of him now, curious, sniffing at him, arching her neck. Tartan recognized the behavior. Her knees had closed, her withers touched seventeen hands if one. "How old is this mare," he asked the air, turning his head to one side.

"Eight summers," the groom informed him. "She's the oldest of Blizzard's Eldadorian sire – the only older is a mare in the Long Mane's tribe."

The one that Lupus had created for Shela's bride price.

"What does she do?" Tartan asked him.

The mare actually put her soft nose into Lurien's hand now. The young squire rubbed it in a circle. She sidled closer, letting him rub, sniffing.

Jean wrung her apron like it was wet.

"She runs," the groom said. "Fast as I've seen, faster than Blizzard himself. She runs so fast, as the bravest of us, even the Emperor, can't stay on her. She don't stop, she don't turn. She runs full out, and Adriam help you."

"She wants to go away," Lurien informed them.

Then, without notice, he took a fist full of her mane, and the mare yanked her head up, and Lurien flipped up onto her proud arch like a rag doll.

Tartan and the groom lunged for the poor boy. Jean shrieked and tore her apron in half. The mare reared, and the boy slid down her neck to couch his bottom on her withers.

She spun and mule-kicked the gate to her paddock. It exploded in a storm of steel and splinters.

She was out before they could stop her, the boy clinging to her mane, the look on his face one of pure joy. The mare tore through the stable for the outer gate.

"The gate's closed," the groom told Tartan as they sprinted after the mare. "She'll kill 'im shore when she finds it."

"I wouldn't be too sure of that," Tartan informed him without turning. Around him, grooms were calling out the 'horse loose,' and sprinting to the outer gate.

That gate consisted of a forty-foot double-door of banded timbers, which stood open, and a six-foot high steel gate, which had been closed.

Tartan arrived just in time to see the mare clear the gate without even hesitating. Lurien's behind rose higher than his head, his little fingers clinging to her mane, as the huge equine touched down on the other side. The boy seated himself with a jolt as the mare turned south, tossing her long mane, her tail upraised behind her.

Tartan turned to the groom. The Uman stood with his mouth open.

"It's the last you'll see of 'im, my Lord," the groom said. "Is a miracle he clung on for the jump – ain't no man can hold on to that beast in full speed, and 'im without a saddle."

Jean ran to the gate, pushed her head through the bars, then pulled back, her green eyes searching for Tartan, her apron hanging in rags below her waist. She dared not communicate directly to Tartan but, when her eyes finally found his, they spoke volumes.

***

Tartan didn't bother sending a troop after Lurien and the mare – the horse ran too fast to catch, and the boy clearly hadn't fallen off. He might later, but when and where could be anywhere between here and the Wild Horse Plains.

Jean, of course, spent the day frantic. Tartan ordered her excused from her duties – she haunted the stables and the ground outside. Certain of the grooms and other stable hands sought to engage her, and the unluckiest of them returned to their duties with blackened eyes.

The day passed slowly. Tartan returned to the stables after a private dinner to collect Jean, when the boy finally returned.

The lather on the mare's sides dripped from her like the foam of a rough sea. Her tongue lolled. The boy drooped on her back, both hands on the ridge between her withers, blood flowing from between his fingers where her mane had cut him, his head down. Jean ran to him, pushing past the mare's head to collect her son alongside of her, Lurien collapsing into her arms. Two grooms put a rope around the mare's neck. One raised a crop.

"On your life," Tartan warned him. The Uman turned.

"She's got to learn," the male began.

"You'll learn a lesson worse than hers," Tartan told him, his hand on the sword at his side.

The grooms looked to each other, then at Tartan, and both nodded. Jean collected her son and fled back inside of the gate with her head down.

"Rub her down, water her and feed her what she'll eat," Tartan said. "Be 'ware she might colic. Be 'ware, also, that if you think to beat that horse while my back is turned – if I find a mark on her come morning, you'll drag from her pommel, one after the other."

Both nodded again. The poor, exhausted animal had returned home with her rider. Beat her now and she'd never make that mistake again. Little Lurien had tamed himself one of Blizzard's get, and Tartan wouldn't see that ruined now.

He watched the two Uman put up the exhausted mare. They rubbed her down and chatted in their own language, which he spoke. They didn't like Tartan's instruction but they'd follow it – when the Duke was sure of that, he went looking for young Lurien.

He found the boy in his own rooms, already tucked away in bed, a bowl of thick stew half-eaten by his bed side. Jean sat next to him, still wearing the torn apron. She turned on Tartan as he pressed the door to the boy's room shut behind him.

"*This* is how you teach him?" she demanded.

"This is what he learned," Tartan countered. "I don't know a thing about what I taught him, to be honest. I didn't do much more than give the boy his opportunities."

She turned away from him and hovered over her sleeping son. The boy snored lightly, barely moving. His crippled foot poked out from the sheets, a twisted, bent claw.

"You should be protecting him," Jean told him.

Tartan shook his head. "Protect a boy and he won't grow up to be a man," he said. "The Emperor put me in combat before I thought I was ready. I killed a man and puked down the side of my horse. His wife had to rescue me when the horse ran wild.

"I lived, and Lurien will live."

Jean looked into Tartan's eyes, then looked away from him, at her sleeping son, then back into his eyes.

"If you could go back?" she asked him. "If you could do it again – would you let the Emperor –"

"Would I watch myself go back into that battle, in Andoron,

against the Wet Bellies and the Drifters?"

She nodded but didn't say anything.

Tartan looked down, then looked back up again and met her eyes.

"Would I do it to myself?" he asked her. "No – I don't think I would. We aren't always strong with ourselves. That's why we have mentors.

"Would I do it with Lurien?" Tartan asked her. "Would I put him in a battle, if there were one to fight right now?

"Damn right I would," he said. "You're teaching that boy to be a cripple, and he's more capable than most of the Men I know. I'd put a sword in his hand and put him to my left side, and I'd tell him to survive as best he could, and I'd expect him to do it, like he did when those killers in Wolf Soldier garb attacked us."

Jean nodded. She stepped up to him until her breasts touched the front of his tunic, and she slid her hand into his hair.

"That's what I wanted to hear," she told him, and she kissed him deep.

Chapter Eight:

Roosters

Duke Tartan Stowe awoke the next morning to a barely whispered, "Your Grace, your Grace," coming from his doorway. He cracked open his eyes to see two of his Angadorian Knights, dressed out in their full armor, peeping into his room. The look on their faces showed a mixture of embarrassment and concern.

Jean stirred next to him, curling up in the warmth of the voluminous quilt. Tartan sighed – no way this wouldn't be making its way back to his wife now, he knew. Even the most loyal warriors were notorious gossips, and this was too good to keep a secret.

"What?" he grumbled, pushing himself up in bed.

His blurry eyes cleared slowly. Jean's insatiable passion had kept him up through the night. He'd actually begun to worry that there'd be get from his adultery. He knew his wife preferred her Uman servants because the two species couldn't breed.

"A call from the stables, your Grace," one said, stepping into the room, the other right behind him. "That mare that the boy ran off on has turned up lame."

Tartan swore and threw the covers aside. The Uman groomsman whom he'd forbidden to beat the horse had gotten even with him by not putting her up properly. She needed a hot mash now and to be rubbed thoroughly with wool blankets, or she could hang up a tendon in her legs and be ruined.

Beside him, Jean shifted where he'd exposed her behind, drawing back under the quilt. One of the Knights grinned openly and looked at the other who, better disciplined, kept his looks to himself.

They'd called him, 'your Grace,' it occurred to him. One was closing on him while the other had his back to the bed, moving toward the stand where his armor and sword hung. Tartan swung his legs over the side of the bed and felt Jean's billowy palace dress at his feet.

He'd never make it to the sword, but he knew what Jean kept hidden just below her bodice. Dressed in nothing but the twist of cotton wrapped around his loins, he squatted down next to the dress as if he was about to lift the garment off of the floor.

The closer Knight took a deliberate step toward him as the Duke's hand found the hilt of one of the daggers in her bandolier.

"Your Grace," the man began, reaching out his hand to take the dress.

It was Shela, not the Emperor, who'd taught him the dagger. She'd made it one of her favorite weapons, light and easy to hide. Curling his index finger over the weapon's crossguard, the weapon seated comfortably into his palm. He turned his head up toward the approaching Knight, pushed out as hard as he could with his legs and drove the weapon directly up into the flesh under the man's jaw, through the mandible, the roof of his mouth and then the brain.

The other Knight spun on one heel, drawing his sword in the same motion and kicking the door closed behind him. He stood armored and ready with the door and the Duke's weapons behind him. Tartan ripped the dagger from the dying man's jaw and planted his feet apart, his chest slick with blood and the weapon red in his right hand.

He'd never win against even a moderately well-trained warrior – and this one had been good enough not only to take the armor from one of his Knights, but to do it without marring the steel and giving himself away. Tartan flipped the weapon in his hand, took hold of the blade and threw it at the other man's face, seeking the eye.

He failed. The warrior ducked and the dagger planted itself in the door behind him. Tartan lunged for the other man's sword, taking hold of it at the crossguard with both hands. If he could wrest that from the false Knight, he'd take back the advantage.

The Knight's armored forearm crashed down on his shoulder, then against the back of his head. Tartan saw stars and his knees wavered.

Then the Knight slipped away from him, another dagger in his eye, and a third in the side of his neck, his life blood pumping out over his shoulder. Jean had joined the fight and stood beside him, red blood splashed across one breast and her stomach, panting. Tartan, his ears still ringing from the battering he took, pushed her behind him and snatched up the dead man's sword, approaching the door. It would make sense for there to be a guard outside of the room, he reasoned, and if one stood by the door, he might have mistaken the sounds of the fight for the sounds of a slaughter.

At the last moment, Tartan spun the heavy sword in his hand, pointing the blade back over his shoulder and leading with the steel knob on the weapon's pommel. He whipped the door open and revealed one more man, his back to the door, turning with his mouth open.

His eyes went wide as the steel pommel took him square in the forehead. One more blow to the side of the head dropped the man at the Duke's feet. Tartan had survived his second assassination attempt, once again with Jean at his side.

He'd been taught by the Emperor not to like coincidences.

***

In another part of the dungeons, a second assassin hung naked in a second cell, with a second apparatus for 'laughing gas' at the ready. Once again Tartan stood watching him with a dour-faced Radmon Rukh and an even more visibly-disturbed J'her and M'den.

Clearly there were problems with the security of the Imperial Palace at Galnesh Eldador.

"All he did was to call you, 'your Grace,'" M'den asserted. J'her nodded, standing next to him but focused on the prisoner.

On the day of Lupus' coronation as a King, an assassin had approached him with a glamour to disguise him as J'her, and given himself away by calling Lupus 'your Grace.' Wolf Soldiers all called the Emperor 'Lupus,' and by no other name. For that reason alone, Tartan had schooled his Angadorian Knights to call him, 'Tartan,' and it had actually paid off.

It probably wouldn't be long before all of the nobles in the Empire did the same thing, and then it would be pointless, but for today Tartan Stowe lived, and that was a good thing.

"This time there is no doubt that these were former Bounty

Hunters," J'her informed them all. "They infiltrated the city, as far as we can tell, as caravaners, then the palace as porters from the market place, then killed Uman servants in the supply depot, and waited there for days until two Angadorian Knights came seeking supplies. That many steps – only Bounty Hunters move like that."

"One more man and they would have been successful," Tartan admitted. In fact, it probably would have taken two more. Jean probably could have held her own against one more attacker, but one after that would have come in and defeated them while they were engaged. As far as J'her and M'den knew, Jean was in her quarters, frantic with shock. In fact she'd probably already slipped out and was trying to learn more throughout the city.

"We'll gas this one, then, and see what he knows, that the other wouldn't tell us?" M'den asked them both.

Tartan nodded. They thought they had a better argument for torture now, but Tartan still wouldn't hear of it. In his mind he still held that you don't beat your enemy by becoming worse than him, no matter what the Emperor and his vassals believed.

"I doubt very much that it will bring us more information," J'her asserted. He already had one of Jean's daggers in his hand. He hadn't released it since he'd personally pulled it from one of the Bounty Hunters' eye.

Such an experienced warrior should have seen right away that two had fought, not just the Duke alone, but J'her kept such opinions to himself.

"I must agree with that," they heard from behind them.

All four warriors turned, surprised, to see a cloaked figure standing in the shadow behind them.

The dagger flew from J'her's hand, but hung in mid-air before the individual's face. The lone stranger took a step forward, plucking the weapon from the air, as if it were an interesting thing that he'd encountered and not a weapon thrown to kill him.

Rukh reached across his waist to pull his sword, but Tartan put a hand on his shoulder to stay him. He took a step toward what he recognized as a Druid and extended his hand, even as the two Wolf Soldiers spread out to his left.

The Druid dressed as his kind tended to, in white robes with a brown over-cloak and cowl, a staff in his hand and sandals on his feet. A shadow from the flickering torch light fell across his pale skin, however Tartan still could see the brown eyes and the curly, green hair.

"Green One," he said, addressing the Emperor's trusted friend and Daff Kanaar ally, "you are welcome here, announced or otherwise."

The Druid smiled, revealing his thin lips and small, white teeth. He extended his free hand and the Duke took the other's wrist, feeling nothing but the arm beneath his sleeve. Dilvesh the Green One needed no weapons other than his staff and his magic.

"A benefit of being Daff Kanaar is not having to move through the court, unless I want to," Dilvesh informed them. "J'her, I must admit that I am wounded that you didn't recognize me."

"My apologies, your Grace," J'her said, inclining his head. "I don't know if you're aware, but we've had problems with assassins –"

Dilvesh waived his hand and stepped around Tartan to the cell bars behind which the prisoner watched him. "Not assassins, I think," he said, "but Roosters in your midst."

The prisoner straightened but said nothing. Tartan had never heard of Roosters before, other than the male bird, and from the look on their faces neither had J'her nor M'den, but Rukh's eyebrows rose and he nodded.

"I hadn't even thought of that," he admitted, looking first into the Duke's eyes, and then at J'her and M'den. The two Uman looked at each other then back at the Knight Lieutenant. "Roosters are a group of former Bounty Hunters who left the guild when they made peace with the Emperor. There aren't many of them and they are far from the best in the Guild, however they're noticeably more ruthless and less expensive to hire, and because the Bounty Hunter's guild considers them an enemy, much more focused on their own secrecy."

"And so, perfect for one noble who sought to remove another," J'her opined, nodding. "I agree – this explains why we're unable to find who hired them."

Dilvesh grinned and said, "Well, why you're unable, anyway."

He pushed his cowl back and placed a hand on the cell door. The latch popped open for him.

"Green One, with respect," J'her began, but the Druid held up his hand for silence. J'her stood stock still, M'den next to him, whether affected by one of the Druid's spells or just his presence was impossible to say. Tartan knew Dilvesh as only slightly less powerful than the Empress herself – a master of the Elements and a worshipper of the gods Weather, Earth and Water. If Dilvesh had decided that he wanted to interrogate their prisoner, there was little any of the people here could do to stop him.

"Your name, sir," The Druid asked the naked prisoner. The man tried to look away, but kept turning back to face Dilvesh. Tartan had looked into the deep brown eyes set under those pencil-thin eyebrows before. Much like the Emperor, he possessed an inquisitive stare that seemed to bore into one's brain with its intensity.

"Your name," the Druid repeated.

"Alek," the prisoner said finally. "Alek of Angador."

"Of the Roosters," the Druid pressed him.

"Of the Roosters," the man agreed.

"Come here to do what?"

Alek lowered his head and squeezed his eyes shut. Tartan saw the muscles in his throat move.

"He's trying to swallow his tongue!" he warned. Some Bounty Hunters were trained to do this – they would actually strangle themselves in bondage rather than betray their clients. Once begun, the process was nearly impossible to stop.

J'her and M'den lurched forward, but the cell door slammed shut of its own. Dilvesh raised his right hand, glowing green with power, the fingers twisted into a claw. The prisoner's head snapped back up, his mouth opened and his tongue protruded.

"I wouldn't advise trying that again," he said softly.

Alek just nodded.

"Come here to do what?" the Druid repeated.

This time, Alek couldn't look away.

"Eliminate the Duke of Angador," he said. "Make it look like someone from Galnesh Eldador arranged it."

Tartan watched the looks exchanged between M'den and J'her. Neither of them liked hearing that. Tartan had been toying with the idea that one or both of them was behind this, and felt inwardly relieved that neither could be a likely candidate if blaming someone in the capitol was the goal.

"And who is paying you for this?" the Druid pressed the bound man.

Alek twisted in his chains, a trickle of blood running from the steel cuff around his left wrist, down his arm. Tartan absently noted that his man was likely left-handed, the warrior training that he'd received since he'd been able to hold a sword never leaving him.

The prisoner twisted, he groaned, he grit his teeth. The Druid straightened, his right hand at his side and his left still holding his oak staff. The two Uman shuffled nervously and Rukh unconsciously moved behind his Duke.

After tortuous moments, the prisoner threw back his head and shouted, "Shellene! Shellene of Vreck! That red-haired temptress paid us nine thousand Tabaars to set up the Duke."

The Druid stepped back, the prisoner hung limp in his chains, his naked body slick with sweat. Steam actually rose from his back, although so faint that Tartan couldn't be sure that anyone other than the Druid would have noticed it. Somehow, he didn't think Dilvesh cared.

M'den regarded J'her. "Do we know this person?" he asked.

J'her just shook his head. Both of them turned to Rukh, but the Lieutenant was baffled.

Tartan wasn't. It had been a long time, but he could still remember the comely woman from the Emperor's coronation celebration, the red-haired noble lady so beautiful that, watching her, he'd actually walked into a column in the great hall, embarrassing himself in front of hundreds of emissaries.

Shellene was the uninvited guest and then-paramour of Ceberro, Duke of Vrek. Ceberro at that time was retaining the woman as his consort, but after two children by her he had decided that she didn't suit him. Ceberro had distinguished himself first as a political enemy of Glennen's Heir, Rancor Mordetur, and then as his staunchest ally when he became King. That rapid transition had filled Lupus with suspicion.

Ceberro had come to Tartan as Duke of Angador on more than one occasion to check the loyalty of Glennen's son. Tartan had never given him any encouragement. He had no illusions of restoring the Stowe's to power in Galnesh Eldador. He himself didn't want to be a King, much less an Emperor.

Ceberro had finally decided that, if Tartan couldn't be turned, that he must be done away with. This offhand relation represented Ceberro's thinking perfectly. He'd promise her some reward, quite likely her sister's place at his side, and if she were caught, the relationship was so tenuous that no one could seriously connect him to the girl. The Emperor would be able to make no case that would satisfy the rest of the nobility of Ceberro's treachery. Eldadorian nobles, especially the Dukes, were by their nature too paranoid for their own safety to come after each other on behalf of the Empire unless treason was clear. Most of them still resented what had happened to old Yerel, and that was more than a decade ago.

"You seem pensive, your Grace," the Druid remarked to him.

Now the deep brown eyes were focused on him, the pencil-thin eyebrows arched and accusing. Tartan looked into the Druid's face, intent on saying nothing.

He didn't want to keep this information from the rest of them for its own sake, but he couldn't afford to release the information half-hatched, either. He knew in his heart that he was correct about Ceberro, but he couldn't have more than half of the puzzle.

Fine – the other Duke wanted him dead. He didn't like that, but he could accept it. Under his father, Eldadorian Dukes attacked and raided each other as a matter of course.

But once he'd been eliminated what could Ceberro have planned then? How was his brother or his wife ruling in his stead any better than he?

One of them had to be involved in this, and no matter which, that news wasn't going to make Tartan Stowe any happier.

Chapter Nine:

Revelations

"So, your wife or your brother," Jean asked him, in the privacy of the Heir's chambers. She'd brought him his afternoon meal once again, the sammiches with the dressing he liked and a sweet white wine. She'd replaced her palace dress and, of course, the room had been scrubbed from blood and body parts.

There were no carpets by the bed to replace – perhaps Tartan had stumbled upon why the Emperor didn't like them. The ones on the far side of the room had not been stained.

"It appears that way," Tartan informed her. He picked up a diagonally cut half and bit off the corner while Jean poured the wine. "Terran has never been very ambitious, but sometimes those are the people who need to be watched most closely. Those without ambition might be more willing to take what seems to come easily."

"Killing you hasn't come very easily," Jean noted, handing him the wine.

He took a swallow, the flavor exploding in his mouth against the tart dressing. He had to learn where the radish that was the basis for this grew, and start a whole plantation for it in Angador.

If he managed to return there on the outside of a coffin.

"Shall I take off this dress?" Jean asked him, frank as ever.

He smiled and shook his head. "Too much on my mind right now," he informed her. Her love making was sweet, her passion exciting, but he needed to think.

She seemed almost disappointed. He could guess that no woman wants her favors turned down. His wife usually tried to disguise her relief when he didn't want her.

More and more, this was looking like Yeral's handiwork. He couldn't help feeling a little rejected.

"And what did you manage to uncover?" Tartan asked Jean, as she sat down next to him with her own sammich in her hand.

"Other than my own skin, which doesn't seem to interest you anymore," she said, arching an eyebrow, "it seems your friend is correct about the Roosters. There are signs of them in the city if you know what to look for."

"There are?"

She nodded. "They like certain breeds of horses and certain types of living conditions," she said. "Common apartments in the inner city, near water and sewer access. They tend to wear brown outfits and not cut their hair. When you have all of that to go on, they aren't that hard to find."

Tartan felt his eyebrows knit. "You certainly know a lot about a guild that's supposed to be secret," he commented.

Jean stared straight ahead, fixated on her sammich. "When a group tries that hard to be secret," she said, finally, "it draws attention."

To certain groups, it does, Tartan thought to himself. But to which of those groups did Jean belong?

***

After the afternoon meal, Tartan sent Jean out to find her son with orders to send him to the stables. He'd had enough time to recuperate from his rough ride, and now it was time to see how Thunder Cloud would tolerate a bit and saddle. Tartan dressed himself in his riding leathers and sheathed a sword over his shoulder. He also concealed a dagger in his boot, another in his left shirt sleeve and wore another blatantly on his belt.

He normally didn't ride this way, but it wasn't normal for anyone to try to kill him, either. He reflected on how that fact had really changed this year.

Six Angadorian Knights accompanied him to the stables now. They'd reported to him that the bodies of four more had been found near the palace's supply depot, meaning that there was still a suit of armor unaccounted for. He resolved to send Jean out to find it and to make sure that Rukh verified, man by man, every Knight he'd brought here with him.

The stables were abnormally busy. J'her had Wolf Soldiers and Eldadorian Regulars from Duke Gelgelden's holdings sweeping the plains around Galnesh Eldador for evidence of anyone who might want to take advantage of there being no Duke in charge of the capitol. That hadn't occurred to Tartan even remotely as a reason to assassinate him, but then that's likely why people like him employed people J'her.

Or like J'her's son, J'lek, the former Wolf Soldier who served as Tartan's own Supreme Commander of his Angadorian Knights. If Central Communications were still working, he'd have already sent a message to J'lek to keep an eye on both his wife and younger brother. As it was, he'd have a squad of Angadorian Knights make the long trip back, the moment Rukh informed him that he was sure of all of them.

Tartan approached the paddock and found Lurien already waiting for him, a groomsman with a saddle and bit ready.

Thunder Cloud pawed the earth and snorted. She wanted to be next to Lurien, but she didn't want to approach the groom. The boy hadn't tamed the mare, he'd merely reached her.

"Can you do anything to calm her down?" Tartan asked the boy as he approached. He'd never actually asked Lurien to put his abilities to use – however they were undeniable, and then needed to be explored.

Lurien looked into his face with those cat-eyes. "Let me try," he said, then turned toward the paddock and put his little hands on the second lowest bar.

The boy's face screwed up as if he were trying to use a muscle that he didn't have a good understanding of. The mare turned her attention to him right away, then approached him. She lowered her nose almost to the level of his, then suddenly raised her head, then quickly trotted twice around the paddock before returning her nose to his level.

He reached out and stroked the side of her nose and mouth. Without turning away, he said, "Try and put the saddle on her now."

Tartan nodded to the groomsman who entered the paddock through the newly-repaired side gate. The mare's ears pinned back to the noble crest of her neck but she didn't move, just stood stock still as the groom brushed her coat down, laid the saddle blanket on her and then the saddle.

"Pick her hooves," he said.

"M – my Lord?" the groomsman asked him. No one who worked here didn't know how dangerous an animal Thunder Cloud was.

"If you can't clean her hooves, there's no point in riding her," Tartan said. "She'll pull up lame eventually. Looks to me like she's barely ever been clipped, much less had her hooves cleaned."

The groomsman swallowed, then put his side to the mare's and tapped the heel of her hoof to get her to raise her fetlock for him. The mare snorted, making the man jump, then on the second try complied and let him clean her.

"She likes that," Lurien said to the open air. "She had a pebble, I think."

"She *did* have a pebble," the groomsman commented. "Lucky as she wasn't lame already, by the size of it."

"She's used to her hooves hurting her," Lurien said. "She wants shoes like the other horses now. I'm telling her that I'll make sure she gets them if she promises not to hurt the blacksmith."

"So you can talk to her?" Tartan pressed the boy.

He still didn't look away. "It isn't talk," he said. "It's more like pictures. She doesn't know a lot of words, and most of them she associates with pain. I think of the groomsman putting the saddle on her, and her being happy, and then of the groomsman picking her feet while she stands still. I think of carrots when she's doing what I want and I think of the crop they've used on her when she isn't."

That made as much sense as anything else, Tartan couldn't help thinking. More than if the horse understood the language of Men but just couldn't speak it.

"Let the blacksmith know that I want her shod in the morning," Tartan informed the groomsman as he picked up a rear hoof. "Lurien, you'll want to be here for that, so you can miss court."

"Yes, your Grace," they each said. Then Lurien added, "She's thinking of you in the sunshine, standing in the grass. I think that means 'Thank you.'"

"She sounds like a very polite horse," Dilvesh said from behind Tartan.

Taken completely unawares, the boy jumped and the horse

reared, screaming her challenge. The groomsman vaulted the iron paddock wall with amazing speed, leaving the mare alone in her containment. No sooner did her front hooves hit the ground than the backs were kicking air as she spun in a circle.

Tartan turned on the Druid. "If that was supposed to be funny, you've missed your mark entirely," he accused the Druid.

"My apologies," the Druid said, inclining his head. "I forget myself in my own thoughts sometimes, I fear."

Tartan fought back his own anger. Surprise moves around skittish horses were a recipe for disaster, but not everyone knew that. Lurien had already reached out for the mare, and the groomsman had taken hold of the paddock bars in preparation for another attempt at her, this time with a bridle over his shoulder.

Tartan was very curious to see if she'd take a straight bit or what the Emperor had called a 'snaffle.' Blizzard's get usually preferred the jointed bits reserved for draft horses. The Duke had made a study of these with his own horses since hearing of the experiment with a stallion called 'Little Storm,' and in fact he found that, with a few weight adjustments, he liked how these jointed bits performed.

Dilvesh stepped up next to the Duke, their shoulders touching, and reached into his robes. As both watched the groom try to get Thunder Cloud to take the bit and bridle, the Druid drew a dagger Tartan recognized as one of Jean's.

"May I ask, your Grace," he said, clearly more interrogating than asking, "where you came by this weapon?"

A wizard could take a weapon and know through his magic who had ever held it, going back decades and more. A Druid, a master of the Elements, could probably tell even more, Tartan reasoned, but could he tell if someone was lying to him?

Tartan decided that it was better not to find out. Dilvesh would likely see the Emperor before Tartan could, and a bad report could carry Imperial ramifications.

"I have an agent working for me in the palace," Tartan admitted to the Druid. "She is investigating, among other things, these attempts against me, and has saved me from them both times. That dagger is hers."

Dilvesh narrowed his eyes and looked sideways at the Duke. The groomsman slipped an index finger into Thunder Cloud's mouth, against the side of her tongue. Tartan had always considered that a last resort to put a bit in. The horse's mouth had wide spaces where there were no teeth, and an experienced groomsman could easily put his whole hand in the horse's mouth if he were careful, however some horses could turn their heads with amazing speed, and their teeth could crush a finger.

The mare popped her mouth open and the experienced groom slid the bit in behind her teeth. The bridle immediately went over her head and around her ears before she could reject it. Lurien kept a protective hand on the mare's foreleg. Tartan half-expected her to bob her head and rear, but she simply accepted the bit and let the groomsman adjust it.

Tartan decided right then that the boy should be able to have another ride, this time with a few fleet horsemen to watch him.

"Would you tell me this person's name, please?" Dilvesh asked Tartan.

This was not good, Tartan knew. There was something about Jean that clearly worried the Druid. "Is it important?" he asked. "I've been using this person's services since the Battle of the Vice on the Eldadorian plains – I assure you, she's trustworthy."

The Druid sighed and handed the dagger to the Duke, who slid it up his right shirt sleeve. He'd never carried this much steel on his person before.

"This woman, I assume, is a striking red head who keeps a bandolier of daggers and is quick to use them?" the Druid asked him.

Lurien slipped between the paddock bars and, despite his club foot, climbed them from the inside with the dexterity of a squirrel. Before the groomsman could cross behind the mare to the right side, Lurien leapt for the horse's saddle, caught the pommel with both hands and was pulling himself up into the seat. Another groomsman vaulted the closed paddock gate to get a hand on the mare as it backed away from the bars, and together the two took hold of the saddle's stirrups in order to adjust them for the boy's height.

"You know her, then?" Tartan asked the Druid, watching the boy. This could be a good day to ride. He motioned to another groomsman. His own horse would be too slow but he had no doubt that Shela kept some for their speed.

"I'm certain you've heard of 'Clear Genna,'" the Druid informed him.

That got Tartan's attention. A member of the Daff Kanaar, Genna had been one of the Emperor's lovers before he met Shela. The more tawdry troubadours sang songs of her pursuits and embarrassments of the Emperor as he sought to leave her and begin his life with Shela. His wife, Yeral, particularly loved these songs.

"Clear Genna died at the Battle of Tamaran Glen," Tartan said.

The new groomsman arrived and Tartan told him to bring him a fast horse, saddled light. This man, an Uman, nodded and ran off.

"I was at the Battle of Tamaran Glen," Dilvesh said. "I was in communication with Genna, just as I was with the Emperor. After we all saw Shela fall, Lupus' mind so filled with bile that it drowned out all others for me. When the battle finally ended and I could clear my mind, there was no sign of Genna, and I could not contact her."

"And so," Tartan said.

"And so," Dilvesh repeated, "we thought her dead. He had to flee from another army – there was no time to search for her body."

"And once this dagger belonged to her?"

"No," Dilvesh said. "Before the Battle of the Vice, the Empress herself, and two of her children, were taken captive by Bounty Hunters – more of these Roosters, we think – and one of these identified herself as Clear Genna."

Lurien ordered the two men in the paddock with him to open the gate for Thunder Cloud. "A moment!" Tartan ordered him, and turned his full attention on the Druid.

"I should have been made aware of this," he said to Dilvesh.

"You were made aware of that capture," the Druid responded. "You know that Vulpe saved his mother and his sisters."

"But not from *who*," Tartan insisted.

"Neither were you informed that, a short time later, Nina of the Aschire was captured in the port city of Kor, now Lupor, again by Clear Genna."

"No," Tartan said, angrier now. "I certainly was not."

Clear Genna on the loose made for a serious threat to anyone associated with the Emperor. While anyone's reputation could grow after her death, Genna's certainly spoke of delivering as much ill luck as she could to Lupus, her former lover.

"In Kor, Genna informed Nina that she had left the Daff Kanaar and hidden herself in Conflu, and that she'd done so to raise Lupus' eldest son."

Lurien ordered the groomsmen once again to open the gate to the paddock. The mare stood pawing the ground impatiently. If he wanted to, Tartan and Lurien both knew, he'd be out of the paddock and out of the city and no one could stop him.

The third groomsman was already returning with a long, lean horse in tow, a small racing saddle on its back. The horse must have already been ready for someone else when Tartan asked for it.

But now Tartan's attention was all on Lurien, on his cat-eyes, his jaw and nose, so much like his mother's.

His eyebrows, his thick bones, the determination in his face, so *very* much like the Emperor's.

"I thought as much," the Druid informed him.

"Your Grace..." one of the groomsmen in the paddock reminded him. The boy and the horse were ready to go.

The boy – the son of Lupus the Conqueror by someone he'd bedded prior to his Empress.

In Eldador, the Emperor chose his successor. King Glennen, their first monarch, had chosen Rancor Mordetur to succeed him over Tartan Stowe, his own son. He'd died leaving Tartan at Rancor's mercy – it had been the then-King's decision to elevate Tartan to an Earl and put him in charge of Angador. On his own success, Tartan Stowe had made Angador so important to the Empire that it made sense to elevate him to Duke, parceling out his land to Earls vassal to him.

Lurien, or whatever his name might be, would have no 'claim to the throne' under Eldadorian law, any more than Tartan did.

However – how many had come to Tartan acting otherwise.

Tartan took the reins from the groomsman next to him and mounted the horse, then raised his hand to the groomsmen in the paddock. No sooner did they open the gate then the mare tore out for freedom, making a beeline for the outer wall. Tartan kicked the light horse into motion behind her, already losing ground. If Lurien couldn't rein the animal in, then the best the Duke would be able to do is follow Thunder Cloud's trail.

Perhaps, he thought to himself, that might give him the opportunity to think that he desperately needed.

Chapter Ten:

The Green One

The Druid Dilvesh of the Daff Kanaar stood alone in the room called 'Central Communications,' in the upper-most chamber of what was called 'the family tower' in Galnesh Eldador.

This had been a good idea, he couldn't help thinking. Knowledge is power, communication spreads knowledge. Using the magic of an Uman-Chi Wizard called D'gattis, the Druidic Triad and Shela's Andaron sorcery, they'd created energies thinner than a spider's silk, travelling between the key points in the Empire to this place, and invoked a permanent power point here to keep them all alive. The most uneducated Wizard could tap into the power they'd harnessed and communicate along the threads, leaving no one the wiser because the threads didn't even exist in this reality, but in the *space between* which separated the world of things from the world of magic.

The Emperor had come up with the idea, the Empress had conceptualized it for D'gattis and for Dilvesh. Both Daff Kanaari allies of the Emperor's, they'd come together with Shela and they'd made Central Communications a reality.

No one could have guessed that Angron Aurelias, the Wizard King of Trenbon and 1,000 year old Uman-Chi, would take the magic to another level and use it to travel right into the palace. Dilvesh wouldn't have believed that the King could detect the conduit at all, but Trenboni spies could have found out about it. That accomplished, Dilvesh wouldn't have thought that the King could have made his own thread and connected it to the central conduit, but there could be no doubt of that now – Dilvesh could see that thread now with his own eyes. To a normal man, an Uman or a Dwarf, this was a glowing sphere turning purple and white, floating in the center of the room. To Dilvesh, probably to any Wizard or Sorceress as well, this was a shining sphere turning in on itself with tendrils running off in all directions. Dilvesh could see those tendrils all the way to their ends if he focused on them – one of them clearly ended in Outpost IX, the capitol of Trenbon.

Shela would have seen this new connection, but Shela had removed herself from the capitol and gone out onto the campaign trail with her husband. The Princess Lee probably barely saw the tendrils if at all, and certainly wouldn't know what to do about a new one, if a new one caught her attention.

The question now was, "What to do about it." Someone had disturbed the central magix which held the conduit in place and fed it. Someone had tried to let the power free, and someone else had repaired it with surprising little grace. Now the tendrils writhed and crashed in to each other, creating what the local Wizards described as 'noise.' This had been left alone by the palace Wizards, who weren't allowed to know the secrets of this magic. Just as well – they couldn't have fixed it, and in fact the condition of it all now was particularly dangerous.

From what Dilvesh could tell, when Princess Lee realized that she couldn't escape the King, she'd attacked the room. Aurelias probably knew as much if not more than Central Communication's creators about the power here and what it would do if unleashed, and repaired her damage. He didn't care if it ever worked again, he just didn't want it to incinerate him.

When Lee couldn't damage it enough to drive the King off, or maybe because she'd been outnumbered by warriors and Wizards, she'd leapt into the conduit itself, or been pulled into it. Black Lupus, Dilvesh' Daff Kanaar ally, would have stood toe-to-toe with the King and his warriors and either prevailed or died trying. His daughter knew what a terrible weapon against her father she was as a hostage, and one way or another she'd removed the threat.

Dilvesh' mind ran down each remaining thread. None of them

terminated with the Princess. None of them bore a mark of her identity, that specific Mordetur *alienness* which the Emperor and his children carried with them. He checked the one back to Trenbon twice – he felt certain that the Uman-Chi didn't have her.

The girl must be destroyed, Dilvesh concluded. That was sad. He liked that girl.

Reconciling himself, he applied his own energy to the conduit and quelled the noise it made. His mind ran down the threads again and re-aligned them. He couldn't do anything with the damage in the room itself which the Princess had caused – that would require D'gattis to return here.

At least it wouldn't explode.

Dilvesh forced his mind down the conduit for Thera, the city where the Empress' brother ruled as its Duke. Even if they thought the conduit wasn't working, they'd still be manning it.

Dilvesh found a wizard at the other end.

Hello, he said, simply.

He sensed the surprise, then the caution. While he could make the communication portion work, he couldn't move the images with it. That had been Shela's inspiration.

Who is this? he was asked.

Dilvesh of the Daff Kanaar, he said. *I'm in Galnesh Eldador.*

A little relief. *Is this working now?*

Well, that wasn't a very intelligent question, considering he was using it. *It works after a fashion, but it isn't stable. After this communication I'm going to disable it just in case the Uman-Chi are monitoring it.*

Just a sense of the affirmative. This wasn't conversation as much as it was communication, and it happened on a different level closer to emotional.

Have you the ability to contact D'gattis or the Empress?

The wizard considered. *I believe I can.*

Very well, Dilvesh emoted. He sent a message for each of them, then terminated the communication.

He'd done that as much for Uman-Chi ears as for Eldadorian. While he'd been communicating, he'd been weaving another spell, and as soon as he was done, he cast it.

A second sphere much like the original communications conduit appeared in the room, much smaller than the first, and Dilvesh immediately connected the thread from Outpost IX to it. A moment later, he weaved more threads from it, each no longer than a man's height, and left them waving without termination.

In fact, that was incredibly dangerous to do in and of itself. If the King decided to whisk his way into here again, he'd be drawn off into one of them by its special gravity. That could end him if it caught him unawares, and at the very least would leave him weakened saving himself.

Dilvesh doubted that Angron Aurelias would try that maneuver again, but if he did they'd be ready for him. That was all that he could do for now.

He had to get himself to Outpost IX, to the Fovean High Council. The Emperor had a plan which required the Druid to surrender to the rest of the Fovean nations on behalf of Eldador. He also had to deal with this new news of Genna.

In fact, *that* had him more worried than any of this.

Chapter Eleven

Reunion

"Take her by the bit, Lurien!"

"Harder!"

"Turn her! Turn her to the left! To the *left*!"

"No, you blockhead, to the *other* left!"

Lurien grit his teeth and pulled back with his left hand. Thunder Cloud responded by kicking out behind her, again and again and again, until her head almost touched the boy's knee and she finally turned.

Most horses 'follow their head,' in that the rider turned them and that was the way they ran. Thunder Cloud would keep running in the direction that she wanted to go unless Lurien pressed the issue.

Eventually she would learn that she had to follow her head, but that would take a lot of work from the boy, and that boy was both small and a cripple.

For three weeks, since the Druid's revelation as to Jean's and Lurien's identities, Tartan had been working with the boy to master the mare, Thunder Cloud. She'd slowly improved in some ways, but become significantly worse in others. She didn't immediately bolt out of the gates the first opportunity that presented itself any more, but

Tartan reasoned that this was due more to the regular exercise that she'd been receiving than Lurien's control of her. Once in the open, she wanted free rein to run full speed, over or through any obstacle that presented itself, to jump everything from small carts to other horses, to kick without warning and rear without concern for her rider's safety. All of that needed to be addressed.

One of the senior handlers had tried his hand with the mare without their permission after she'd been put up with the night. He took off out of the stable gates and wasn't seen again until dawn, three hours after the horse returned. Since then no one but Lurien tried to ride her.

The boy was convinced that he could reason with the horse as if it were his friend. Tartan had to get into the boy's head that the horse's mind didn't work that way. It was 'rule or be ruled' in the herd, and it had to be 'rule or be ruled' between horse and rider.

Lurien was being ruled.

"Very good, Lurien," Tartan informed him, from the back of another of Shela's fastest horses. "Now straighten her out, make her walk. She'll want to run, don't let her."

"She wants to run!" Lurien complained. The problem was that Lurien also wanted to run. He loved to run that mare, and who wouldn't? Her speed was nothing short of amazing.

"She runs when she proves she'll stop," Tartan informed him. "She does that by walking when you tell her, and stopping when you tell her."

The mare tried to surge forward and Lurien yanked back on the reins without having to be told. She snorted but she commenced a walk in a straight line, right toward Tartan.

Once before she'd done this and then leapt forward and jumped him and the horse he rode. Tartan's mount had gone into a bucking fit. He'd changed horses since, but he tensed himself and, beneath him, the horse's muscles quivered as if he'd heard the rumor.

Lurien walked the mare right past Tartan, turned the mare and walked her back to where he'd started. He turned her around and stopped her.

"Now make her do it again," Tartan ordered him.

Lurien opened his mouth to complain but a stern look from the Duke shut him down. Thunder Cloud balked a little at the beginning, then did as she was told.

"*Now* run her in the same route, and make her stop."

Lurien grinned wide and the horse took off without being told. She ran a close circle around Tartan's horse, an equine threat as to what she was capable of, Tartan was sure, then back to its starting point again, stopping but pawing at the ground, wanting more.

Jean watched her son from the gates to the stables. Tartan hadn't confronted her with what he knew yet – he knew it wasn't time.

That Jean could be Genna was affirmed in his mind, but this left other questions open to him, not the smallest of which had to do with J'her.

The Supreme Commander of the Wolf Soldier guard had been at the Battle of Tamaran Glen. He'd seen Genna before. A keen-eyed, intelligent male, why hadn't he recognized Jean right away and, if he had, why had he said nothing?

In three weeks, Tartan hadn't come up with an answer to that question, and it bothered him.

Training went on until the noon hour, on a day when no court had been scheduled. Dilvesh would have made his speech for peace to the Fovean High Council a week ago and there had been no news. Having become reliant on Central Communications for its speed, using conventional methods of riders and messenger birds seemed gruelingly slow. No wizard had been able to overcome the 'noise' as they called it from the damaged tower, and then no wizard could communicate with any other while still in sight of the capitol. Tartan had diverted a little gold from the war effort to commission a tower out on the Eldadorian Peninsula and a road to it, but that wouldn't be ready for more than two years.

A lot would be different by then.

"Your Grace!" someone shouted to him. He turned to his left, where a squad of his Angadorian Knights guarded him and Lurien to see one of his Knight Sergeants pointing to the north.

A squad of riders appeared from the direction of the docks. Normally this would mean less than nothing to the Duke – Galnesh Eldador was the busiest port on Fovea and riders came to and from the capitol all of the time, however this squad was different from the others.

Its standard bearer bore the Wolf's Head standard. This meant it brought someone from the Imperial family.

Had Lupus returned home?

***

Tartan let the squad come to him, lining up his Knights behind him and his charge next to him. It didn't take long to see that this was not, in fact, the standard of the Emperor. His bore a wolf with red eyes. This one's eyes were plain black.

One of the children – must be Vulpe, Tartan knew. Vulpe had been campaigning successfully with his father in Volkhydro. There could only be one reason for him to come here.

It had come time for Tartan to return to Angador.

"Greetings, your Highness," Tartan addressed the Prince as soon as his squad stopped their horses before the Knights. "All of Galnesh Eldador will rejoice to have you back."

Vulpe had twelve years to his name. He regarded Tartan more like a warrior measuring a threat than as a boy with a favorite uncle or cousin. His eyes flickered across the Angadorian Knights and came to rest on Lurien, then narrowed.

"Who is this?" he demanded.

"A Volkhydran boy," Tartan lied. "Come to squire from the north, after the fall of Hydrus."

"What city is he from?" Vulpe demanded. His Wolf Soldier guard shifted behind him.

This wasn't right, Tartan thought. No salutation – and the Mordeturs *loved* their formalities. Vulpe had been made Lord High Commander of the Eldadorian Regulars, yet he'd come accompanied by Wolf Soldiers. He'd come through the rear gate like a messenger when he should have marched through the main gate, a conquering hero like his father.

Tartan immediately suspected a glamour and another attack. Without being too conspicuous, he released the strap over the crossguard of his sword in its sheath.

"From Teher," Lurien repeated the lie as Genna had first told it. "The home city of the Hero Of Tamara. We seek to – "

"Take him," Vulpe ordered one of his Wolf Soldiers, cutting the boy off. The Wolf Soldier kicked his horse in the ribs, Thunder Cloud began to back up as the other approached.

In a moment she would bolt, and it would look like whatever suspicions Vulpe had of this one were confirmed.

"Your Highness, please," Tartan began.

"You stop right there, boy," Vulpe demanded, placing his hand on the pommel of his sword, then grimacing and removing it.

That settled it for Tartan. No one who knew the boy didn't know of his love for *Fury*, the sword that had been made for him by the

Dwarves after he was born. The glamour clearly couldn't include it, meaning that the whole image was false.

This was not Prince Vulpe.

"It's an imposter," he shouted to his own men, drawing his sword. The Angadorian Knights pulled their swords as one. One took off for the main gates, to summon the guard.

The look of disgust on Vulpe's face did not belong to a child. "What is *this*?" he demanded.

Jean was already sprinting toward them from the main gate, pulling at her bodice as she did so. Either she'd sensed the same thing, or she'd seen something he'd missed. Ten Wolf Soldiers faced ten Angadorian Knights on horseback, but Wolf Soldiers fought on foot.

If they were Wolf Soldiers at all.

"You will put up your swords, all of you," Tartan informed them. "We will take you to the palace wizards, and we'll find out who is who."

Vulpe or the person wearing his glamour straightened in his saddle. "You forget yourself, Tartan Stowe," he informed the Duke, again much more like a veteran general than a boy of nine. "I am a *Mordetur*, and you are a vassal to my father –"

"But not to you, as any Mordetur would know," Tartan countered, even more convinced. "We've had problems here with glamours before. Either you come with us, or we'll drag your bodies from our horses."

This was it – Tartan knew. If they were imposters, then they had to fight or run. If they were the real thing, they'd just settle this with the palace wizards and the Shem Hannen.

Vulpe sighed. "Sheath your swords," he said. That took Tartan by surprise.

"We can out-wait the paranoia of one self-important Stowe," he informed the Wolf Soldier guard. Then he turned his head toward Lurien.

"As for you," he said, "don't think I don't recognize that horse, and there's a penalty for riding it. If she's taken you as her sole rider then you had better be the most important person in Volkhydro, or summon a scribe for your last words."

The Wolf Soldiers slammed their swords into their sheaths as one. The Knights traded looks and said nothing. This was all coming too fast for Tartan. Either Vulpe Mordetur had changed radically or an imposter had protection from Wizards like no other. Either way, he'd know soon enough.

As for the penalties for Lurien – he had a feeling that this was about to work itself out.

***

The situation had resolved itself before Jean had shed her palace dress, but not before she'd pulled a dagger from her bandolier. She followed the two squads of riders from the side, her head down but her eyes focused on her son, her bodice torn and a black leather undergarment revealed beneath it.

Jean's disguise had lasted her since the beginning of the month of Chaos. Now at the end of the month of Water, it was wearing thin. A lot had changed in the capitol city in two months. Arguably, the same could be said of Fovea.

Once inside the city, Tartan ordered all but his Angadorian Knights to dismount, and groomsmen took their horses. Most were confused by this treatment of the eldest son of the Emperor and his Wolf Soldier guard – stable hands first brightened to see them, then frowned when it became clear that they were in custody. Sideways glances found themselves directed at the Duke, and he didn't miss them.

If Vulpe Mordetur wanted to rally the people, he'd be able to do so, and probably bring the Wolf Soldier house guard with them. Tartan hadn't been here nearly long enough, neither had he done enough to win any loyalty from House Mordetur.

Tartan sent for J'her and for the palace Wizards with him. "We'll just wait right here, then, your Highness, and see what magic has to say."

Vulpe just rolled his eyes and shook his head, then watched Lurien put Thunder Cloud up with a groomsman's help.

"The boy's a cripple," he noted.

"He has a clubbed foot," Tartan informed the Prince.

"And yet, he's mastered Thunder Cloud."

"He has a gift with certain horses," Tartan admitted. "Thunder Cloud took to him almost immediately."

"I don't think that my father meant that mare for some Volkhydran squire," Vulpe said, then turned his attention back to Tartan, "by what right do you assign her?"

Tartan straightened. "I've been ruling here in your father's absence since both your sister, Duke Hectar and his son Hectaro were lost," he said. "I've kept gold flowing to the armies, I've kept peace in the Empire –"

Vulpe just waived his hand and turned from Tartan. The Duke found himself scowling. This person acted *nothing* like the Vulpe Mordetur he'd known and seen on many occasions. War changes a man, but not *this* much.

J'her was not long in coming, two Dorkan wizards in tow. Both of these were bald men, overweight, gold loops glistening in their ears, dressed in Wolf Soldier greys. J'her's face brightened when he saw the young Prince but darkened when an Angadorian Knight put his sword in front of the Supreme Commander of the Wolf Soldier guard.

"When we know for sure who he is," Tartan informed the Uman. J'her frowned.

"Were I myself not the victim of an intruder…" he apologized to Vulpe. The Prince just shook his head.

"My Lords," Tartan said to the Wizards, and pointed to the Prince and Wolf Soldiers.

One raised a hand, the fingers spread, in the direction of the Wolf Soldiers. A few of them winced but none reacted overly much to the spell. Common people fear Wizards, Tartan knew, and soldiers on the battle field had a special reason to hate them, but Wolf Soldiers worked more closely with the Empress, who acted rather freely with her magic.

"I am – we are," the first Wizard sputtered, then consulted with the other.

Tartan rested his hand on his sword. J'her did the same. Vulpe straightened.

The other Wizard raised a hand in the same way, this time his hand glowing white with his power. Certain spells required more energy, Tartan knew, but releasing or just detecting a glamour usually seemed relatively easy for an accomplished Wizard. There were even some of Lupus' 'barely gifted' who were trusted to do this.

The Wizard's hand wavered, then the light went out. Beads of sweat appeared on his shaved head, and he put his lips to the other Wizard's ear.

"What is this?" J'her demanded.

Both raised their hands together when one of the Wolf Soldiers stepped out of rank from the others, pulling his helmet from his head and throwing it on the ground. The others stepped away from him, Vulpe included, and J'her and Tartan pulled their swords, the Angadorian Knights in attendance pointed theirs at this man.

"Bother all foolish Dorkans," the Wolf Soldier swore, and then his Wolf Soldier greys shimmered and dissolved. The man grew nearly a foot, his clothes melting like wax from pants and a tabard to white robes, the hair lengthening out white behind him, a beard sprouting from his chin. The sword at his side lengthened, the nose grew a little more pointed and the eyebrows arched over penetrating silver-on-silver eyes set on pale skin.

The ears became pointed finally, as where a warrior had stood, a Wizard replaced him.

An Uman-Chi Wizard, one wearing the yellow hook and dot symbol of the Daff Kanaar on his breast.

D'gattis, one of the most powerful wizards on Fovea, had come with the Prince.

Chapter Twelve:

Gifts

Jean took one look at D'gattis and sprinted for the main gates. She hadn't covered a quarter of the distance before she stopped in mid-stride.

Dilvesh the Green One had not completely trusted Tartan Stowe to handle this situation, apparently.

The two Wizards seemed relieved to see D'gattis as the explanation why their magic didn't work as they expected. Vulpe, clearly not surprised by the Wizard in his midst, pushed past him to little Lurien, who watched his approach with his strange, cat-eyed expression. Vulpe looked the boy up and down once, his eyes finally resting on his dagger.

"Pull that," he told the boy.

Lurien pulled the blade from its belt sheath and offered it handle-first to the Prince. Meanwhile the remaining Wolf Soldiers ran at D'gattis' order to collect Jean.

Tartan dismissed his Angadorian Knights. J'her crossed through their numbers to D'gattis' side, but D'gattis was focused on the two boys.

The two sons of Lupus the Conqueror.

Vulpe took the proffered weapon, regarded the black blade and even ran his thumb on its edge. He handed it back to Lurien, who sheathed it, and then pulled his own sword.

Not Fury, Tartan noted immediately. The blade was a foot longer and black, like Lurien's dagger. A Y-shaped bone formed hilt and crossguard, but had been wrapped in leather to look more like the Prince's former sword. Vulpe cradled the blade in his arms and offered the hilt to Lurien.

"Take it," he said. "It isn't heavy. Tell me what you think of it."

Lurien put his hand on the sword. It was too large for either boy. A man could swing it and barely touch the ground, but either of these would end up wielding it like a two-handed sword of the six foot variety that some Volkhydrans loved.

Lurien looked into the Prince's eyes, then took his hand off of the blade. Vulpe sheathed it right away.

"They are the same," Lurien said.

Vulpe nodded, D'gattis with him. The Wizard turned to the Duke.

"We need to move all of this into the palace," he said, then looked sideways at Jean – now clearly Genna. The Wolf Soldiers had stripped off her palace dress and taken her bandoliers. In the process they'd managed to strip her leathers down to her waist and to tear the arm and leg sheaths where she usually kept more daggers.

"In fact," D'gattis said, "I think the Imperial dungeons would be appropriate."

***

A third trip to the dungeons, a third cell, a third person hanging naked from chains.

This time it was Clear Genna, her toes barely touching the floor, her head down and sweat already beading on her upper body. The passionate lover Tartan had known was now an older woman with grey streaks in her hair and stretch marks on her belly, revealed to all.

"We never knew she was a member of the Bounty Hunter's guild," D'gattis explained to J'her and Tartan. The three of them were alone with Genna, save for a squad of Wolf Soldiers from the house guard. Lurien had been removed to his personal chambers under the care of Angadorian Knights, and Vulpe had retired to his new chambers, selected for him by his sister Lee, in the family tower.

"It appears that she has ties to the guild *and* to the Roosters," he continued. "It also appears that she's forgotten the consequences of breaking the bond she made to the rest of us, so long ago."

"You broke that bond yourselves," Genna snarled at him. "You broke it when you left me for dead in Conflu."

"In fact, it was you who left us," D'gattis reminded her.

"I couldn't stay with *her*," Genna insisted. "She wasn't a member, she was a slave, but she had more rights than I did. She was in your favor more than me."

This was *not* the same woman whom Tartan had known since before the Battle of the Vice. Competent and cunning, that was Jean, and this was Genna.

"What we actually need to know from you," D'gattis informed her, "is who hired you to take the Empress and her children, and whom you're working for now."

"Why, the House of Stowe, of course," she said, a smile on her lips, a look almost like vengeance on her face. "Why don't you ask him?"

J'her and D'gattis both turned their attention to Tartan. He shook his head.

"Ridiculous," he said. "Yes – she works for me now, and as a scout before, but only because I found her on the road – "

"You said already," J'her interrupted him. "Impressive convenient, that."

"To what end are you employing her here?" D'gattis asked him.

"She wanted her son trained as a young noble and as an equestrian," Tartan said. He forced himself to be blatantly honest – he had no doubt that the wizard was working his magic. "In return she became my eyes and ears in the palace. I wasn't getting any information or help from J'her and his Wolf Soldier guard, so I accepted. She's since been there both times I was attacked, and saved me both times."

J'her turned to the Wizard, who nodded.

"But you didn't hire her to take the Empress," D'gattis pressed him.

"Of course not," Tartan scoffed.

"Well, this is interesting," D'gattis said, and stepped back from them, crossing his arms over his thin frame. "Because neither one of these two is lying, and yet they can't both be telling the truth."

"Unfortunately, we can," Tartan said, and stepped up to the gate to the cell.

"Jean – Genna," he said.

She kept her head down.

"It was my wife who hired you to take the Empress, wasn't it?"

J'her grunted behind him, but Tartan ignored him. Genna kept looking down.

"I will take an oath to protect your son as if he were my own," Tartan said, knowing her greatest concern, "but only if you'll tell the truth –"

That got to her. She raised her head, her eyes wild with anger. "But he is *not* your own, is he?" she demanded. "He is *not*! He is the son of the Emperor of Eldador. He is the son of Lupus the Conqueror. The eldest son, the Heir to the throne!"

"No," Tartan said, "even allowing that he is Lupus' eldest son, you know as well as I do that his future isn't assured. I was Glennen's eldest son, but Lupus became King.

"In fact, I became an Earl, my sister the wife of a Duke, and my younger brother is still a common. My youngest sister – I think she's a lady of the Princess' court. None of us –"

"Fine," she said. "Fine. Fine, fine, fine. On your life, this Wizard as your witness, your protection for Lupennen, as if he were your own."

"On my life," Tartan swore.

Genna searched for the Wizard's face and found it. She smiled to herself and said, "His wife."

"The attempt on the Empress?"

"That," she said, "and the attempts on his life here. Anything that she can do to bring down the Empire. Her father had a great cache of gold from his days as an adventurer with Glennen, and she's been drawing on that. The Guild wouldn't take gold to kill a Stowe until they could be sure that Lupus was taken care of, but the Roosters are less… discriminating."

Tartan had guessed all of this, but hearing it still cut him like a knife. His wife, not just a traitor to the Empire but to him. His wife, whom he'd tried to give his love to, whom he'd felt had a common link with him as a fellow fosterling of the Mordeturs, whose family was all but gone.

He straightened. If the Emperor and his own father had never told him anything else, if they both believed in nothing else, it was that the past, no matter how recent, no matter how painful, was set in the stone of the ages, and denying its existence marked a man as a fool.

"I'm still Regent," he said aloud. "I'm still under orders from the Emperor to hold the capitol and the Empire."

"Yes, your Grace," J'her said. D'gattis remained quiet.

He could have loved this woman. Her mind, her passion, her fire – he knew what Lupus had seen in her. He could have wished that he'd found her before his wife.

"Cut her throat," he said, to the open air. "Throw her body into Tren Bay."

"Yes, your Grace," J'her replied, stonily. He heard a dagger slide from a sheath.

"I'll deal with my wife myself," he said. "With me, Wizard."

***

D'gattis and Tartan navigated the passages through the Eldadorian palace to Lurien's personal rooms.

Lupennen, he reminded himself. A combination of the names Lupus and the masculine of Genna, unfortunately similar to his father's, Tartan reminded himself.

What to do with Lupus' bastard, if indeed he was?

"Congratulations, your Grace," D'gattis said, of a sudden.

"Eh?"

The Uman-Chi wizard stepped up next to Tartan. He stood an inch taller, but for his bearing it might have been a foot. D'gattis commanded magix that would challenge the Empress, Tartan knew. He'd been alive for hundreds of years. Tartan had heard of his exploits even as a boy, before the Emperor had built the Daff Kanaar with him and a few others.

"Congratulations," he repeated. "You've managed to do what neither Lupus nor any of the rest of us have accomplished."

"What is that?"

D'gattis smiled. "You've finally killed Clear Genna," he said. "The woman may have been instrumental to… certain aspects of the Daff Kanaar's founding, but in fact has accomplished far more in opposing us than she ever did to our benefit."

Tartan didn't actually feel very much like celebrating Genna's death. He'd found a real peace with her, a security in her advice, always so on-point for him.

"Of course, this leaves the difficult situation of the son," D'gattis pressed on, echoing the Duke's own thoughts. "Now that you've done away with the mother, you may find it difficult to manage the son."

"The son of Lupus the Conqueror, Emperor of Eldador," Tartan said.

D'gattis nodded, his silver-on-silver eyes appearing to stare straight forward. "I have no guidance from Black Lupus on what to do with this one."

Black Lupus – the Emperor's Daff Kanaar name. Tartan stopped dead in his tracks, his eyebrows dropping in a scowl over his brown eyes.

"You don't?"

"Why would I?" the Uman-Chi countered.

"I thought it was the Emperor who sent you here."

D'gattis shook his head. "I witnessed the Emperor's suit for peace through Dilvesh at the Fovean High Council," he said. "No sooner was it made, then the Andarons called for relief against his invasion of Chatoos."

"So the Emperor *did* invade Chatoos," Tartan said. They'd stopped in a passage way, lit by torches. Tartan leaned against the stone wall and crossed his arms over his breast.

"And how did *that* go?"

D'gattis smiled to himself. "How do all of the Emperor's adventures go?" he asked. "He sent his son before him to assemble and to move an army, but then it seems the son had no stomach for what he found there. The advance crumbled, but Black Lupus took the field and set it right."

"So he took Chatoos," Tartan pressed the wizard.

"Of that, I'm uncertain," he said. "My intelligence comes from the son, and the son quit the field. He's been very dour as to why. I found him on a Daff Kanaar ship moving between Chatoos and Eldador via Trenbon. He asked that I follow him here, and I did so."

"So you haven't seen the Emperor," Tartan said.

"I believe not as recently as you, sirrah," D'gattis said.

"And what about that sword he's carrying?" Tartan pressed him. "I haven't seen that blade before. He was very attached to the one his father received from the Dwarves."

D'gattis smiled again, the silver on silver eyes almost flashing. "Well, that," he said, then straightened.

"That sword was a gift to me from a friend of mine named Arath, who is Daff Kanaar and one of Eldador's Earls now. He found it when he chased what was left of the Confluni invasion force into the Forgotten Sea after the Battle of the Vice. It is no normal blade, and he didn't want it. I found that, although its manufacture is flawless and it fit into my hand as if it had been molded for me, I couldn't stomach carrying it for long. When the boy informed me that his own sword had been lost in the battle for Chatoos, I made a gift to him of it. He seems to be content with the blade and to suffer none of the ill-effects that Arath and I felt."

"I've held Lupennen's dagger," Tartan said, and turned on his heel, proceeding down the passageway once again. "I didn't tell anyone of this, but afterward it gave me nightmares. I've seen the boy wield it – you can see his mother's training in him. He touched the sword and said they were the same."

"So I heard from him," D'gattis responded.

Tartan looked sideways at the sarcastic Uman-Chi. One could never know what was behind those silver-on-silver eyes, or where they were looking. "My point," he said, "is that whatever the older son saw in the blade you gave to the younger, the younger son was immediately drawn to that of the older."

D'gattis' eyebrows dipped. "I will admit that I hadn't considered that."

"Did you inform Vulpe as to the possibility of this older brother?" Tartan asked. They'd come to the stair to the family tower, and Tartan stopped again. An Angadorian Knight with a pike, guarding the entrance to the stairs, made a fist over his heart in salute to the Duke.

"I did not," D'gattis told him.

Tartan couldn't read the Uman-Chi's face and he had no magic. It wasn't beyond his type to lie, and he had no loyalty to an Eldadorian Duke.

"It seems to me," Tartan said slowly, almost to himself, "that we need to have a conversation with both of these young Men."

Chapter Thirteen:

Boys and Men

A squad of Angadorian Knights stood outside of the door to Lupennen's personal chambers, located in the family tower, a level above Vulpe's, on the same floor as his sister, Lee. Like the guard at the base of the stairs, they stood at attention in their armor, pikes in their hands.

Tartan accepted the salute from their sergeant. Like the Wolf Soldier guard and the Eldadorian Regulars, Angadorian Knights broke out into squads of ten with a sergeant responsible for them, who reported to a Knight Lieutenant.

"Where are the rest of your Knights?" Tartan asked him.

The sergeant gave him a blank stare.

"Sir?"

"Your other Knights?" Tartan repeated. "I ordered you to guard the boy – where have you deployed your other Knights?"

"They're all here, Tartan," the Knight said. "It's just one crippled boy –"

Tartan pushed past him and into the chambers, beyond. The boy had been given a smallish suite with a single bedroom and separate sitting room. Tartan saw thick pile rugs on the floor and books in shelves on the walls. A meal had been partially eaten at a small table with one chair, and an overstuffed couch sat in a puddle of sunshine under the room's one un-shuttered window.

There was not, however, an occupant, not that Tartan was surprised. As soon as he'd realized that they weren't going to watch him, Lupennen had gone out the window, his clubbed foot not-withstanding.

"Stupid!" Tartan growled. "When I say to guard a person –"

"Call the alarm!" the sergeant interrupted him, barking at his fellow Knights.

"Belay that!" Tartan overrode him. The Knights, already breaking up to follow the sergeant's orders, stopped as one in mid-stride, looking to the Duke for his orders.

Tartan started with the sergeant. "You're relieved, sergeant," he informed the Man. The latter took the bad news with a wince. "Report to your Lieutenant to be re-assigned.

"The rest of you," Tartan said, turning his back on the former sergeant, "all but two of you, with me. You, and you," he continued, pointing at two of the younger Knights, "stay here, search the room, make sure that he's not just hiding."

The two Knights saluted and pushed past the others into the room, casting sidelong glances at their former sergeant. No squad, even a bad one, likes to be broken up. Warriors get used to each other for better or worse and form a bond.

Tartan turned on his heel, D'gattis next to him, and quick-stepped to the stairs. His mind told him to run, but he knew better. A Duke dashing through the halls would raise an alarm more assuredly than his own warriors might have, and he didn't want there to be an alarm. Lupennen had his mother's training – the only way to catch him would be unwarned.

"Your Grace?" D'gattis asked him, leaving, "What could you be thinking?" unvoiced.

Tartan didn't slow down. "He's for the stables, if he isn't there already," he informed the Wizard. "He's tamed one of Blizzard's get, named 'Thunder Cloud.' She's probably the fastest horse alive right now. If he's leaving, he means to be gone on her or he's a fool, and that boy's no fool."

"I am surprised that you allowed him – " the Uman-Chi began.

Tartan achieved the bottom of the stairs and returned the surprised salute of the Angadorian Knight stationed there. He turned left down a passage that he knew was the quickest route to the stables.

"I didn't *allow* him," he interrupted. "The boy was drawn to the horse no differently than Vulpe was drawn to his dagger.

"If you haven't noticed," he said, keeping up his fast pace, the Wizard beside him and the Angadorian Knights struggling to keep up in their full armor, carrying their heavy pikes, "we seem to be living in extraordinary times, where paupers become princes and children call on strange beasts and magical weapons."

"Yes," the Wizard noted, dryly, "I seemed to have come to the same conclusion, all on my own."

***

The grooms at the stable had seen Lupennen leave with the Duke and a squad of Wolf Soldiers. They hadn't been told that the boy was going to a house arrest, mostly because it shouldn't have concerned them.

When the boy returned a short time later and demanded the horse that he rode daily be saddled for him, they thought of nothing other than whatever problem had included him being resolved. The fact that he wanted it in a hurry was just him being a young noble.

Tartan sprinted into the stables to see the boy mounted and leading his horse away from the paddock, toward the city gates.

"Luri – Lupennen!" Tartan shouted.

The boy turned in the saddle, his mouth open. He'd dressed out in the boots that Tartan had fitted for him, in worn leather riding pants, a red gentleman's shirt and white vest with a thick blue riding cape that would double as a blanket. He had saddle bags behind his saddle.

He wasn't coming back.

"Lupennen, dismount that mare," Tartan ordered him.

The boy dropped a hand to the dagger in his belt. "I think not, my Lord," he said.

"Where do you mean to go?" Tartan pressed him. On the other side of the stable, two wise hands were already taking cautious steps toward the gates.

If they could close the outer doors, they'd trap the boy. The horse had proven before that she could jump the iron inner gate.

"Tell me something, and be honest, my Lord," Lupennen countered.

"Very well."

"Did you kill my mother?"

Just like that, the Duke thought. He'd been raised knowing

what his mother did for a living. Her death had been a real possibility in his life. Clearly, she'd trained him to handle it.

"She took a contract to kill me," Tartan countered.

The boy scowled. "No," he said. "She just knew of the contract. She came here because of it, and because of what she wanted for me."

"Let me finish that, then," Tartan offered the boy, taking a step closer. The two Uman hands were less than forty paces from the gates. In a few minutes they'd beat the mare to the outer door.

Lupennen shook his head. "She was worried that you'd discover her," he said. "She told me what to do if you did. And she told me one other thing."

"And what was that, Lupennen?" Tartan asked. He needed to draw this out just a little more.

"She informed me that, if you killed her, then you should know you also killed your unborn child."

Tartan could have been pole axed right there, and it would have stunned him less. A child? His own wife had denied that to him. In fact, it now looked very much like a child wasn't going to be coming from that quarter at all.

Lupennen turned on his horse and must have seen the two Uman, because he drove his heels into her sides and the mare leapt forward, pushing out with both back feet. Faster than any horse should move, she ran for the outer gates, the two Uman stablemen racing to get between her and it, one of them waving a work towel in an effort to make the mare shy and gain more time.

It didn't work. The boy nearly ran down the one Uman and passed the other before he could even get his hands on the pulleys that closed the outer door. Lupennen broke free of the stables and turned south along the city wall. He'd be gone before the seven Knights Tartan had brought with him could even mount a chase.

He'd lost this boy. He'd have a hell of a time making good on the last promise that he'd made to Genna. He'd ordered the execution of his own heir without knowing it.

"Your Grace, I grieve for you," the Wizard offered.

Tartan looked into the silver-on-silver eyes.

Yes, he thought. He'd lost a lot this day.

***

Of course, there was always the chance that a warrior like

Genna had found a way to elude her captors and escape, but that hope was dashed as soon as he saw J'her.

"And the body?" Tartan asked. D'gattis still attended him, quiet to one side, watching everything like Uman-Chi do.

"I was about to assemble a party of Wolf Soldiers to go dump it," he said. "We usually do that farther out on the peninsula, so that the body doesn't float back into the wharves."

"Give her a proper burial instead," Tartan informed him. "There's a cemetery west of the city where my mother is buried. I grant her a space in there."

"Sir?" the Uman pressed him. That cemetery had been set aside by Glennen himself for nobles and their families. Duke Hectar had been laid to rest there, and a marker laid for Hectar's lost son, Hectaro.

"Just do it," Tartan ordered him. They'd met half way to the dungeons. The Duke pushed past him and traveled the remaining distance to see with his own eyes what he'd done.

He found Genna left hanging, still naked, in her cell, a red flow of blood down her body and pooled on the floor. D'gattis stepped past him, stepped delicately around the puddle and pulled the woman's head back by the hair.

The wound had been quick and deep, taking the woman at the base of jaw and cutting almost to the bone. She hadn't screamed because she couldn't have. She'd probably bled out in under a minute.

"There is no saving her," the Wizard informed him. "She is with her god or goddess now."

"I thought as much."

"Still, it was important to be sure," D'gattis allowed him.

Tartan shook his head. He remained on the outside of the bars. Genna's death face showed a serenity that he'd never seen in her in life, even sleeping in his arms. Her eyes were closed, her mouth relaxed but the lips shut. Although Tartan had seen dead bodies before, even seen what the torturers had done to his mother, that he should hate them more, it took all of his courage to touch one, if he could manage it. He had no desire to feel Genna's cold, dead flesh or press his lips to her forehead for a final good-bye.

Genna was gone out of his life, and his heir with her, and it was his fault with nothing he could do about it, save to accept that he had ordered it done.

"A girl," D'gattis said.

"Eh?"

The Wizard stepped away from the dead body. Three older women of the palace staff filed into the room outside of the cell and were surprised to see them. Each curtsied then stood to one side, waiting for the two to leave.

Strong-willed people, or those being disciplined, to clean the body for the grave.

D'gattis drew closer to the Duke. "A girl child," he said, "that's how I read her. She couldn't have been more than a week conceived. You are blameless, your Grace. I'm surprised that even she knew –"

But she had known, and she'd said nothing, Tartan thought. He turned his back on the Wizard and returned to the stairs that would take him out of the dungeon. He might as well see Vulpe now.

"From beyond the grave, she smites at me," Tartan said aloud, drawing a stare from the palace women. It was a line from an old poem – Tartan didn't know the author. He'd been interested in such things after his mother had died.

He repeated the words for the Wizard, who looked quietly on.

"From beyond the grave, she smites at me,
"Fair skin grown cold,
"Red lips puckered in death's kiss.
"She raises not a hand, yet strikes at me,
"Raising red welts under untouched skin.
"A woman's wroth, it travels,
"Time and space unhindr'ed.
"And finds unhappy solace,
"In the souls of shabby kindred."

It was an old poem that an old Uman had supposedly written for his wife, but the words suited the Duke now.

***

Wolf Soldiers, not Angadorian Knights, stood outside the door to Vulpe's room. They weren't there to keep him in, they were there to keep others out, and as far as they were concerned, that meant Dukes and Wizards.

"You *will* let me pass," Tartan said, drawing himself up to his full height and looking the Wolf Soldier in the eye as he'd seen the Emperor do. The sergeant of this guard bore the Mark of the Conqueror, a scar from the corner of his eye to his jowl. This marked the highest honor that any Wolf Soldier could receive, given to only the bravest of Wolf Soldiers.

Tartan already knew that he had nothing to intimidate this man.

"I have my orders," the Wolf Soldier informed the Duke, not moving.

"Botheration," D'gattis cursed and waved a hand, looking almost like he'd swatted a pest out of the air.

The nine Wolf Soldiers shimmered and stood still, two with their mouths open, one reaching for his sword. Tartan knew of a spell that Uman-Chi liked, that froze a person's muscles and rendered him or her still. This must have been that.

Tartan stepped past the frozen sergeant and rapped on the stout wooden door. For some reason, he wondered why there were nine. Wolf Soldier squads numbered ten – even if one had been D'gattis in disguise, then where was that tenth member whom he'd replaced?

The Duke waited for a moment and, when he heard no response, knocked again.

"Come," he heard from within. The tone sounded more like a man's than a boy's to Tartan. He took a single look over his shoulder at the Wizard and then opened the door.

Vulpe was dressed in black leather riding pants and an open black shirt, his feet bare, and sat on one corner of his bed. His new sword lay unsheathed next to him. Vulpe's head rose from the floor to greet him.

His scowl was that of a man, not a boy, Tartan thought. Well, he'd been the son of a king. He'd grown up before his time, as well.

"Your Highness," he said to Vulpe, entering the room with D'gattis behind him.

D'gattis closed the door. Vulpe shook his head.

"As regent, you're 'Your Highness,' my Lord," he said. "I'm just a son of the Emperor."

It must have been ten years ago that Tartan had said the same thing to Tartan's father, and under similar circumstances. The Emperor had said something to him once about history repeating itself, but he couldn't remember it.

"Very well, my Lord," Tartan said, forcing a smile, "I was wondering if I could ask you for a few updates from the outer world?"

The door behind them burst open, armed Wolf Soldiers charging into the room, ready to fight. D'gattis raised a hand white with power, but it was Vulpe's word that stayed the Wolf Soldiers.

"Enough," he said. "Back to your posts."

No one had told Vulpe what had happened, and it would have been the last thing that Tartan would have guessed, however Vulpe had grown up under different circumstances and in different times. The Wolf Soldier sergeant fixed the Duke with an angry expression, but then ordered the squad out, following them and closing the door behind them.

"What would you know?" Vulpe asked them.

"Your campaign in Chatoos?" Tartan asked. D'gattis stood up next to the Duke.

Vulpe shook his head. "The Emperor took it over," he said. "I left before it was complete. I think I would have heard, though, if he'd failed."

"One might think the same if he'd succeeded," D'gattis said, but Tartan tended to agree with the Prince. A failure of the Emperor's would be more famous.

"Orders from the Emperor?" Tartan continued.

"I have none for you," he said. "I don't think my father knew that I was coming here."

"And the dagger in the boy's hand?" Tartan went for what he really wanted to hear.

In response, Vulpe turned on the bed and picked up the sword next to him. He laid the black blade across his lap, and turned his attention back to Tartan and D'gattis.

"You're aware that my father has a very special sword," he said.

Everyone knew that. The 'Sword of War,' he rarely strayed far from it. He'd born it into every battle. In his rage, he'd struck and broken even stone with it. Tartan nodded, the Wizard next to him said nothing.

"This sword, is every bit as special as that one," he said. "I knew it the moment I held it in my hand. That boy's dagger, it is just as special as this one, but in a different way."

"Is it?" D'gattis asked. Behind the silver-on-silver eyes, it wasn't hard to tell that the mind was racing.

Vulpe nodded. "I don't know if you're aware of it, but that boy is a son of my father's," he said.

Tartan looked at D'gattis, then back at Vulpe. "I'd just learned that he was the son of Clear Genna, of the Daff Kanaar."

"And where is Genna now?" Vulpe asked.

Tartan couldn't look the boy in the face when he said, "I had her executed for trying to kidnap your mother, yourself and your sisters."

"The woman with the red hair?" Vulpe asked.

Tartan nodded.

Vulpe nodded with him. "I remember," he said. "I assume that her son, my brother, is long gone now."

Tartan nodded again. "He took off on Thunder Cloud. I assume you know the horse."

"I do," Vulpe affirmed for him. "My father won't like that. That's two of Blizzard's children that he's lost control of. "

Vulpe sighed, then stood, and swung the sword before him, the point down, almost touching the stone floor.

"You know," he said, "I shouldn't be able to wield a sword this big."

"We'd conjectured on that," D'gattis informed him. Tartan didn't recall it.

"There's more than one sword like this," he said. "And there's more than a dagger. I've seen a spear, as well. Nina of the Aschire informed me that there might be even another sword, and a shield. There is even a staff."

"I did not know this, my Lord," D'gattis said.

"You probably also didn't know that there's already a member of the Daff Kanaar to replace Genna," he said.

The Uman-Chi's eyebrows rose up on his head. "No," he said, "and I rather feel that I should know that immediately, should it happen."

"We were all shocked to meet him," the Prince said. "You'll need to go find this new member, D'gattis, because I think his addition changes all of my father's plans, and he isn't going like that, either."

"What could you mean by that?" Tartan asked him.

But Vulpe would say no more. Eventually, he informed them that he was tired and asked them to leave.

They exited the room past the frowning Wolf Soldier guards, down the stairs to the main level in the palace. Tartan and D'gattis said nothing until they came to the throne room.

"I'll need to leave and find Black Lupus," D'gattis informed him. Tartan expected no less.

"Do you need anything before you go?"

"Nothing I can't get myself," he said. As far as he could tell, D'gattis looked Tartan right in the eye.

"You have a lot of loose strings to untangle, your Highness," he said. "That boy bears watching, and you have to deal with your own immediate family. Your wife cannot be allowed to kill you or to threaten the Imperial family."

"I will take care of that," Tartan said.

"I would be careful, as well, for the Princess Chawnee," he said. "If your wife wants to disrupt the Empire, and she can't get at you, and she failed with the Empress, that is a logical place to strike."

Tartan hadn't thought of that, but he nodded. In his mind, he was already planning the defense of the nursery hall.

D'gattis surprised Tartan by reaching out and taking his shoulder in his hand. "Your Highness," he said, "if there is a new member of the Daff Kanaar to replace Genna, then that first speaks to Genna being a founding member of the Daff Kanaar, and even an hour ago I would have said that this was not true. In fact, there has not *been* a new member to the Daff Kanaar since Karel of Stone, who replaced Drekk, and it was Drekk that died and then Karel replaced him, not the other way around.

"I think that many ideas that we held true about the Daff Kanaar are just our own suppositions," the Wizard said, "and if this is true then the Emperor's plans are set on an idea that does not work."

"I'll make sure that the Empire is ready for anything," Tartan promised.

The Wizard released him. "What I think that you might find," he said, "is that it is you, not the Empire, that should be ready for anything. And anything, I think, might be closer than you might think."

The Wizard and the Duke took each other by the forearm, and then D'gattis turned on his heel and left down the throne room's central aisle.

Tartan had to agree – he had a lot to think about.

Chapter Fourteen:

Daff Kanaar

The rain fell hard that night, lightning crackling 'round the towers that framed the palace in Galnesh Eldador. Rain pattered against the stones and on the rooftops, audible even within the solid round walls of Central Communications, where a lone Uman-Chi regarded two communications conduits with silver-on-silver eyes.

D'gattis had been called here years ago as an excited ally and his witch-wife had described to him a great plan for a communications system which would span their growing Eldadorian Empire. It had been D'gattis' idea to include The Green One in the plan, to tap into the Natural Trinity of Earth, Weather and Water, so that the thing would operate without a Wizard constantly having to recharge it.

He, Shela and Dilvesh had worked for months, changing out stones, realigning the floors and the roof to achieve the right shape for the thing. Black Lupus' Dwarven allies had come in at one point with specially mined stones for key points. The whole thing had been a tremendous undertaking of the Emperor's tech-no-gee and native magix.

The real surprise in all of this, other than an end result where it worked at all, was that the mind of one of the race of Men had conceived it, but Black Lupus' thoughts had always run strangely. As far as he knew, alone among the race of Men, and certainly alone among those who had no magic, Lupus had derived 'the ultimate truth of things,' the concept that the most powerful thing in the world was a thought.

Not a sword, not a nation, not a noble, but a thought. A thought had been the thing to start it all and, in the end, a thought would be the thing to end it. If an Uman-Chi came to this conclusion on his or her own, usually after centuries of contemplation, then he or she was immediately elevated to the caste of Casters, and taught the ways of magic.

No other mind sufficed to sustain the rigorous training.

At the time that Central Communications had been conceptualized, birthed as a concept and brought screaming into the world, Yellow D'gattis – called *The Far Travelled* by his people – had known that this attack by the Uman-Chi King was not just a possibility, but in fact an inevitability.

Angron Aurelias would first wonder how word passed so quickly between the important cities of Eldador, and between Eldador and the island city of Wisex which was the foreign holding by Black Lupus at the junction of the Safe and Mid Rivers.

He would derive the magix, and next he would derive the source.

When he knew the source he would exploit it. With the patience of his kind, who lived centuries where mortal Men lived decades, he would wait for the best time to employ that knowledge, or he would create that time, and he would invade the palace at Galnesh Eldador.

Had it been D'gattis, he would have entered with legions, not with a handful of soldiers and some few casters. Just that tax on the magix would have cracked the tower and destroyed the conduit, but then the city would have been Trenbon's, and the Eldadorian Empire demoralized from within while the Emperor campaigned in Volkhydro.

Angron Aurelias ran more careful, because Angron Aurelias had been defeated too many times by Black Lupus. Angron Aurelias had come through the portal to kidnap the Princess expecting to see a grinning Emperor and his witch-wife waiting for him. Angron had risked no more than he was prepared to lose, himself included, because in fact if he were defeated again, the old King was ready to depart this plane in favor of the final gifts of Adriam the All-Father, his god.

D'gattis shook his head. He didn't like to think of his King as an old fool who'd seen too much of Life to benefit his wisdom, however a Wizard lives by logic, not emotion, and logically speaking, Angron deserved his failure.

D'gattis couldn't have set him up any better than he had without betraying his oath to Black Lupus, as he'd sworn it more than a dozen years ago in the depths of lost Outpost X. Yellow D'gattis had sworn not to betray Black Lupus or any other member of the Daff Kanaar lest he suffer the wrath of Adriam.

He hadn't sworn not to let Black Lupus cut his own throat.

D'gattis reached out with his own mind, among the best of this peoples' all for its less than three centuries experience, and rewove the magix that the Princess Lee had undone here, and that Angron Aurelias had stayed. The Princess must have considered herself done in to have resorted to this tactic – if she'd been successful then Galnesh Eldador would be a smoldering crater filling from Tren Bay when the magix ran free. Here was the only known meeting of the influence of five gods on known Fovea, one of them dark Power. Arguably there could be six as Lupus existed as the earth-bound representative of War. This had all begun as his idea after all.

D'gattis nearly grunted at the effort to repair the twisted magix. To his silver-on-silver eyes the power ceased to writhe like so many snakes, and began to pulse through the walls with some semblance of order. The power aligned itself – the conduit once again flowed a healthy white and purple, spinning gently on its axis.

D'gattis lowered his head, his beak of a nose pointing to the ground. Some Wizards preferred staves, and the Uman-Chi would certainly have appreciated leaning on one now.

Ancenon, his Uman-Chi cousin and the rightful leader of the Daff Kanaar, and he had long ago decided that the best course of action was for the Uman-Chi people to be a friend to Lupus the Conqueror, Emperor of Eldador as Rancor Mordetur. In the relatively few decades that it would take the Man to die, either of natural causes or of his own reckless ambitions, the Uman-Chi could wait, and then when the time came step into all of the power and all of the glory that Eldador had brought to Fovea. If Lupus were successful in his conquest of the rest of Fovea then all the better – the Uman-Chi would reign when drawn into the vacuum of power left by Lupus' eventual, inevitable passing.

Angron Aurelias would have none of it. Too many Uman-Chi balked at the idea that any Man was capable of *anything*.

D'gattis shook his head. At one time Ancenon had been heir to the throne of Trenbon, but he had lost that position for his association to Black Lupus. Now that the Uman-Chi who had replaced him had fallen, and in this very room, it was time to re-present Ancenon's case.

And when that happened, perhaps it was time to focus the Emperor's attention on the current King of Trenbon. D'gattis regarded the second conduit, a trap left by the Druid for an unsuspecting invader. D'gattis applied his magix and enhanced that trap, strengthening the tendrils that dead-ended around it. What was a pitfall became a snare. Any being that wandered into that end would find itself a victim of its own magic skills and doomed.

D'gattis turned on his heel and exited Central Communications. As soon as he'd left the anteroom where a squad of Wolf Soldiers and a palace Wizard guarded the place, he lifted the spell that had frozen them in space and time and left them unaware of his coming. He didn't bother to tell anyone that he'd come here – a sorceress would still be needed to re-invigorate the magix and start the conduit operating. Until that happened, the thing would work but would push itself back out of alignment and require his coming back here.

Slipping silently down the circular stairs to the tower's ground floor, past a Wolf Soldier guard who looked right through him none-the-wiser, D'gattis knew that the last thing he wanted to do was to return here if he didn't have to.

D'gattis passed like a ghost through the stone hallways within the palace. Soon he would reach the royal stables, and from there he'd be on his way on a fast horse to Thera. He didn't necessarily like the Empress, but she kept an admirable stable and he had to allow her that.

In fact, this new protégé of the Emperor's, old King Glennen's son Tartan Stowe, was himself quite an equestrian. He'd arranged to buy a few dozen Angadorian horses a few years back and he truly enjoyed all of them. D'gattis approved of Tartan's regency in Eldador, if only because, for a Man, the boy kept a somewhat level head on his shoulders. He'd neither detract from the Emperor's efforts nor add to them. Tartan Stowe, he knew, would keep the home fire.

Not like the Princess Lee who'd as soon incinerate the capitol and everyone in it as be captured. If Lee had simply allowed herself to be taken, the Uman-Chi would have a worthwhile vassal in the Emperor and D'gattis' life would be simpler.

D'gattis' life had not been simpler for a long time.

Chapter Fifteen:

Family

The last day of the month of Water saw heavy rain falling in Galnesh Eldador. It hadn't rained in so long that it caught the palace by surprise. Windows had been left open and now passages and personal rooms were left with water in them, a dangerous and sometimes deadly combination when most of the floors were made of stone.

Tartan awoke to a polite knocking on his door and an Uman maid begging permission to come in and shutter his open windows. Already the divan under the room's open window where he'd sat to take his morning meal from Genna had a dark stain from rainwater on it.

Tartan groggily bid the woman enter and propped himself up with his back against the head board, watching her. She looked about thirty, barely a woman by Uman standards. Her hair hung long and green down her back, pushed past her pointed, lobeless ears. She dressed in a palace gown no different from Genna's, tight in the bodice and billowy in the skirts, blue and white with lines of bows from the waist to the floor. When she stretched out the window and into the rain to pull in the shutters, she revealed her palace sandals.

If that hadn't been enough to warn the Duke, the clear outline of a dagger against her mid section under her dress would have. He wouldn't have noticed either before his close association with Genna, but perhaps she had made him a more cautious man.

He waited for her to be over-balanced, her fingers just finding the edges of the outer shutter against the palace wall, before he sprang from the bed. He'd hidden one of Genna's daggers under his pillow, now he had it in his right hand as he leapt naked at the unsuspecting Uman pulling the shutter closed.

She turned open-mouthed to see him flying toward her, his feet off the ground, the dagger before him. She barely had time to raise her hands in defense before his full weight hit her and slammed her light Uman body into the back of the water-logged divan.

That much force would have broken her bones against the stone wall. The divan absorbed most of the impact and left the naked Duke straddling the stunned woman. It didn't take more than a few seconds for Tartan to have his knife at her throat and her wrists enclosed in his strong left hand, pinned to the arm of the divan above her head.

"My- my Lord!" she gasped. Her eyes shown wide, but her breath remained even. She wanted to appear surprised while her mind worked out an escape.

Tartan pressed the dagger harder to the skin. A thin trickle of blood ran down the side of her neck and stained the couch. His naked thighs across her middle told him of at least three daggers beneath her palace dress. He squeezed them.

"Don't 'my Lord' me," the Duke said as the Uman's eyes widened. "You thought to catch me that easily? Two attempts in the same place, Rooster? That's just sloppy."

The look of surprise evaporated and the cunning spy took over. "My apologies, your Grace," she said, her voice an octave lower, more confident despite her situation. "However I'm a member of the Guild, not one of *those*."

"Forgive me if that doesn't make me any happier," Tartan said. When Glennen had been King, he'd remained on good terms with the Guild, and in fact there had been a member on the King's council. Lupus had tolerated the same man for a while – a red head whose name escaped the Duke now – but as the war between the Guild and the Mordetur's had grown, that position had dissolved, the Emperor had replaced the man with a standing order that *no* member of the Bounty Hunter's Guild could enter the palace without the Emperor's specific permission which, as far as Tartan knew, Lupus never gave.

"Nor should it," the Uman said. She twisted her body as if she expected to slip out from under the Duke now, but he pressed the knife even harder. It wouldn't take much more to start a real flow of blood and end this woman, and Tartan had to assume she knew it.

"You've killed a master in the Guild, your Grace," she said, looking him straight in the eye. "We take that very seriously."

Tartan found himself in a predicament now. He could call for his Angadorian Knight guard, but then spend the rest of his time in the palace listening to the half-whispered snickers of the house staff as to the situation he'd found himself in. He could trust to the woman's good behavior, but a lifetime of experiences told him better. He couldn't squat naked over her for the rest of the day and he didn't want to kill her – at least, not yet.

Genna kept her knives sharp. Tartan took the edge from the woman's neck and slipped it under the laces in her bodice. From the bottom to the top, he cut the crossed white string one loop at a time until the bodice fell open and revealed her pale white skin beneath it.

She stared straight into his eyes as he took the dagger in his teeth and reached his right hand into the upper portion of her dress. He had to scoot his thighs down her thin body to her blousy skirts, but he satisfied himself that he was safe when he'd removed three daggers from her.

He'd be stupid to think there wasn't something hidden in the blousey skirts, he knew, however he couldn't feel anything there, and knew for sure that whatever it was, she'd have to hunt for it. He took the woman's daggers in his right hand and pitched them out the window, then took Genna's out of his mouth and stood up off of the Uman.

She remained where she was, her hands over her head, staring up at him with her breasts exposed. The blood has stopped flowing from the wound he'd left on her neck.

While still facing her, he stepped backward to his bed, found his robe on the floor and squatted down to pick it up. She didn't move until he'd stood, donned it and tied its belt.

"Feeling less vulnerable now?" she asked him.

"I know what I'm dealing with," he said. "I know you can kill with your hands and feet, even your teeth or with simple things from around the room if you need to. So, no, I don't feel less vulnerable, however I'm ready to listen to whatever you came here to say."

She sat up on the couch and made no move to close her bodice. Her training had probably told her that a distracted opponent made for an easier kill. Tartan wanted to crack a smile, thinking of it, but controlled himself. He had to focus on the dangerous woman before him, because she was waiting for that focus to shift.

He still couldn't be sure that she hadn't come here simply to kill him.

"You know your wife tried to pay us to kill you, I assume," she said.

"I do."

She nodded. "If you knew of the Roosters, then you knew that much. We didn't take the contract because we didn't want to eliminate Glennen's son and empower the Emperor further."

"You'll never forgive him, will you?" Tartan asked her.

She just smiled.

"So why come here, if not to eliminate me?" he asked. He saw no point in any banter with her. She hadn't come here to make friends.

"We suspected that you knew of your wife's activities," she said, "and if not, we planned to tell you. We have no allegiance to the Roosters. Knowing of what she plans, perhaps you have plans of your own?"

Again, Tartan wanted to smile but controlled himself. No, he thought, not your friend, not your ally.

"I'd think I do," he said, simply.

"Then perhaps you'd like to make use of our services."

That made for a surprise, he thought.

"You'd like me to pay you to do away with my wife," Tartan said. He sat on the edge of his bed, the knife still in his hand. Absently, he counted the number of steps that he'd need to get to her, and decided that she couldn't beat him to the door.

"Well, not necessarily pay," she said.

She pushed herself up onto the arm of the divan. "We watched you as you worked with Genna," she said. "It seemed to us that you benefitted greatly from her help and from her company. We would like to offer that to you again. There was a time when one of our number kept your father's council, and we believe that this time should return."

They wanted back in, he thought. They wanted a Bounty Hunter in the council of the regent of Eldador. What better place for them to spy from? What better way for them to return to their former influence? Even if they lost the position when the Emperor returned, that might not be for years, and then there was the chance of returning to Angador with him.

This time he couldn't help a little curl in his lips. "And you're here, because you know what services Genna was providing."

"I would be entirely at your disposal, your Grace," she informed him.

They wanted this position badly, Tartan thought.

"I'll have to consider this," he said. "In the mean, I assume you've inserted yourself in the palace staff?"

"Since before you came here," she informed him, standing. She looked down on the open bodice then back at the Duke.

"Are you sure you aren't going to sample the wares, prior to your decision?"

She didn't know how being unfaithful to his wife haunted him, he saw, and that meant that she hadn't actually been talking to Genna, just observing her. As careful as Genna always was, it surprised him that she could miss another Bounty Hunter working so closely.

Perhaps she hadn't? Too much was left up to guesswork.

"I'm sure your wares are fine," the Duke informed her. A flicker in her eyes spoke perhaps of disappointment. No woman wants to offer herself and be turned down.

"Very well, your Grace," she said. She pulled her bodice closed and quickly tied a few of the severed ends back together. It wasn't pretty but it would get her down the passageways. Tartan had no doubt she'd blame him for the broken strings, regardless.

The Emperor had once said something like, "Good behavior is its own reward, mostly because no one else ever appreciates it."

Again, he had to fight back a smile.

"I'll be back in touch with you, your Grace," she said.

"I shouldn't need more than two days," he informed her.

"Very well, your Grace."

And she was out the door. Tartan closed his own shutters, reminding himself that the divan would need to be removed and aired out before it made the room smell.

***

Tartan had gotten out of the habit of eating a formal breakfast. When he returned to the Imperial Dining room, he was reminded why.

A huge, heavy table stretched almost the length of a room no less than fifty paces long. Stout wooden chairs surrounded it, and palace barons filled most of them. There had been lesser nobility around the palace from the days of his father, persons who had been elevated without land by the King, who then had nowhere to go and no services to offer, who ate the palace food and gossiped the palace politics. Tartan knew that it was rare for any of them to miss a meal.

The head of the table had been reserved first for the King, then for the Emperor, and in his absence the Heir. Tartan had occupied it as regent, and on entering was surprised to see the Prince in it now.

This could change everything, he knew. If Vulpe meant to rule in his father's place, as his older sister had, then Tartan needed to leave. No writ had been signed by the Emperor to support him, and the Wolf Soldier guard under J'her would not obey him with a Mordetur wanting the throne. Tartan straightened, painted on a smile and saluted the young Prince.

To everyone's surprise, Vulpe stood and surrendered the seat, moving to the left where the Empress normally would sit. Tartan moved quickly down the length of the table, behind the chairs filled with barons and a few visiting dignitaries, including some of Lee's ladies in waiting, all of their waiting now focused on being recalled to their homes, to the seat belonging to the Emperor. He sat and summoned the Uman girl who carried the water pitcher.

"We did not expect you, your Highness," Vulpe informed him. He switched the empty plate before him for the one he had left in front of Tartan. "I was informed that you rarely attend the morning meal."

"I didn't want to eat alone this morning," he said.

"I can't blame you," the Prince said. "Half of the palace is drenched and the rest smells like old dogs." Palace barons around the table smiled and chuckled at the joke. Rain pattered against the huge bay window that looked out over the harbor from the dining room. Dark, dreary grey clouds hung ominously over the few Imperial Sea Wolves and the many merchant vessels bobbing at the docks.

The Uman servant poured his water. Tartan picked up the two-pronged fork next to his plate and reached out for a platter of ham. The Emperor had turned his nose up at the traditional beef haunch and vegetables for the morning meal in exchange for ham, eggs, cheese and strong tea. While the practice might be slow coming along with the common people, the palace happily converted to the newer, fatty fare.

But then, the Duke mused, the Emperor stood taller than almost any other man, and when he walked across a wooden floor the room shook. Palace barons had become paunchy and sallow on what seemed to fuel Rancor Mordetur's strength.

"Court in less than an hour, your Grace," another Uman reminded him, sliding three fried eggs from a serving tray onto his plate. Tartan looked up and recognized the Uman Bounty Hunter, her front laces replaced, a smile on her lips.

"Your name, girl?" Tartan asked her. It occurred to him that she hadn't bothered to tell him that in his chambers.

"Kirren, your Grace," she informed him, and dipped a curtsy.

Tartan nodded and attacked his food, ignoring her as he would any other servant. She left to her duties with a smile on her lips.

If she thought this would impress him, Tartan reflected, she'd made a mistake in her tactics. If Tartan hated anything it was to be pestered.

"How have you enjoyed court, your Highness?" Vulpe asked him, not looking up from his plate, where his knife and fork butchered a thick slice of ham, and a smear of yellow spoke of where his eggs had been.

"Tea, your Highness?" another Uman girl asked him. He nodded and she filled his mug.

"I don't care for it, much as your father and, I'm sure, your sister did not care for it, and as I know my father, before them, did not care for it," Tartan informed him, then took a mouthful of ham from his fork. Around it, he added, "But the alternative is even more distasteful."

Vulpe smiled. One of the Shem Hannen cocked an eye at him but said nothing. Next to that man, his Knight Lieutenant sat, quietly eating.

"You're quiet, Radmon," Tartan noted.

"As befits a junior officer," the man replied with a smile. The baron sitting next to him snorted.

Tartan couldn't help feeling like he had stepped into the middle of a conversation about him. While no one was less than cordial, no one seemed to want to give back anything, either. The evening table had a reputation as being more formal – the morning table began the day and most attendees, even palace barons, had something to share.

"I regret that I will be missing that," Vulpe added, and took another bite.

"My Lord?" Tartan said, by way of asking him what he meant.

Vulpe put the knife and fork down. "I have duties to perform for the Empire," he said. "I'll be taking a Sea Wolf and a full crew back to Volkhydro."

The whole room fell quiet.

"I knew nothing of this," Tartan said, scowling. He would have expected the Prince to remain at least for a week, out of good manners if nothing else.

"I would be surprised if you had, your Highness," he said. "I doubt that you knew, as well, that the Lady Nina of the Aschire has left the Imperial service, either."

Eyes darted back and forth around the table. *That* was a surprise. Nina of the Aschire, known by such monikers as "The Emperor's Personal Squirrel," "The Imperial Watch Dog" and more ominously, "Mistress of Pain," had overseen the safety of Lee and then Vulpe and Chawnee for ten years. Her rule had been merciless – even Wolf Soldiers feared the slight girl from the Aschire forest. In his last years here, learning to be both an Earl and a man at the Emperor's side, he'd both loved and hated Nina of the Aschire, but he'd never thought she'd leave.

"What prompted that?" Tartan asked.

Vulpe looked once around the room before answering. "She's been in my father's service since before I was born," he said. "I think that any woman, especially one who raises the children of others, will eventually want to pursue her own."

Tartan saw that as unnecessarily cryptic but reasoned that Vulpe didn't want to make what would already be burning gossip into a wild fire. "She will be missed," Tartan acknowledged. "I found a great friend in Nina of the Aschire."

Sneers passed among the palace barons, and even a few of Lee's former ladies.

Yes, he thought, there were good reasons why he minimized his time here.

***

Court droned on. Earls and wealthy commons came before him complaining of the damage done by the invaders from Conflu, seeking relief from their taxes or loans at little or no interest from the Empire. The command in Uman City, where most of the Empire's troops were being trained and almost half of the Eldadorian Regulars still resided, needed more and more gold to pay for the incredible expense of feeding so many. The Imperial coffers were emptying at an alarming rate, and Tartan saw a mere trickle coming in to refill them.

Soon they might have to go the duchies, looking not for taxes but for loans against the future. Tartan couldn't imagine driving the nation into debt on behalf of an Emperor who hadn't authorized it.

At the end of a court session that had run unusually long, a commotion came from double doors at the entrance to the throne room.

Tartan sighed. This used to happen with his father, he remembered. Someone was demanding audience and the palace guard felt otherwise. J'her's Wolf Soldiers were more likely to seek their own solution if pressed too hard, and Tartan doubted that they'd improve anything.

"What is this?" he demanded. The Earl who had been speaking to him about getting help from the Eldadorian Regulars to find or to replace his herds, which the Confluni had run off, made an exasperated expression and stood to one side.

Tartan had been considering actually helping him. It would be an easy way to send a few hundred Angadorian Knights back to Angador to be replaced, perhaps bringing his wife with them.

"Your Highness!" a man with an Andaron accent called to him. "Your Highness! We come seeking our reward!"

Reward? What reward? Tartan hadn't heard of this. He motioned to the Wolf Soldiers surrounding the unseen Andarons to bring them before him.

Twenty Wolf Soldiers formed a box around five Andarons as the group of them marched down the red carpet that ran from the entrance to the throne room to the Circle of Judgment before the throne. Each of them bore a sick trophy in each hand.

The horned head of a Swamp Devil. Skin dark as night, mouths open and forked tongue's lolling over red teeth, some with red eyes still open, some with them closed or gone. Tartan's heart actually froze in his chest – he'd heard of this.

The Emperor had promised one of Blizzard's get to the person who brought him ten pair of Swamp Devil horns. During his father's time, the Swamp Devils had travelled up from their swamp in the north of Toor into southern Eldador, murdering and raiding. Standing over eight feet tall and most of them endowed with their own evil magix, they had been the scourge of the southern kingdom.

With the creation of Angador, the raiding had become worse as the spoils were sweetened. In answer to this, the Emperor had built a bridge over the Great Mid River, which formed the boundary between Eldador and Toor.

On the bridge, at its apex, a basket could be found. In that basket, on the first day of every month, a representative of Angador, under heavy guard, replaced every Swamp Devil horn he found with a gold coin. Horns had been deposited there from Eldadorians, from Toorians, from the occasional wandering warrior; but for the most part, these horns came from other Swamp Devils, who killed their own kind gleefully and welcomed the gold coins.

That alone had curtailed the Swamp Devil invasions. This latest invention had led to wholesale slaughter, mostly by Andarons who wanted to improve their herds with Blizzard's bloodline. The tribes had all but invaded Toor to get at the Swamp Devils, and the side effect of that had been that Toorian/ Andaron relations stood at an all-time low.

Plots within plots, traps within traps – this was the mind of the Emperor. Tartan didn't know if he actually meant to honor the promise, and he'd said nothing to Tartan about it. The Duke knew one thing, however:

There wasn't a ridable horse that Blizzard had fathered in the Imperial stables.

The Andarons stomped forward and dropped the heads into a pile before Tartan, a defiant look on their faces. Tartan could tell – they expected to be cheated. Even one Swamp Devil could be so formidable, how could *anyone* kill ten?

"How many lives did this cost?" Tartan asked, his voice ominous even to himself.

The Andarons straightened. "Nearly one hundred," he said. "We had a huge tribe once. Now, we are mostly women, children and old men."

"How do you hope to keep the horse I give to you, once you have it?" Tartan asked.

"That is our concern."

Tartan nodded. Fair enough. The Emperor would probably have charged down the steps to the throne with a sword in his hand if anyone dared to speak to him so plainly, however the Emperor wasn't here and these Andarons knew it.

Tartan turned to his Shem Hannen. "My Lords," he said. "What is the status of finding a foal to reward these brave men?"

"A foal, your Highness?" old Datreve repeated. "No such was promised."

Scowls ran over the Andarons' faces like clouds over an angry sea. Tartan straightened. If the game was to deny that the promise had ever been made, then it was no wonder Vulpe didn't want to be in this seat, or even in the capitol, now.

"The promise was for one of Blizzard's bloodline," the Andaron who'd spoken before said, through gritted teeth.

"And you shall have it," the Shem Hannen said. "But not a foal – certainly that wouldn't be fare to you, to take your chances with a foal."

Tartan's eyebrows lowered.   True – foals could be risky. Especially in the plains of Andoron, where wolves still roamed.   He himself wouldn't want to travel that distance, across that many different climates, with a new born.

"We're to receive a full grown horse, then?" the Andaron asked.

Datreve smiled.   "In fact," he said, his right hand sweeping before him, "you may have your choice of five."

That's when Tartan got the joke.   He didn't think it was particularly funny.

Chapter Sixteen:

Results

The first time that Rancor Mordetur had ever mated a mare to his famous stallion was in Andoron, for the Long Manes tribe. Everyone knew this story, because the price for his stallion's services had been his then-slave, the Empress Shela.

That mating had resulted in a mare, which went to an Andaron war lord, Shela's father, whose name meant, "Kills with a Glance." Where Blizzard was the veteran of almost as many battles as the Emperor, the mare had fallen to an enemy spear the second time Kills rode her into battle, and never produced offspring.

Since then Blizzard, who as a stallion should have produced hundreds of foals, in fact barely produced dozens, and most of them proved unridable. Tartan had seen one stallion named 'Little Storm,' which the Emperor had gifted to an old man rumored to come from his homeland, another named 'Bastard,' which belonged to the Prince Gelgelden and had apparently been stolen, and of course Thunder Cloud.

Another mare had been named, "Doomsday," which Tartan had always thought a funny name. The Empress herself had worked for years to try to tame the mare, but to no effect. Almost from birth, the horse hated all other life, other horses included, and had to be put down. A few of Blizzard's colts had been gelded and then barely served as drafts.

Because Little Storm had come from a draft mare, the Emperor had bred to other mares similar to her. The problem unfortunately was not finding the mares, but in getting Blizzard interested in them. Blizzard came from far to the north, from what people called "The Herd that Cannot Be Tamed." In recorded history, the Emperor alone had ridden a horse off of those plains. Those horses didn't breed outside of their own herd, and Blizzard rarely made an exception.

Outside of the palace walls, where a medium stone wall enclosed an open-air compound, the Andaron warlord and his four countrymen stood at the fence of a corral where Blizzard's unridable scions kept each other company. Three mares and two stallions between three and six years old, barely tolerating each other and certainly no other living being.

Tartan hadn't even heard of these horses, or he'd have spent more time here. When Thunder Cloud galloped out of the Imperial stables, he'd honestly believed that with her went the last of Blizzard's offspring.

"You may have your choice," Datreve informed the Andarons, indicating the small herd with an outstretched arm, the wrinkled index finger sporting a long fingernail. "You've certainly earned it."

The Andarons all crossed their arms over their breasts and frowned. Clearly they had expected to be cheated, and were finding how easily this reward came difficult to believe.

Tartan stood quietly to one side and shook his head. Little did they know, he thought. This was going to be a bloodbath.

"May we ride them?" one of the Andarons asked.

"None of them are broken," Datreve said. "We leave that to you."

The Andarons exchanged glances. There had been no promise of a trained horse, of course, but horses were usually at least broken to the saddle by the time they reached three years of age.

Any Andaron would want a stallion, Tartan knew, just because of the status of owning one. As well, a mare could produce as many as six or eight foals, while a stallion could mate to every mare in their herd. A stallion made more sense.

Without warning, one of the Andarons leapt up on to the top rail of the corral fence, then off into the actual corral where the horses nibbled at the dry ground and random patches of grass. One mare's head came up as the Andaron sprinted to the larger of the two stallions, a palomino standing opposite the herd from a dapple grey with a long, black mane and tail. That stallion seemed to ignore the Andaron until he came within a man's length of his side.

The stallion's head came up, its eyes wide. His tail rose in alarm. The Andaron leapt, stretching his body, reaching for the stallion's long, white mane. He caught the stallion just above the withers and threw a leg over his broad back. The palomino, just under 17 hands tall, stood stock still, as if unable to comprehend what had just happened to him.

The equine eye narrowed as reality set in.

The Andaron screamed out his war cry as the stallion reared in anger. The rest of the small herd ran to the far side of the corral, led by the dapple grey. To his credit, the Andaron gripped the stallion's barrel with strong legs and slipped both hands into the base of the thick black mane. The heavy horse, well over ten times the Andaron's weight, dropped to all fours and then immediately kicked out with his back legs, turning on the fronts, reaching back over his shoulder trying to bite the Andaron. Again and again, kicking and turning, the bucking stallion worked to shake the Andaron from his back.

When bucking didn't dislodge him, the stallion went to leaping straight up in the air, all four hooves leaving the ground as his back arched. Called a 'crow hop,' the horse used his mass to force the lighter Man off of his back.

The Andaron jerked back and forth on the stallion's back but didn't shake loose. Next the furious horse combined crow-hopping with kicking, adding to the force delivered to the tenacious Man. Now Tartan could see the Andaron starting to come lose, moving first to the left then the right, his tired legs slipping as the horse's barrel started to slick with sweat. Tartan was actually surprised that anyone could hold on for this long. If he lived, Tartan resolved to offer him a position among the Angadorian Knights. He'd make an excellent trainer.

Unfortunately the stallion had other plans. The great beast reared again and, as he started to return to the ground, kicked out with his back legs. The result was to fire the unlucky Andaron like a crossbow bolt over the stallion's shoulder, driving him into the ground. The Andaron didn't even have time to scream as he crashed into the hard-packed dirt almost twenty feet away from the horse.

The Andaron hit the ground, bounced and then hit the ground again. The stallion charged. The other Andarons leapt for the fence and to their fallen comrade's aid. Tartan shook his head.

Not a chance, he thought to himself.

Like a bull might, with his head down, the stallion ran down the Andaron lying on the ground. Like a bull, he spun on his hind legs, turned and ran him down again. Huge hooves crushed bones and threw blood as the helpless Andaron tried to crawl to one side, then to curl up into a ball and shield himself from the angry beast.

On the fourth pass, the man moved no more. The stallion allowed itself to be distracted from the ragged pile of skin and protruding bones which once had been a proud Andaron male. The one who had returned unscathed from so difficult a challenge found himself killed by the prize.

The irony wasn't lost on any of them, Tartan felt sure.

The four surviving Andarons stood around their fallen comrade, then one started chanting. Tartan had seen this before when he'd gone to Andoron with the Emperor. The chant went on for twenty minutes, then ended as quickly as it started. In Andoron tradition, they left the man where he'd fallen. As far as they were concerned they'd sent him off to be with his goddess, and what remained belonged to Earth, and not to them.

They returned as one to Devarre. Tartan knew the Shem Hannen would order the remains be removed and interred when these warriors left. Right now there was the issue of what they would consider unfairness, of the Emperor cheating them. They'd risked their lives for a reward that turned out to be more deadly than the challenge.

"We will have that one," the warlord said, the others nodding. "We will come for him in the morning."

"Your will, my Lord," Devarre said, lowing his head. He made a fist of his left hand and enclosed it in his right, then made a circle in front of him with each. "The deal is sealed."

The Andaron mimicked him and nodded. Without another word, the four turned and left.

Tartan shook his head. He turned away from all of them, toward the hills past the stone wall to the west of Galnesh Eldador, and to his surprise saw three more horsemen near the monument to his father, King Glennen, marking the first King of Eldador's grave.

One was a tall man in a blue travel cloak and brown leather pants, riding a huge grey horse. Next to him another rider, also in a blue riding cloak, but wearing black leather pants; small and thin and possibly a woman, sat a much smaller sorrel. His or her maroon blouse gave no clue, but the hair caught the wind - long and brown and light on the breeze.

The third was a tiny being, all in black on another large horse that Tartan recognized at once as Thunder Cloud. He straightened. If he'd been mounted or if there were a horse near, he'd have ridden out after them right now, but they'd surely be gone before he could be properly mounted.

For whatever reason, Lupennen hadn't strayed far from Galnesh Eldador, and had instead found allies here.

*****

The month of Law stood sacred to those who worshipped the god for whom it had been named. Tartan counted himself among them, although his father had worshipped Adriam. The Emperor, of course, worshipped the god War. The closest thing that that god had to a holy day was the anniversary of the Battle of Tamaran Glen.

Glennen had established the church of Law before he'd even finished his own palace. High holy mass began on the first day of the month with the rising sun and the church stayed full even after the sun set. The faithful would come in, attend, listen to the different priests and then leave. The Stowes, Tartan's family, owned a balcony in the church that even the Emperor wasn't entitled to, not that he ever came here. War had his own obsidian shrine in the city.

Tartan cancelled court and spent the morning here, trying to find some sort of serenity. He hadn't expected life to be easy in the capitol but he hadn't expected it to be this hard, either. He hadn't expected to lose so much. His father had warned him once that while the commons saw the nobility as leading a life of leisure, in fact there came great weight and responsibility with the birth right.

Tartan hadn't appreciated that before now.

"Beloved," he heard from behind him.

He turned in his padded chair, in the balcony that overlooked the podium where the priest of Law spoke of the power of steadfast devotion, to see the red velvet curtains at the entrance to the Stowes' sanctuary parted, and his wife standing there, dressed in white, a gold chain around her neck with the closed fist amulet of Law dangling from it, her long brown hair bound up to reveal the cut of her pale neck.

Her over-large bosom rose and fell, her low-cut dress revealing her. Two Uman servants in the Stowe livery flanked her, their hair pony-tailed behind their heads, their faces down in respect. There she stood, Duchess Yeral Stowe, his wife, the woman who had worked so hard to betray the Empire and to kill him.

"I've missed you," she informed him.

He stood, took her hand and kissed it. He guided her to the wooden chair beside him, padded in red velvet to match the drapes, and held her finger tips as she sat. He took his own seat beside her, keenly aware that they'd drawn the attention of the congregation and of the buzz of gossips remarking on the unexpected appearance of the Lady of Angador.

"Have you just arrived?" Tartan whispered. An Uman restored the curtain behind them. Tartan couldn't see the squad of Angadorian Knights who had accompanied him here to guard just outside of the balcony, but that didn't mean anything had happened to them. Yeral could have ordered them away but Tartan didn't think it likely that they'd listen to her.

"Only this morning," she said in a hushed voice. "We stayed at a dreadful hostel south of here and came early. I've left Terran in charge of Angador and brought another thousand of your Knights with me."

That left less than 2,500 at home, Tartan considered. Proper for the Lady of Angador to be protected, not so to leave the home garrison bare. Angador stood responsible for the southern Empire, and so few Knights would barely cover his own duchy adequately.

"You're pleased to see me, I hope," she said, and batted her plain, brown eyes.

He kissed her hand again and forced a smile. "Of course, my dear," he said. "Surprised and concerned is all. The weight of the Empire is on my shoulders."

"So typical of the Mordeturs to go off on their own adventures, and leave us to keep the home fire," she sniffed. "Even the death of their own daughter couldn't bring them back."

The residents of the attached balcony looked sideways at the duchess but said nothing. Tartan recognized the Earl of Tonkin and his family, come to the capitol to discuss shipping futures. Tartan had bought Sentalan grain and livestock heavily in anticipation of Eldadorian shortages and most of that product had moved through Tonkin.

"In confidence, my dear, not in church," he reprimanded her

gently.

"I'm merely proposing –" she began.

"*Not* in church," Tartan repeated.

She cast him a dark look but said nothing. The priest at the altar introduced the choir, which began a hymn. The sweet sound flowed over Tartan. He knew even now that his wife was creating a vengeance to serve on him, but didn't worry overmuch. She'd done so before, and lately gotten more serious.

Beside that, he mused, she wouldn't be around long enough to put it into motion.

***

"A missive from the Duke of Vreck," the squire informed him.

Tartan had retired to his room with his wife, who'd spent the last hour complaining of the inadequate furnishings and the Emperor's poor taste. He was the *Regent*, after all, and some opulence seemed to be – well – demanded!

She perked up to hear the name of Vreck. The Duke had been one of the most adamant in insisting that Stowes, not Mordeturs, belonged on the throne, until Tartan himself had informed him that he had no interest in it. He also seemed to be an accessory in the Duchess' treason.

Ironic how that had worked out.

"What does Ceberro have to say?" Yeral inquired, just *slightly* too eagerly.

If Yeral had thought to incriminate the Duke, she couldn't have done better. His avarice knew no limits.

Out of habit, Tartan checked the seal on the scroll before opening it. Nobles would usually seal a scroll with a glob of wax and then the imprint of their own signet ring in that. Although there were magix that could lift such a seal, most of them couldn't put it back exactly right, and then the stain from the wax would be slightly off from the stuff on the paper.

Such was the case here. Tartan held his face bland and noted that the seal was just the tiniest bit off from the red stain in the parchment. Someone had been good, but not masterful in replacing the seal.

Tartan's mind raced.

"Well?" his wife demanded.

Nothing for it. He popped the seal and unrolled the parchment. He recognized Ceberro's handwriting from the dozens of messages he'd received before. Ceberro hated to use a scribe, claiming that his best eloquence resided in his fingers, not his tongue. Tartan's eyes scanned the yellowed scroll as he sensed his wife behind him.

The thought unnerved him. It was as if the weight of the dagger were already in his back.

"He claims," Tartan said, "that the south is overrun with unruly Andarons. Word spread fast that someone had come north for the prize, and then the Toorians and the Swamp Devils have worked almost in cooperation to drive out every Andaron. Most are choosing to cut through Angador and Eldador rather than the Slee Swamp to get back to Andoron."

"Ghastly," Yeral exclaimed.

Tartan shook his head, his mind already racing. She didn't know *how* ghastly, he thought. A good portion of those Andarons would try to brave the Aschire, the forest between Eldador and Andoron which filled the only land route directly between the two nations. The purple-haired Aschire who peopled the forest not only killed anyone who entered their forest uninvited, they were the staunchest supporters of the Emperor other than his own Wolf Soldier guard. Time and again they'd come to the Eldadorian call for expert archers, some of the best in the world. Not only could this create a problem with the Andarons as the Aschire slaughtered them, but the Aschire would surely take offense that Eldadorians allowed Andarons to approach their side of the Aschire forest in the first place.

This made for an excellent opportunity for profiteers. Ceberro himself had argued many times that the Emperor took too soft a hand with the Aschire. Eldador had claimed the forest under Glennen's rule, and Tartan's father had looked with disdain on what he called 'the squirrels' of the Aschire forest. The Emperor, in turn, had made the Aschire a duchy under the one Aschire Duke, his nanny Nina's father, and made him the official liaison between the Aschire and the Fovean world, almost independent of the Empire itself.

Tartan leaned back in his chair and smiled, dropping the letter into his lap. Where Ceberro had thought to add to his headaches, he had in fact provided him with a solution, not just to one problem but to many.

His wife picked at him over his shoulder- she wanted the letter. He let her have it. It didn't matter what she did now.

This had turned out to be a good day.

Chapter Seventeen:

Actions

Tartan Stowe awoke in the Heir's chambers on the second day of Law to a gentle knocking at his door. His wife snored peacefully at his side, wearing nothing, her loose hair framing her plain face.

She'd resisted his advances the previous night – a surprise to him because she normally either encouraged him or at least laid peacefully and waited for him to be tired of her. Considering the recent assassination attempts he'd really only made the effort in order to appear normal, and apparently she'd given up even that fiction.

In fact, she held no interest for him. She'd never be Genna. He'd never had a lover of that caliber and he felt in his heart he never would. This reminded him that Genna would be interred this afternoon, and that thought brought a wash of melancholy over him.

The knock came at the door again, more insistent this time. It had to be important if they dared to disturb his rest – not that it seemed there were too many worried about that lately.

He slipped out of the covers and into his robe, his bare feet finding no slippers on the cold stone floor. Yeral had seen the state of them and ordered them removed the day before, as a part of her redecorating flurry which Tartan could only assume was her way of making her presence known. No matter what his plans for his traitorous wife, he didn't want to foreshadow them now by acting like her desires didn't matter.

He padded over to the door, reaching into the robe's left pocket and assuring himself that one of Genna's daggers still lay hidden there, and put a hand on the door, standing directly behind it.

"Who is it?" he whispered. A cautious glance informed him that his wife still lay sleeping.

He half-expected the door to fly open and armed assassins to force their way in. Unlikely, he knew. He'd doubled the Angadorian Knight guard not just here but in the nursery and at key points in the palace as well. He just couldn't bring himself to trust Wolf Soldiers.

"Kirren Navesh," came the response. "The Heir's chambermaid."

He'd enlisted no chambermaid, he knew, but he recognized the Uman Bounty Hunter's voice. He'd asked her name at breakfast the day before. He doubted very much that this was it but if she meant to visit him with his wife in attendance, then this was as good a disguise as any.

He opened the door to see her and twenty Knights in full steel in his anteroom. She lowered her head demurely and moved to enter, but he laid his left hand on her hip, staying her and earning a look of surprise that for some reason gratified him.

"The Duchess still sleeps," he informed her, stepping into the anteroom. The Knights all came to attention, some groggy from the night watch. Tartan knew from experience how excruciating it could be to stand in full armor for hours, waiting for an attack that never came, not allowed to speak for fear of waking one's charge.

"Don't do what they do," the Emperor and his father both had told him, "but point to when you've done it in your past. You don't want to be one of the men or they'll never respect you, but if you've suffered as they have, they'll come to believe you understand them, and they'll follow you anywhere."

He needed to talk to this woman, but not in front of his warriors. The whole palace knew of his dalliance with 'Jean,' so he might as well use that to his advantage.

"With me," he informed her, and without a sideways glance left the room in his robe and bare feet, the Uman woman in attendance behind him. He caught the glances between his Knights but of course they said nothing.

From the Spartan anteroom to a passage with a bare stone floor and walls, Tartan saw sconces holding half-burned torches set so that someone could move from one puddle of light to another, and the occasional iron-bound door to either side. He turned to his left without a glance at the Uman. He'd grown up here, and he knew where he'd find privacy.

Past three doors, he came to one on his left no different from the others. He took the cold steel latch in hand and lifted it, hearing the scrape of rust on steel. No one came here and hence no one used the latch.

He pushed the door open on dirty hinges, hearing more of a grind than a squeal. Within the room measured barely eight feet by eight, lit only by a small window barely large enough for a hawk to push through, barred to keep exactly that from happening. There had been furniture here once, but it was gone now, and dust covered the floor.

He entered, the Uman behind him, and he closed the door.

"My *Lord*," she said, mocking surprise.

He shook his head and grimaced at her, feeling no humor in him. This wasn't a place for humor.

He felt like he could still smell the blood in this room, the sweat, the fear. No one came here because no one had a reason to – this was the room where he and his siblings had been born. Glennen had set it apart for that purpose alone, and apparently the Emperor hadn't bothered to change it. He may even have used it himself, though he doubted it. Shela, an Andaron, would have wanted to see the sky as her children came into this new world.

"Have you come to a conclusion, then, your Grace?" she asked him, trying to look into his eyes.

"Strip yourself," he ordered her. Even his own voice sounded strange to him.

"Your – your Grace?"

He back-handed her. Even her lightning-fast Bounty-Hunter reflexes didn't serve her. He caught her square below the left eye with his knuckles. She managed somehow not to drop the serving tray that she'd brought with her, her head lurching to one side, the cheek already pink.

"You wanted to replace Genna," he informed her. "Do it, then. Strip yourself."

"Your will, your Grace," she said. She turned and set the serving tray down in a corner next to the door, then returned to her place before him. She unlaced the front of her palace dress and slid the top over her shoulders.

"Continue," he ordered her, watching. In the end, his father had pursued a replacement for his mother. He'd descended into a drunken meanness that his children all had difficulty watching. Glennen hadn't even been safe around his eldest daughter.

He wondered if what he was feeling now, the rise of lust in him mixed with an undercurrent of self-loathing for violating his vow to his wife, mirrored what his father had felt.

Kirren wriggled out of the blousy skirts of her palace dress, revealing herself in leggings and two daggers at her mid section, held by a belt. She unbuckled that and dropped the daggers next to her, leaving them clearly within reach, and then slid her thumbs under the waistband of her white, cotton leggings.

Looking up into the Duke's eyes, she removed those, as well, revealing her smooth skin from nose to sandals.

Tartan dropped the robes he wore and more fell on her than laid with her. She grunted as she slipped backwards to floor, his body against hers. He pushed her legs apart and violated her, taking no consideration for her pleasure, feeling more as if he were punishing her by doing this than sharing it with her. His body reacted with more energy than his mind would have attributed to the act.

Although a young man in his prime, he didn't last long. He forced his eyes to remain open as he reached his climax because he didn't really trust her. A thin sheen of sweat on his body, he simply rolled off of her when he was finished, leaving her lying on her palace gown.

"I have to admit that this was unexpected, your Grace," she informed him.

"Were you aware that my wife was on her way here from Angador?" he asked her, pulling on his robe. He didn't want to be naked in front of her now.

He could feel her eyes on his profile, trying to read him. He gave her nothing, forcing his eyes forward.

This meanness in him seemed both new and familiar. He'd seen ally after ally leave or abandon him since he'd come to the capitol. He had to do what he had to if he wanted to keep order here.

And he couldn't do that if he was dead.

Dead like Genna.

"No, your Grace," she informed him.

He turned his head and looked her in the eye. Hers were a greenish brown, common in Uman. He just stared, keeping his face blank, as he'd seen the Emperor do when he tried to wring the truth out of someone.

He'd received that look, that feeling like the Emperor was actually sniffing around his brain. He got that now – understood what the Emperor had done. His eyes might be focused on hers, but he took in her reactions, the tiny changes at the corners of her eyelids, the flare of her nostrils, the movements of her lips. She wanted to force her face to be plain.

She was clearly lying, and in a few seconds, he could tell that she knew he'd found that out. The face sank a little and relaxed. She'd been revealed.

She looked away.

He lay to her left. She turned her right shoulder just a little.

Quick as a wink she snatched up one of the daggers and drove it for his heart. She must have decided that he'd want to kill her for lying to him. That is what the Emperor would do.

Tartan Stowe caught the Uman woman's wrist in his right hand. Her right formed a claw and went right for his eyes. He caught that hand in his left, his hand enveloping hers, one of her slim fingers slipping between his. Next came her knee as she twisted her body, going for his more vulnerable stomach and groin. If she could get on top of him then she could bring her teeth to bear. A trained bounty hunter, he knew, could kill in one thousand unlikely ways, as cunning or as vicious as any predator.

Tartan tucked his legs up underneath him, catching her knee on his, then hopped up onto the balls of his feet. He turned both of his forearms in, forcing her elbows to lock and keeping her at the distance of both of their arms, and planted his right foot. Kirren's eyes widened as she saw what he would do.

The Emperor had taught him this. The man might be a devil with a sword but his first love seemed to be wrestling and he had never met his match. Where Rancor Mordetur might use his size, a slimmer, shorter Tartan Stowe needed to rely more on dexterity.

The Duke crossed his wrists and turned his back on the Uman woman. Feeling her naked body against his back and drawing her arms over his shoulder, he yanked her body forward and sent her flying across the tiny room.

She hit the wall flat against her back and crumpled to the

ground. Tartan pounced on her, pulling the belt from his robes to bind her wrists and ankles.

He might as well not have bothered. With a weight advantage of nearly one hundred pounds, he'd knocked the woman out cold and, for a moment, worried that he might have killed her. He laid her out on the floor and saw her naked breast rise and fall. He hadn't killed her, but he didn't doubt that he'd broken a few ribs.

He picked up her daggers and slid them back into their sheaths, then took their belt and strapped it around his waist under his robe. He waited and she didn't wake. He crossed the room and picked a bite of fried egg, a crust of buttered bread and a sip of tea from the serving tray. Chewing, he let what he felt must have been half of an hour pass before her eyes fluttered open and she took a ragged breath.

Her eyes found him and narrowed. He stood leaning against the far wall, his arms crossed over his chest. If she lunged for him, he knew he could kick her back down to the floor.

"You haven't killed me," she informed him.

"Apparently not."

"I assume I owe you an apology," she said, still not moving.

"You owe me a whole lot more than that."

She pushed herself up onto her elbows, wincing. A purpling on her rib cage showed him he'd been right about the damage done.

"What of mine have I left to give you, that you haven't sampled?" she asked him.

He wanted to smile but he didn't. She'd lied to him. He'd caught her. She'd challenged him. He'd beaten her. He had to hope he had enough respect from her now that she didn't think there was any future in opposing him. If she believed she had to negotiate with him to get whatever it was the Bounty Hunters wanted, that would be his best chance not to wake up with a knife in his chest tomorrow morning.

"How long had you known about my wife's coming?" he asked.

"We approached you as soon as she passed the Lone Wood," Kirren answered him. This rang more like the truth. "We knew about her attempts on your life from Genna. Even Genna didn't know that Duke Ceberro had encouraged those attempts. Right now he's buying every Angadorian war horse he can afford to keep them from the Emperor."

That made no sense. After his victory in Volkhydro and the defeat of the Andarons, the Emperor had more horses than he could find riders for. The loss of Angadorian war horses…

Would make it seem that Duke Tartan Stowe had withheld them, Tartan completed his own thought. That would put Tartan's loyalty in question and prompt the Emperor to replace him in the capitol. Tartan would return to his duchy, feeling slighted.

Plans within plans, plots within plots. Wouldn't Tartan then have wondered if the Emperor was behind those attempts on his life?

And why had the Bounty Hunter thrown him that little piece of information? He hadn't asked about this. He didn't think that she was lying, though he'd check on it, but he didn't doubt that she was filtering the truth, either.

Enough of this.

"Make it look like an accident," he informed her.

"My Lord?"

He reached into his robe and unbuckled the knife belt. The two sheaths clattered to the floor, shockingly loud in the tiny room. He had his own plots to weave now – plans that he finally had enough information to make.

"My wife," he informed her. "Make her death look like an accident. Keep in mind that we have Wizards who will examine her in death."

"Of course, your Grace," she said, smiling. In her mind, Kirren had gotten precisely what she wanted.

The Emperor had taught him that when your enemies believed that, then that put them at their most vulnerable.

Before he left the room, he picked up another crust of buttered bread from the serving tray. Everything else had gone cold. The cooks in the capitol, at least at the palace, were decidedly better than his own.

Walking back to the Heir's chambers, he contemplated and chewed. His father had taught him certain aspects of ruling, either by his words or his example. Tartan Stowe wanted to embody that man's legacy of honor and nobility, but he had to live in the world as it existed today, as well. Say what one would about the Emperor, he'd changed Eldador, changed Fovea, and been more successful than Glennen Stowe.

This wasn't his father's Eldadorian nation anymore.

***

Tartan returned to the Heir's chambers and found his wife awake and dressing. Normally she had no fewer than three maids attending her, but she'd come here without them and was dressing herself now. He closed the door quickly behind him after entering in order that she not be exposed to the guards in the anteroom.

"Business so early?" she asked him without turning, her hair running down her bare back and only her blousy white under skirts to cover her from the waist to the floor.

"Running the Empire has more duties than running Angador," he informed her. He crossed the room to its far corner where his clothes hung on a stand. He shed the robe to the floor, the dagger in the pocket clanking against the stone, and with his back to her reached for his leather pants.

"What was that?" she asked him.

"What was what?"

"You dropped something?"

"Just my robe," he said, and stepped into the warm leather.

"Is your robe made of steel?" she sniped at him.

He looked over his shoulder to find her watching him, still topless, her hands on her hips. He recognized the focused expression and knew that, for some reason, she'd latched on to this and wouldn't let it go.

"There's a dagger in the pocket," he informed her, and turned back around.

"Of your robe?"

"Yes."

"A dagger, in the pocket of your robe?" she insisted.

He sighed.

"Why would you keep a dagger in the –"

He spun back around. "Why do you *think* I would keep a dagger with me? Are you aware that there have been three attempts on my *life* since I arrived here?"

He watched her, open-mouthed with surprise from his outburst. He focused on her eyes, her mouth, her long, pale neck. He'd lied. There had been two attempts, not three, but if she'd arranged for them, she'd know that.

If she'd arrived innocently in Galnesh Eldador, she'd know nothing.

Her eyes shot down and to her left, her neck flushed. She collected herself and met his eyes, more demure, tears held back but just barely.

"So – so many," she informed him. "I was unaware, husband."

He could have called off the assassination if he'd wanted to, he knew. He could have found Kirren and informed her that he'd changed his mind. Then the Uman would have had to die, once he felt sure that she'd gotten the message out and recalled the order.

There'd be no need for that now. Yeral had revealed herself with her answer. *So many*, she'd said.

How did she know that there were any at all?

She'd die for betraying him – then he'd deal with Ceberro.

Chapter Eighteen:

Results

Tartan took breakfast in the palace dining room again, not because he wanted to but because the alternative was a breakfast alone with his wife, and since he'd reconciled himself to having her done away with, he really didn't want to spend that much time with her.

Done away with. Assassinated. Tartan mulled over his morning porridge and a cup of strong, black tea that had become a breakfast staple since the Emperor had introduced it. To his left Yeral worked on half of a melon with a knife and a two-pronged fork. The normal rumble of gossip around the table between visiting dignitaries and court barons remained subdued as they gauged the Duke's mood, dark as it was.

He didn't like the idea that someone would be killing his wife for him soon, but he liked even less the idea that the same situation didn't seem to bother his wife.

"May I be excused from court this morning?" she asked him, of a sudden.

The question shook him from his revelry. He turned to his left and found her carving on her melon with a concentration fitting a surgeon. When she spoke to him and didn't look at him, that usually meant she was up to something.

"I see no reason why not," he informed her. He'd have been more surprised if she'd come to court with him. In Angador she shied away from such things in favor of spending time with her maids.

"I wish to see some of these horses that Blizzard has sired," she informed him. She stabbed a piece of melon and raised it to her lips. Regarding it, she added, "Perhaps the Empress has missed something that we can take advantage of."

If Yeral thought that she was leaving Galnesh Eldador with one of Blizzard's scions on a tether, Tartan decided that she must have grossly overestimated the Emperor's generosity. But then, why was she telling him this at all, when he'd already given his leave.

A more suspicious man would think that she meant to establish an alibi.

So he said nothing and continued eating. Looks passed between the nobles at the table. Some of these meant to be before him in the court, and when his father had ruled, it would not have been uncommon for them to make their case here. The Emperor, on the other hand, refused to hear them except formally and didn't allow what he referred to as 'back room deals,' which made no sense because the back rooms in the palace were used for storage.

Breakfast passed with little further incident. Tartan finished quickly and watched the other attendees eat for a little while. The three Shem Hannen advisors hadn't made an appearance, which was strange. Outside of court, he couldn't remember the last time he has seen them.

Finally he stood, nodded to the other occupants and exited down the bay side of the table, giving himself a look through the room's huge windows at the open port beneath the palace, the wharves teaming with activity and lined with ships.

War or peace, there was business to be done, and goods needed to find their way to eager hands.

Out of the Imperial dining room and into the passageway beyond, it struck the Duke that another of his responsibilities was to tend to Princess Chawnee, and he hadn't seen her, either, in more days than he cared to count. Knowing he'd be late to court, he turned on his heel and made a direct path to the wing of the palace that had been reserved for the nursery.

He smiled thinking of the time that he'd spent there with his brother and two sisters. Little known to the Mordeturs, the Stowe children had convinced the original builders to install multiple passages between the different rooms, and even one false wall that concealed a passage out of the palace to the stables. Terran, Tartan's younger brother, had spent countless hours instead of sleeping or at his studies with the old smith who once had shod King Glennen's horses. That man had filled the royal children's ears with incredible tales of his life at Glennen's side, a man at arms caring for the adventurer's horses before he'd become a king. Terran had loved that old man and wept openly on the day his labors took him. The Emperor, at the children's request, had buried him in the royal cemetery.

There existed only one public access to the nursery wing. Ten Angadorian Knights in their full armor guarded it, pikes in their hands. They watched as their Duke approached.

"All quiet?" Tartan asked one of them.

"All well," the sergeant of the guard responded, an older Man with grey hair showing from under his helmet. "One of the Majors of the Wolf Soldier house guard is with the princess now."

"Really?" Tartan stopped dead in his tracks. He hadn't approved this – he didn't even know about it. What were the Wolf Soldiers doing with his charge?

The sergeant made eye contact with him. "My apologies, Tartan," he said. "Agmar of the Second Wolf Soldier Legion. He visits with the Princess no less than once a week."

The other Angadorian Knights exchanged a glance that Tartan barely caught. He wouldn't have needed to, to be on his guard. Suddenly he felt very much naked and very much alone, having come here with no personal escort, feeling himself safe within the palace walls. He hadn't even brought his sword.

That had been a bad mistake.

Tartan nodded and took the door's handle in his left hand. The Angadorian Knights snapped to attention as he passed. The door pulled open to his left, the armored nights standing to his right.

Tartan drove the heel of his right hand up into the sergeant's chin, ramming his head against the wall. The man released his grip on his pike and Tartan snatched it up as it fell, leaping through the door and pulling it shut behind him.

He twisted the handle and drove the head of the pike in between it and the door, bracing the end of the weapon's shaft against the stone ceiling. This door locked from the outside and its hinge pins were on the same side as these pretend Knights, but at least Tartan would have as long as it took them to pry those out to find something to defend himself with.

The handle shook but held. The door resounded with the sound of an armored shoulder thrust against it, but it was made of stout wood bolted in place through bands of steel and wasn't going to give in that way. Tartan turned on his heel and sprinted for the nursery.

It wasn't like the Guild to make the same mistake twice. None of these 'Knights' had called him, "Your Grace," nor would they. The Roosters had realized the mistake but hadn't had the time to study it. He let his Knights call him, "Tartan." That didn't mean that he'd let them grow familiar.

None of them had saluted him. They hadn't snapped to attention until after he'd wanted to pass. Angadorian Knights, like any other regulars, don't make mistakes like that unless they were very new or trying to prove something.

Vulpe Mordetur's sword, 'Fury' had been hidden in the nursery once, but it was gone now. The Prince carried a different weapon and, by now, had left with it. Where could he find something to defend himself with?

Not in the actual nursery, clearly. Leave anything sharper than a wooden spoon there and the children would manage to decapitate each other with it. The nursery as he remembered it broke off into an adjoining room on either side, then across the hall from it the nanny's and the wet nurse's rooms. Farther down the hall there'd be a storage for the diapers and other things that children needed, a pantry and a simple kitchen, a larder, a class room, and then rooms for the children of visiting dignitaries.

If these Knights were telling the truth then there were Wolf Soldiers already here – but what if the actual plan had been for *them* to attack him? Traps within traps, lies within lies, and no weapons in the nursery wing of the Imperial palace!

The door behind him shook in its mountings. They'd have the pins out before he could bash through a locked door. He had to hide himself in rooms belonging to the wet nurse or the nanny, or he'd have to do the best he could with his bare hands against armored warriors.

Then it struck him – this wasn't the nanny he'd grown up with, this was Nina of the Aschire who guarded the Emperor's children. Tartan had grown up with Nina in the palace after his father had died and Rancor Mordetur had assumed the throne. She was probably the most paranoid, overly-protective individual who'd every changed a diaper.

Two quick steps brought him to her door. He flung it open – no lock on the nanny's door. It was her duty to be accessible, and in fact it galled Nina to be enclosed and alone.

She kept her room like the Emperor kept his – Spartan in all ways. Simple cot, simple stand next to it with a lamp. On the wall a bandolier of daggers, all polished and ready for use. A simple stack of shelves stuffed with books, an open window to let in the air.

"Oh, Law bless you, Nina of the Aschire," Tartan said as he pulled the bandolier off of the wall and threw it over his shoulder. Nina was death with her daggers, but the Empress had trained them both.

He turned to face the door. They'd have to come in one at a time – he had a chance in close quarters if they meant to use their pikes. More likely they had short stabbing swords over their backs, more suitable for close fighting and more lethal. Even then, at least he could face them one or two at a time.

For a moment he wondered if he might not have a better chance out the window, but disregarded it. Shela wouldn't have left so obvious an escape route unguarded and, if she had, Nina wouldn't. He'd survive a drop of three palace levels to the stones below if he had to, but not whatever witchcraft waited for the person who crossed those eaves. He didn't even dare to stick his head out and call for help.

He heard the door shake in its jamb down the hall. They'd have it off in a moment. Hopefully they'd come for him before they tried for the Princess. In fact, if they wanted her they'd have her already.

Tartan took a breath and lowered his head, a dagger in each hand. *Collect yourself,* he whispered. Go into the fight with a clear head. How many times had the Emperor told him that the fight usually went to the one who wanted it more, whose mind didn't give the lead to his muscles?

He opened his eyes and then he saw it – a half-circle of steel under Nina's cot.

He knelt down and tugged on the edge. Lo and behold – Nina had hidden a round shield under here. *That* would give him quite an advantage. The Emperor had never favored the shield but Tartan's father had and his trainers as a boy had taught him its uses. This one was three feet wide and emblazoned with the face of snarling dog, its wrinkled face looking like those that the Emperor had spent time training, paws reaching for its enemy under giant fangs and an extended tongue.

Through the leather loops on the inside of the shield, meant for the user's forearm, a broadsword almost four feet long, with a plain steel cross guard and a handle wrapped in leather.

This brought advantage! What could Nina have been doing with weapons like these? Tartan put his arm through the leather straps and hefted the sword. It felt deceptively light, perfectly balanced in his hand. His fingers tingled to hold it, a surge of power moving up through his arm. Suddenly he found himself full of rage – a cold, angry determination that the whole world had been arrayed against him, and this steel was his only avenue to justice.

The first of these fake Angadorian Knights crossed in front of Nina's door, then caught sight of him from the corner of his eye.

Whatever the man might have expected, it wasn't that the Duke would find himself armed and armored, standing on the offensive. Tartan cast aside his original plan to face these Bounty Hunters or whomever they were one at a time. There were only ten of them! He'd face greater odds than this!

With a war scream that rang strange in his own throat, Tartan leapt through the open door, the shield raised and leading with the out-thrust sword. He skewered the first man through the rib cage, the sword slipping between the man's breast and back plates. The 'Knight' screamed and fell against the far wall. Tartan turned and planted his feet apart, facing down the hall where nine still remained, lined up almost like Wolf Soldiers with the front four charging two at a time with short swords, the last five standing behind them two and then three at a time, their pikes raised to strike over their comrades' shoulders.

Tartan squared off on them, his feet spaced apart precisely under the breadth of his shoulders, leaning forward, his breathing even. Wolf Soldier formation – they'd come in high and at mid range all at the same time, seeming impossible to defend from, unless someone had spent *years* designing a defense to just that sort of attack.

Tartan ducked his head behind the shield and rammed the front line of their 'squad,' feeling the scrape of steel weapons on the face of his defense. The first two warriors gave way, one losing his footing and falling on his back, the other stepping backwards into the next line of swordsmen, entangling them as they sought to keep their comrade on his feet. Tartan switched his grip on the sword in his right hand and brought it down like a hole-punch on the unprotected inner thigh of the prone man, cutting the vital artery there.

He stepped back as blood gushed from the wounded man. He'd

be dead in a few minutes – no one could survive that injury. The armored warrior who'd been standing next to him righted himself just in time for Tartan to change his grip again and thrust with the broad sword, punching clean through the man's breast plate and into the heart beneath it. The man groaned and slumped back against the second line once again.

The pikes came in at head level – Tartan met them with his shield. The warriors were all striking for the same target at the same time – a fatal mistake. If they'd have staggered their attacks they'd have had him.

A Wolf Soldier squad had a sergeant to make sure that happened, but this group wasn't so fortunate. Tartan's sword lunged forward again to find the chin under a warrior's helmet, driving for the throat behind. What began as the man's scream was choked off by a fountain of blood as that warrior fell.

The last remaining swordsman swung his sword straight down for Tartan's outstretched arm. Tartan pulled back and met him steel for steel, the pikes clattering again against the shield he held just above head level. When the pikes withdrew, Tartan slammed the shield's metal edge against the bridge of the swordsman's nose, dropping him with blood already starting at the corners of his eyes.

Five swordsmen lay dead at his feet. Five pikemen took a step back from him as one. Normally the pikes would outmatch the swordsman with a shield, but here stood Duke Tartan Stowe defiant and not beaten.

The two pikemen in front lunged forward together with their weapons at mid-range, seeking his gut. The three behind followed up with their weapons at the head level. No way could Tartan meet them all.

Almost of its own accord the shield tilted back and rose, Tartan's arm still in the straps, to catch the lower then the upper sets of pike heads, sending them harmlessly to his left and entangling their barbs. Trapping the pikes against the wall to his left, Tartan stepped forward and drove his broadsword into the breast of first the man on his left, then the man his right, going right for the heart each time, the sword punching through armor like it was barely there.

Both men fell – the three remaining dropped their pikes and reached over their shoulders for their swords.

Tartan pressed the attack – first chopping down at an exposed thigh on the middle man, then taking the one on his left with the back swing, the sword cleaving across the face. That man fell with his face in his hand, the one in the middle dropping next to him and clutching at protruding bone in his leg.

One remained. He threw his sword down and ran. Tartan slammed the sword into the back of a dead man and reached for one of the daggers in his bandolier. He took the weapon by the blade, calmly felt the balance, measured the distance to his target and threw.

The Bounty Hunter, or whomever he was, made it to the door before the dagger took him in the side of the neck. A nearly impossible shot – the dagger caught the vital artery that ran behind the ear to the brain. He made another four shaky steps before he fell.

Tartan heard a sound behind him and turned on his heel, pulling his sword from the dead man's body. Rather than more Bounty Hunters, he found a brute of a man in Wolf Soldier grays, a baby girl in his arms and a look somewhere between alarm and anger on his face. Clearly a Volkhydran, his beetle brow and thick jaw spoke more of hired muscle than a major in the Wolf Soldier guard.

The little girl pointed to the blood-painted walls and bodies before her and said, "Yucky."

Tartan had to agree.

***

Radmon Rukh regarded the bodies of eight pretenders to the Angadorian Knights, cleaned up and laid out naked on the floor in one of the chambers in the tunnels beneath the capitol city. Two more resided in cells in an adjoining room, wounded but saved from death through the quick actions of Eldadorian Wizards.

The Knight Lieutenant shook his head and said, "I don't understand why it's been so easy for them to get into the palace, replace either Wolf Soldier or Angadorian Knight guards, and attack us," he said.

J'her and M'den looked at each other and then Duke Stowe. They'd come here with the three Shem Hannen to consult with the Duke in the wake of the last attack – each of them concerned now about a problem that had moved from local politics to national. Now a squad of Angadorian Knights and a squad of Wolf Soldiers would guard both the Duke and the Princess at all times. J'her and Rukh were working together on a cross-identification method for the troops to keep track of each other.

Tartan tended to think that this wouldn't be as important pretty soon. He also had other things on his mind.

"This smacks of the Bounty Hunter's guild," he said. "It's pointless to tighten security – I'm sure they're already in, deeper than we could find them.

"Datreve," he turned his face to the three Shem Hannen, addressing their leader, "I want every 'sayer the Bank of Eldador can spare in the palace in the morning, and we're going to go person by person through the staff – "

J'her frowned and old Haldarch raised his hand. Third among the Shem Hannen, he usually represented the treasury and finances.

"Your Grace," he said, "the cost of that will exceed what we have in the coffers right now."

"What?" Tartan knew that the cost of the war had been extreme and returns from the duchies had been low, but he couldn't imagine that they'd already managed to spend the Eldadorian nation into bankruptcy.

"I'm to blame," Datreve admitted. "We're spending money to rebuild Volkhydro faster than we can recover it, and I sent five Sea Wolves full of gold and silver Tabaars to Lupha. The Emperor wants to spread coin with his face on it to reinforce the new cities' status as additions to the Eldadorian nation."

"I heard none of this," Tartan said.

M'den and J'her looked at each other and J'her added, "Daggonin brought the order with him from Volkhydro. I hadn't made up my mind about you yet so I didn't share it. When Prince Vulpe meant to depart for Volkhydro anyway, it seemed natural to send that treasure with him."

Tartan felt his lip curl. He'd have known better than to beggar the treasury against future earnings, had they asked him. J'her ran armies, not accounts.

The Emperor had told him once that every time he found a pot hole on a muddy road, it meant a drink of water to a thirsty dog. No matter what situation he found himself in, no matter how bad, it had some value to someone. His mind raced for something like that here.

"I would like to think," he said slowly, "that we can learn from this disaster?"

M'den chimed up this time. "I am the one who advised J'her," he admitted. "And it's the last time either one of us will do something that affects the nation without first consulting you."

"Until the Emperor returns, of course," J'her was quick to add.

"That should be sufficient," Tartan said, and the Shem Hannen nodded. He'd left it up to his subordinates to decide what to learn from this, and this time it had paid off. He wondered if that would make good council for him in the future.

"I want the two survivors interrogated," he said. "I want to know who sent them, when and why. I leave it to the five of you to manage this for me."

"Your will, your Highness," Datreve informed him.

"Lieutenant, Supreme Commander, I'll need to speak with you individually after court today. Make time for me."

Both nodded.

Without another word, Tartan left them, his Angadorian Knights following him and the Wolf Soldier guard preceding him. Alone although surrounded, he had time for his own thoughts.

If the Bounty Hunters had set a trap to kill him, how had they known to spring it in the nursery? he wondered. That made no sense. Even a moment before he'd gone there, he himself hadn't known he'd be seeing the Princess today. Had some magic been involved to change his mind for him? His Angadorian Knights would have been relieved in the afternoon – this group would have had to either keep killing Knights and standing endless posts until he arrived there, which was ridiculous, or they had some way to know where he was going before he himself did.

Even this new Uman Bounty Hunter wasn't close enough to him to be providing that sort of information.

And what of this fortuitous discovery of weapons in Nina's quarters. These were *not* the sort of weapons the Emperor's Watch Bitch employed – not ever. They resided in the Heir's quarters now so that he could study them, but in that battle he'd fought like a warrior with fist full of victories behind him, and although he wasn't new to battle he'd *never* fought like that before.

Afterward, there wasn't a mark on either of them – not a scratch on the shield or a nick on the blade.

Something important was happening in Tartan Stowe's life, and whoever was making it happen was *not* Tartan Stowe!

Chapter Nineteen:

Progression

Tartan was bathed in the Heir's chambers by Kirren, his new personal maid. He'd been bloodied from head to toe and should have steeped himself in a hot bath, but court beckoned and there were issues that he simply had to address.

"My apologies, my Lord," Kirren informed him, scrubbing his back with a rough cloth. He stood in a copper basin filled up to his ankles in water, his arms spread wide, naked. Kirren had disrobed to her undergarments in order that her palace dress not be ruined with red splatter.

"For what?"

She didn't miss a beat, moving to his legs. "The attack on you – we should have caught that. The Roosters took us entirely unaware this time."

Tartan couldn't help thinking that Genna would have known. Her body had been interred by now. He needed to visit her grave. He needed to inform her that he'd been wrong, that he was sorry, that he was just feeling his way here and he didn't know all of the right answers.

He needed to forgive himself, he knew, but that just wasn't coming. The Emperor spoke of this – the guilt after the battle, the regret that came with killing, robbing wives of husbands and children of fathers.

Tartan wanted to rage and weep at the same time, but he

managed to hold it all in.

"Not your fault," he informed her.

"You're kind, my Lord," she informed him, moving to his front.

The water at his feet ran red. He hadn't realized that he'd been bloodied this badly – yet not a scratch on him.

She looked into his eyes as she moved around in front of him, working on his chest. He kept staring forward. He had nothing of himself to give.

"You were fortunate to find that sword and shield," she added.

That got his attention. He looked at her as she looked away. "You knew of them?"

"They came from Volkhydro with Daggonin," she informed him. "Nina of the Aschire found them somehow and wanted them kept here for her. We know nothing else."

That in itself was a lot, Tartan thought. He remembered now that Vulpe had mentioned something of this. He needed to get a message to Nina of the Aschire. Once again, the loss of Central Communications smarted. The tool that none of them could have imagined five years ago had become indispensable since.

Why hadn't the Green One fixed that when he'd come here? Why hadn't D'gattis?

She dropped the rag, stained pink with blood, and picked up a terry-cloth towel. Another of the Emperor's inventions, it made drying faster and easier. He'd explained to Tartan how it worked several times, but he just didn't get it.

She started at his head and rubbed him down to his legs, then took his feet and rubbed them as he stepped out of the basin, turning the white towel pink as well. She tossed the towel into a pile with the clothes he'd discarded. Blood, he knew, was difficult to get out of the fabric.

"Shall I service you before dressing you, my Lord?" Kirren asked him, looking him in the eye again.

At first he didn't know what she meant, then he realized and shook his head. Some warriors craved the release of sex after killing, but for him it seemed an abomination. In the past he'd ignored his wife for days after a battle, which was how she'd found the comfort of her Uman servants.

He wondered if his wife was still alive now. He thought to ask Kirren, but realized that he didn't want to know.

This was going to be a dark day.

***

Kirren dressed him without another word and he left without thanking her. His two squads of guards saw him to the throne room, where the gallery stood packed with courtiers and dignitaries.

Taxes were on everyone's minds. He needed more, the Duchies wanted to give less, and the Earldoms were screaming, even after reaffirming that they still only paid a percent of their gains, not a flat fee. Entire herds and crops had been destroyed in the Confluni invasion, and two armies had burned a swath through the center of the farm-rich center of the Empire. The common people were once again having to buy Confluni grain and meat and the prices, though lower than they'd been before Lupus' reign, seemed incredibly high compared to what locals had charged.

Guilt panged the Duke as he realized that he'd invested heavily in Confluni futures this year, and that those futures were paying off to him at close to 100 percent now. His distributors were raking in piles of silver, on which he paid his due of tax, but his brothers in the nobility repeatedly informed him that the common people who'd lost everything in the invasion also had no coin to pay for foreign goods.

"While volunteers to the Eldadorian Regulars have never been higher," the Earl of Kreddenton, a territory between Steel City and the Lone Wood, informed him, "we've also never had to support more widows and orphans, neither have we had so many beggars in our Earldom."

The Earl, a Man named Theref, stood at the foot of the throne. Dressed in simple brown tunic and leggings, with brown boots and a red sash around his middle, Tartan could tell that his clothes once fit him tighter but that he'd lost weight. His face looked gaunt, his cheeks hollow and his eyes underlined with faint circles. His skin had been browned by the sun. He'd travelled his lands, and he'd suffered with his people. Tartan knew that when the nobles suffered it usually meant that the people had to be close to death themselves.

He had to take this seriously.

"What have you done already to ease their suffering?" Tartan asked him.

The man stood stunned for a moment. This seemed more typical to Tartan. What should *he* do? Why, he'd come here.

"My coffers are bare from taxes," he began.

Tartan shook his head. "You pay a percent. If you paid fifteen coins to Eldador, then you've kept eighty-five for yourself."

Theref's face twisted – he might have expected resistance, but he hadn't expected Tartan to turn the problem back onto him.

"We've used this coin in support of the Emperor's people –" he began, but then he looked up at Tartan and met his eyes.

No, he knew. Tartan Stowe would not fall for that. His own Duke perhaps – but Tartan had the Shem Hannen right here to inform him. Tartan stared back, as the Emperor did, right into the man's soul. He wasn't going to be lied to, and he clearly wasn't going to be politic.

"I suppose there are roads that need resurfacing," he said, looking away, his hands meeting before him as he fidgeted nervously. "With better roads, then perhaps when things improve, more goods will come to my people more quickly."

"Perhaps instead," Tartan advised him, "you could purchase foreign seed and calves and loan them to your own people against future gains."

This caught the Earl by surprise. "Your Grace?" he asked.

It had just occurred to Tartan, but suddenly the Emperor's teachings began to register in his mind.

He looked up from the Earl and swept the court with his eyes. He had their attention.

Good.

"My own Duchy," he said, "has invested heavily this year in Sentalan futures. "We have reaped a great profit redistributing grain and meat bought cheaply at the start of the season. Lately, I have thought that I have made too much.

"So I will follow what the Emperor has taught me: I will 'lead by example.' I will sell to any of you, to the nobles and the wealthy commons among you, at cost, that you may resell seed, calves and lambs, poultry and other commodities to your peasants.

"But our peasants have no coin, my Lord," Theref informed him.

Tartan nodded. "You will sell to them against future earnings," he said. "You will give a calf worth a gold Tabaar now, you'll ask for a gold Tabaar and two silvers at the end of the season. Your people will have a hand full of silvers then after paying you, and you'll all be richer men."

A gold Tabaar, the coin of the realm, was worth twenty silvers, also called 'Tabaars.' To each silver there were twenty copper pennies.

Lupus had talked to him about this concept of ech-nomics, and talked to him about it, and talked to him about it again, but until just then it had made no sense. You put money into the people, you got more back. If you gave them charity, they'd just spend it and you'd be poorer later to help them again.

Now Theref stood where he had. "But… calves will sometimes die. Crops can fail. Peasants don't want to become debtors and Earls don't want to become banks."

"And we have banks already, your Grace," one of the Oligarchs, old Haldarch, informed him. "Perhaps peasants can in some way go to *them* for small loans?"

Tartan nodded. "Let these peasants," he said, "come to the Bank of Eldador for this money then. Let the bank know that they can loan to these peasants for these goods, and if they will pay the state fifteen pennies, then we will guarantee these loans of one gold."

"Fifteen pennies for a gold?" Haldarch looked as if he'd been stabbed. "The treasury will be crushed."

"No," Datreve interrupted him, "it will not. I see the Duke's logic. If a bank loans out 100 gold Tabaars and expects 120 gold Tabaars back, they'll pay 1,500 pennies or three and three-quarter gold Tabaars to the state."

Theref nodded. "Meaning that if you just guarantee the gold Tabaars, then three of every one hundred peasants could fail and the state would *still* be ahead."

Tartan nodded. The gallery to the left of the throne room was buzzing. He'd be surprised if there weren't wealthy commons in the street this afternoon, trying to take advantage of the same thinking and demanding that the state guarantee their loans.

The possibility for corruption was daunting. "Let it be proclaimed this very day," he said, straightening in his throne, "that this act, the… Emergency Peasant Relief Act, is law. Either the Bank of Eldador or any noble or wealthy common may, if *registered with the state*, make these loans to needy peasants affected by the recent invasion, at two silvers per gold Tabaar, and then pay fifteen pennies to the Eldadorian state to be guaranteed back that gold coin, should crops fail.

"And know that," he added, and his gaze swept the room, "any person who uses this Act in any way to defraud the state shall, when caught or when a truth sayer testify that he or she has been deceptive, be whipped to death against the palace walls, immediately upon conviction."

"Whipped to *death*?" Theref exclaimed. That took even the Shem Hannen back.

He had learned that people break laws when they believe that the rewards for breaking them out-weighed the consequences of getting caught. The consequences to the Empire for wide-spread corruption of this relief act could mean the end of the Eldadorian nation's efforts overseas. The consequences for that corruption, then, had to reflect that severity.

"As Regent," he said, "I have spoken."

The Shem Hannen would put the words into paper, and the state would spread the news, probably two steps behind the gossips. Tartan's own experience in his own duchy told him that about seven out of one hundred farms failed in a given season. The state would then expect to lose a gold coin for every two it invested in this idea.

However the state would tax the profits from the ninety-three out of one hundred who succeeded at fifteen percent. What these nobles and wealthy commons were missing was that the state hedged the bet – the state would make another three pennies on every silver of interest paid by the peasants. The peasants who would have demanded free food or stolen it in desperation, burdening the state either way, would pay tax from their additional silvers as well. Coin would start to flow into the coffers on this act of benevolence.

It had taken Tartan Stowe *years* to get his mind around this, but it opened up for him like a budding rose now. Theref would have hired a few strong backs to rebuild roads that needed no rebuilding. He'd have lost his wealth to workers who would just buy food and eat it, sending gold back to Sental.

He leaned back and smiled. This day had started out poorly, but had evolved nicely for him.

Which was when a Wolf Soldier squad marched in through the double doors to the throne room and stood at attention at the end of the red carpet that ran down its middle. Tartan looked into the faces of the warriors, none of whom would meet his eyes, as they waited to be recognized.

Tartan knew right then – his wife was dead.

***

"My condolences, Tartan," Radmon Rukh said to him, his eyes cast down.

Yeral lay still on a stretcher, on a table in the Imperial Infirmary, in the palace. The room had cold stone walls and barred windows where the light shone through and the air passed out. The floor had been made of cold grey stone with a drain at a low corner, making it easier to wash the blood of the wounded out. A white-robed priest with the open hand of Adriam on a gold chain around his neck, no hair on his head and pale in skin from spending his days indoors, tending the sick, stood opposite Yeral, commending her soul to the All Father. Here was where injured warriors would be brought for treatment by healers, usually priests of Adriam like this one, for dire wounds. It had been the most logical place to take the duchess.

Tartan just nodded, unable to take his eyes off of his wife's lifeless body.

"She insisted on approaching that one stallion," J'her informed him. He'd already taken a report from the duchess' guard and the stablemen who'd accompanied her this morning. "She claimed that she saw a 'good boy,' fighting to get out of him, if she could reach him.

"Your own Angadorian Knights brought her the news of the attack on you," he continued. He exchanged a look with Rukh, who nodded. "They called to her that you were being treated in the Heir's chambers. She turned her attention from the stallion to the Knights, and it struck."

The left side of the duchess head was caved in. Tartan already knew the story from beginning to end before J'her opened his mouth.

Yeral knew better. You can't trust a stallion – not for a moment. A stallion might be reached, might be loved, might seem as sweet as a cool breeze on a hot day. All it took was for a thought to get into its head, and it would act on it without hesitation. What made the stallion a fearless friend on the battle field made it a threat in the paddock.

"We have verified the identity of each Knight and each Wolf Soldier," J'her informed him.

"Eh?"

"It wasn't a plot by the Bounty Hunters," Rukh informed him. Tartan met his eyes. "This was just an accident – an unfortunate unfolding of events."

Tartan nodded, not believing it for a second.

"How shall we attend you, my Lord?" Rukh asked him.

Tartan's eyes darted to the Lieutenant's face, but he decided immediately that he was simply expressing his sorrow and respect as a good subordinate, not a Bounty Hunter revealing himself.

He didn't know if he could handle three assassination attempts in one day.

"I'll eat alone tonight, and pray," he said, finally. "Arrange to inter my wife in the Imperial Cemetery."

"Not Angador?" Rukh asked him. *That* was more like Radmon Rukh.

Tartan shook his head. Not his home for the traitorous wife, he thought. This had been his home once, but it belonged to the Mordeturs now. Angador was for the Stowes, and the Stowes didn't need a traitor in their cemetery.

"Her father is buried here," he said, finally, "and she loved him. Let her rest where their spirits might meet again."

All nodded. The priest began to sing, a final prayer for the duchess' soul. Tartan resisted the urge to shake his head.

To Chaos with you, Yeral, you traitor, he thought to himself. *I never gave you cause to try to kill me. If you were so set to dethrone the Mordetur's, you should have started by giving me an heir.*

Tartan let the song end before he left them. J'her and Rukh spoke softly to each other. They were becoming friends finally, or at least forming an alliance. Military men did better with a common enemy to fight.

He understood that now.

***

"You work quickly."

Kirren had brought him 'sammiches' like the ones that Genna had made for him, with the dressing that exploded in his mouth, and a tart, white wine. She poured generously for him as he sat on the couch.

"The Roosters prompted our actions," she informed him, "though the trip to the outer stable would have been too good to pass up, anyway."

Tartan bit into the sammich. The bread was a Sentalan wheat and he had to admit it tasted better than that from Eldador. Kirren knelt on the floor by his feet, to the left of the caw-fee table, and watched him. She didn't take wine like Genna would have.

"Before I washed you, after the attack, I informed an off-duty squad of your Knights that I was to the Heir's chambers to treat you for the blood on you, and asked if they could move the heavy basin for me, as I couldn't lift it with the water. Of course they spread the word as fast as they could, and the story grew in the telling. By the time your wife was informed, it was imperative that she see you in your chambers."

Not the version he'd received from J'her, Tartan considered, chewing.

"We had an operative among the stable hands," she continued, "and when the news came and your wife was distracted, he did no more than hit the stallion's head with a pebble."

"And the stallion reacted," Tartan informed her.

"Precisely," she informed him. "The best assassins act in plain sight, doing what's expected of them."

"What's happening with the stallion?" he asked her.

"My Lord?" she asked him.

"The stallion that killed my wife," Tartan said. "What is happening with him?"

"I would imagine he's being put down," she said. "He's one of Blizzard's wild ones. No one is going to want him now."

Tartan shook his head, and called for his guard.

His voice must have been too emphatic – the door burst open and three Angadorian Knights rushed in, their weapons drawn. Kirren leapt to her feet – too quick for a simple maid, thought he doubted that anyone else would notice.

"Your will, Tartan," the sergeant among them said, coming to attention once he realized that there was no enemy here to fight.

"The stallion that killed the duchess," Tartan said to him. "Send a squad to the stables, separate it from the herd and put it in a paddock."

The sergeant nodded. It occurred to Tartan that he didn't know this man's name. The Emperor prided himself on being able to recognize every Wolf Soldier on sight. No one knew how he could do it. Tartan Stowe certainly couldn't.

"I want no harm done to that animal," he said. "My wife claimed that she saw something good in him. I'll have the truth of it."

"My – your – Tartan?" the sergeant spluttered.

Any other noble would have vented his rage on the poor beast. Tartan wasn't one of them. His wife had loved horses and he'd learned to appreciate them through her. It wasn't the horse's fault that he'd been sorely used.

Maybe there was something to his wife's judgment after all.

***

While dressing for the stables, Tartan was interrupted by the three Shem Hannen begging entrance to his personal chambers.

The had a scroll where they'd written down his proclamation.

As he dressed, they read it to him, sitting in the hard-backed chairs around the one table in his chambers.

"Is this to your liking?" old Haldarch asked him.

Tartan nodded. "Is there room at the bottom of the scroll, before the signing?" he asked.

The proclamation became law with his signing it. It wasn't uncommon for a ruler to want to make a change to such an edict between its being created and its being signed, and so a wise scribe knew to leave a little room near the end, where another paragraph could be added. This kept the law from being rewritten a dozen times.

"At least a hand's breadth," Guerrin informed him. Datreve pulled a steel quill and an ink bottle out of one of the pockets in his robes. Haldarch pushed the scroll in front of him.

"In order to guarantee the funding," he dictated to them, "let Angadorian war horses not in possession of or preparation for the Imperium be taxed at one gold Tabaar per head."

"Your Grace!" Guerrin gasped. The other two looked up, alarmed. "A tax on your own herds?"

"My herds are all in preparation for the Imperium," Tartan informed them. "I sell to some few landed nobles and retain, of course, my own herds, but they are used exclusively for my Angadorian Knights, all of whom are contracted to the southern border or here."

"Then to what end?" Haldarch asked him. Datreve was satisfied and had already begun writing.

Tartan just smiled, pulling on his boots. To what end, he knew, was that Ceberro was collecting Angadorian war horses in order to keep them from the Empire. When the tax collectors came to his estate this year, the levy for all of those idle beasts would be ruinous. Ceberro would have something else to occupy his mind, other than killing him.

He might also get an idea of the consequences for his actions, but that was up to Ceberro.

Tartan signed the bottom of the scroll with a flourish, then dripped wax and pressed his seal into it. Of course, the Emperor would have to sign under his own signature when he returned to the capitol, but until then this edict would carry the force of law.

Tartan left his chambers grinning. He wouldn't mind being a mouse in the corner of the throne room of Vreck when the Eldadorian tax collectors paid Duke Ceberro a visit.

Chapter Twenty:

Completion

The stallion stood at roughly 17 hands tall, a dapple gray – the only unclaimed male remaining of Blizzard's ilk since the Andarons had left with his brother. His neck arched like his father's, with the wide saucer cheek and the tea cup nose. His legs and barrel spoke more of his dam – thick and powerful, clearly muscled like a draft horse, not tooled like an Andaron steed.

He mule-kicked the steel gate to the paddock that held him, ringing the metal like a bell. The top frame bent a hand's width, even though the stallion was unshod.

The weight of ten men if one, Tartan thought in his mind. Here was power, here was spirit – a true son of the legendary Blizzard, companion to the Emperor. He threw his black mane and pawed the earth with one foreleg.

"Your wife claimed that she saw good in him," an Uman stableman informed him. Dressed in stableman brown vest and pants, his white shirt stood open to his hairless chest, his long white hair tied behind his head in a ponytail, making his pencil-thin eyebrows and wise, brown eyes look more severe. Tartan had known the Uman since the days when he'd worked for Glennen. "I see none. The Emperor and the Empress saw none, either, and they are never wrong, your Grace. Not about horse flesh."

"They're wrong this time."

Although the stables teamed with the workmen who kept it running, Tartan and the stableman had thought themselves alone. They turned and saw three cloaked figures standing behind them. One stood just over waist high, his black cloak draped over his shoulders, the hood over his head shading his face. Tartan didn't need any help recognizing this one.

To his left, a woman by her figure, in a blue travel cloak. Her hood also shaded her face, brown hair spilling out past her collar. She wore stiff riding boots and black leather pants more fit for a man.

On the other side stood a man, as tall as Tartan, short brown hair and hard-set brown eyes peering out at him from under another blue cloak and hood. The sword at his side made an impression on the cloak he wore. He wore brown leather pants much like the Emperor's and a white homespun shirt, open at the neck, where a few black hairs peeped out. This one had just come to man, and by the look in his eyes he'd made a hard journey of it.

Tartan knew Lupennen well, but he barely recognized Hectaro, son of Hectar, the deceased Duke of Galnesh Eldador. Almost four months had passed since he had disappeared into the void created by Lee Mordetur, and Hectaro stood noticeably taller, his brown eyes noticeably harder and more focused. Hectaro left his right hand open, ready to rip his sword out of the sheath if he needed to. Where ever he'd been, he'd cut his path through it to get here from there with that weapon.

"My – your," the old Uman stableman stuttered, lowering his head. "Your Grace! We thought you lost."

"Since when do you address a Duke before a member of the Imperial family?" the woman asked.

Tartan's heart skipped a beat. He hadn't thought this possible – he'd watched the both of them step into the void. That one of them should survive was a miracle – that both should return home spoke more of divine intervention.

The stableman fell to one knee and, around the stables, others followed suit. The woman threw back her hood, long brown hair tumbling out wild around her shoulders. Her skin had been burned olive like her mother's, her eyes held the same steady focus as the young man's.

A Duke, Tartan thought. Not a Duke's son or a Prince. They knew what had happened to Hectar. They had likely not just arrived to Galnesh Eldador. Tartan thought back to the three riders he'd seen on the hill a few days before.

Tartan lowered his own head to Princess Lee Mordetur, first daughter of the Empire.

"My Lady," he said.

She nodded and pushed past him to the paddock where even the stallion looked on curiously. Lupennen and Hectaro followed behind her, throwing back their hoods, Lupennen's cat-curious eyes focused on the huge beast. The stallion lowered his head down almost to the child's level behind the paddock gate, snorting once. His mane hung so long that it actually touched the ground at his feet.

"Brother?" Lee asked Lupennen, turning to face the smaller of the three.

So she knew that, too, Tartan thought to himself. What else had been going on here? He'd thought he'd finally gotten his mind around his current situation, and here it stood all unraveling.

Lupennen didn't look up at his sister, but kept focused on the horse. He stumped up to the paddock gate and reached through the bars to touch the stallion's nose.

The stallion should have relieved him of that hand, but instead first sniffed at it, then actually licked his palm.

"Do you see a future in this horse, Tartan?" Lupennen asked him.

Not *Duke* or *Your Grace*, Tartan realized immediately. Lupennen as a member of the Imperial family felt at ease to refer to Tartan Stowe in the familiar.

So be it.

"Of course, Highness," Tartan said.

"Will you ride him?" Hectaro asked the boy. Lupennen didn't answer for a moment, rubbing the great stallion's muzzle. Finally he took his hand away and turned his head to the Duke.

"He's not for me," the little half-prince said. Lee would have her fifteenth birthday in Life's month – Lupennen would have to be older than she if he was the product of Lupus and Genna, and yet his head didn't rise to her shoulder.

"No," he said, then turned to face Tartan, the cat-eyes focused.

"This isn't my horse, and he's not for my sister," he said. "This horse's name is *Forgotten Son*, and he's waiting for the Duke to ride him, if he can."

"Me?" Tartan couldn't believe what he was hearing.

Lupennen nodded. "He won't be like his father with mine, or

Thunder Cloud with me," the boy informed him. "He'll make you earn a place on his back, but this horse waits for you, Tartan Stowe, if you have the courage to take him."

Tartan had never broken a horse before. He'd worked with those who had, but no member of the nobility would risk his life to break a stallion when there were commons expert in the field ready to be hired. Tartan swallowed, feeling every bit the slender, delicate replica of his mother standing in his hulking father's shadow. Glennen Stowe, he knew, had broken his own horses.

That settled him right there. "Bring me a saddle, then," he ordered the old Uman stableman. "We'll be done with this right here."

It didn't take long to bring the Duke's tack, and with Lupennen right there, it wasn't hard to saddle up the stallion. Tartan had come to the stables in his regular riding apparel out of habit, but he hadn't planned to use them today for anything more than show. He sent a message to the Shem Hannen that court today would be cancelled.

No matter how this turned out, he knew, he wouldn't be sitting on the throne.

"Keep your heels down and your back straight," the old Uman warned him, while younger men brought the stallion from his paddock to the lunging ring where horses were ridden for the first time. "When he starts to bucking, you turn him in a circle. That sounds like you'd put all of your weight to one side and be thrown, but that keeps his power all off of you. If a horse that big bucks you on the straight, I don't care if you're nailed to the saddle, you'll go flying."

"I've seen a horse broken before," Tartan informed him, donning calf skin gloves. These would give him the same grip as bare skin without the reins burning his hands.

"But you ain't *done* it," the Uman informed him. "And this is a hard horse to be your first. Normally I'd give a man a palfrey for his first one, or an older gelding who'd gone green. You're going to get a hell of a ride."

Tartan nodded.

"If he throws you," the Uman continued, as the groomsmen closed the gate to the lunging ring behind the stallion, "push the reins away and kick out your feet. Don't get behind 'im. One kick of that beast and you're sitting for life if you're lucky."

Tartan's heart was already pounding. The Uman was filling his head with doubt from the warning. He knew how to dismount in an emergency – he'd had to leave a wounded horse *and* a spooked one before. He hoped that this would be no different.

He put a boot on the lowest rail of the lunging ring. It stood fifty paces across, the six banks of rails on the inside so that a rider wouldn't hit a post. Each of those stood eight feet high, discouraging a horse from even *thinking* it could jump free. The stable hands and free staff from the palace were already lining up to watch the Duke's efforts. Tartan saw silver changing hands as bets were made.

That gave him a little grin. The stable hands were notorious gamblers. He wondered at his odds.

Tartan stood up on the lunging ring's bottom rail and put a hand on the highest rail of its five. Then he paused, reached into a pocket in his leather pants and fished out a gold Tabaar, clumsy in his gloved hand. He threw it to the old Uman.

"Put that on me," he ordered the man.

The Uman caught it in the air. "My Lord?"

Tartan let himself smile. "Either I'll make this lot pay for stacking the odds against me," he said, "or I won't need it."

Looking on, Lee Mordetur smiled, reminding him again of her mother. Lupennen's cat-curious expression didn't change, and Hectaro seemed focused on the horse. Tartan scrambled up the fence before his courage left him.

In the lunging ring, two Uman held the stallion by the bridle, one on either side. They had a blanket over his head so that Tartan would have a better chance to get on and sit a proper seat. The saddle they used was older, no saddle horn to gouge him, wide stirrups that wouldn't trap his feet. If the horse rolled, as some will, this wouldn't break his back.

Tartan marched straight to the horse and took a fist full of mane. The stallion shuddered as he raised a foot and put a toe in the right stirrup.

"Ready?" he said to the closer of the Uman groomsmen. The man nodded.

In one fluid motion he stepped up into the saddle and threw a leg over the beast's behind, making sure not to make contact and spook the animal. He felt the Uman on the other side take his boot by the heel and seat it in the far stirrup. The stallion already began to gather as the first Uman ripped the blanket from his head and both Uman ran for the wall.

There was a brief pause – a calm before the storm, where the horse realized that there was a rider on his back, and terror gripped the heart of the rider. Suddenly Tartan realized how stupid an idea this was, how unready he felt, how this giant horse, nearly two thousand pounds of muscle, could just snuff out his life as he'd seen the other do to the Andaron rider just a few days before.

Then the moment was over, and Tartan imagined he saw the stallion's eye narrow.

The destrier kicked out with his back legs, Tartan lurching forward, his left hand holding the stallion's reins and the other taking the mane. Again, and again, and again, Tartan pulling to the left, the stallion kicking in a circle, turning on his powerful front legs, head down, snorting, the people watching shouting, Tartan's head whipping forward and back as if he were a rag doll in the hand of an angry god.

Without warning came the crow hop – the horse leaping straight up into the air, all four feet leaving the ground at the same time. Bouncing like a marionette, the stallion threw all of his weight up into Tartan's mid-section in an effort to get him off balance.

Tartan tightened his grip on the mane, his legs closing on the powerful barrel like he'd seen the Andaron do, his head down. "Don't let him go to straight bucking," the Uman had warned him.

He didn't have time for the rest of the thought before stallion landed and, with no warning at all, bucked powerfully forward, launching the Duke over his shoulders to the wall.

If the stallion hadn't worked its way to the far side of the ring, Tartan would have hit the wooden fencing head first. As it was he flew across the middle of the lunging ring and then landed less than a man's height from the lowest rail. His elbows and knees took the brunt of the landing, still when his chest touched the ring's soft sand his breath exploded from him. He rolled over and was back on his feet in one motion before he'd even realized how much pain he was in, the stallion with his head down trying to buck the saddle off of his back. He'd settle down in a moment and then Tartan would remount him.

"You're not doing it right," he heard behind him.

He turned to see Lupennen behind him, the cat eyes focused on him.

"Am I not?" he gasped.

The stallion was already starting to settle. The Uman handlers had come in to the ring with the blanket and were approaching him warily.

Lupennen shook his head. "You're trying to break him," he said. "You can't break him. He isn't going to give in to you."

"I'd thought that was the idea," the Duke argued. This made no sense.

"My father didn't break Blizzard," Lupennen said. "You've heard the story. I know it. I didn't break Thunder. You were there when I rode her."

This was true. "But you said yourself that he wouldn't be like Blizzard or like Thunder Cloud."

Lupennen's expression didn't change. "I did," he said. "Forgotten Son waits for you to prove yourself, even though he knows he's meant for you. You have to do that."

This made no sense to Tartan Stowe at all. He turned his back on the boy and walked back to the stallion, where Uman held him by the bridle and were trying to fight the blanket over his head.

"You can't break him!" Lupennen called out from behind him.

Tartan hadn't taken two steps before he realized that he hadn't come off of the horse clean and had pulled a muscle in his groin. He wasn't going to be able to hold on to the stallion with the full strength of his legs. With any other horse, a strong hold on the mane and the proper posture in the saddle might get him through a rough ride, but Tartan hadn't lasted ten seconds the first time with Forgotten Son, and that wasn't enough to wear the stallion down.

He'd learned that the fight didn't always go to the best warrior – it often went to the one who wanted it more. Tartan had to ask himself if that could help him here.

"My Lord?" one of the stablemen said to him, noting his walk. He just shook his head and winced as he took a fist full of mane and seated his left foot in the stirrup.

He had to bounce once but he got himself back up into the saddle, his heel still not touching the stallion's butt. Again, the groomsman on the other side took his right heel and shoved it into the right stirrup.

That *really* hurt, he couldn't help thinking.

The ripped the blanket away from the stallion's head and ran for the wall. This time there was no pause, the stallion commenced straight into bucking, furious at the Man who dared to ride him. Tartan pitched forward and back, his heels down, his head down, trying to keep the horse turning to the left and his own body from whipping too far forward. When he didn't come right off this time, the stallion changed directions, pulling against the bit, kicking to the right, pitching the rider off of his center of balance.

Once again, he put all of his weight underneath the unlucky Duke and, as the old Uman had warned, bucked straight up into Tartan's center. He felt his heels actually drag the stallion's withers as he flew from the saddle and across the lunging ring.

This time he could have reached out and touched the lunging ring's wall if he'd wanted to. He rolled over onto his feet and turned to see the stallion facing him, pawing the ground like a bull.

Forgotten Son didn't charge him. He snorted and his nostrils flared. Tartan instinctively looked past the stallion's eyes so as not to challenge him, as if that mattered now.

'You can't break him,' the young half-Prince had said.

He looked for the boy now couldn't find him. Maybe Genna's son simply couldn't bear to watch?

Lupennen was right – he couldn't break him.

The Emperor had told him once, "Common sense is rarely common. Most people just don't have it. They look at the world and take what appears to be the most logical reaction to their surroundings, usually forgetting that they don't have enough information for their logic."

The lesson was not to over think the situation, he knew. The lesson was to understand that you rarely had all of that information when you needed it.

Tartan climbed to his feet, then limped to the stallion's side, putting a hand on the shoulder of one of the stablemen who held him. The expression on that Uman's face was telling. These were professionals; they knew what had happened to the Duke. He wasn't going to stay on through another bucking ride.

The answer was not to.

He took the horse by the bridle and pulled the blanket away from his eyes. The giant head shook, the giant right hoof pawed the ground.

"Leave me," he ordered the Uman.

"My – my L' – your Grace?" the Uman stammered.

"Both of you, out," he ordered them.

A murmur rose from the on-lookers. The two Uman exchanged a glance, the closer one shrugged and both released the stallion. Forgotten Son focused his attention on the Duke, a fraction of his size, whom he'd already beaten.

Sometimes the key to winning was to not fight. No one needed to tell Tartan that, he just knew it.

He rubbed the flat space between the stallion's eyes, and let it smell him. He put his forehead against the animal's, as he'd seen the Emperor do with Blizzard a dozen times. He'd been told repeatedly that any other stallion would take the opportunity to bash in a man's skull for doing that, but Blizzard never had.

Forgotten Son didn't, either.

"Don't hurt me," he told the horse. "I'm no threat to you. We need to do this together."

He calmly pushed away from the horse, limped to its side and took a fist full of mane.

The horse turned its body away from him as he tried to raise a foot to the stirrup. His groin protested in agony but he made the motion anyway. He pulled the reins to turn the stallion's head to the right side, then put the foot back in the stirrup. This time the horse couldn't turn and he got his toe in place.

This was either going to work, or it was going to be the last thing he ever did. In any other situation he would have tried either to mount from the fence or use a mounting block to get on the huge beast, but as Lupennen said, he had to prove himself.

He actually cried out in pain as he stood up in the stirrup and threw a leg over the horse. This time he couldn't raise the leg high enough and dragged a heel over the stallion's rump.

He'd done it all wrong. Even a broke horse would shy from a weak mount like this. He felt the stallion gather.

He seated his boot on the far side, he took the reins in both hands.

Nothing.

He sat there. He'd never been on the back of a horse this huge before. He could easily see over the top rail of the fence around the lunging ring. Onlookers stared up at him as if he'd just appeared there, not understanding what they were seeing. The horse that had tried to kill him moments ago just sat passively beneath him.

His groin really, really hurt. So did his back. Red spots dotted the shoulders and the elbows of the white homespun shirt he wore, and its collar had ripped. He had so much sand up his nose he'd have to pick it with a shovel.

"Open the gate," he told the Uman.

"Is that wise, my Lord?" the Uman asked him. "Perhaps a few times 'round the ring, get a feel for his movement?"

In other words, when he gets a smell of freedom and throws you up onto the roof of the nearest stall, we don't want to spend the rest of the day chasing him.

"Do as you're told," he said, and looked away from the Uman. He searched the crowd for Lupennen, Hectaro and Lee, but couldn't see any them.

"My Lord," the Uman protested.

This was getting him nowhere. He must look a wreck, he thought. They were afraid that he was going to hurt himself or let the stallion do it for him.

Like a Mordetur, he met the Uman's eyes.

"*On your life*," he said through grit teeth.

The Uman stiffened, walked to the gate, pulled the latch line and pushed it open, onlookers scrambling out of the way. The stallion saw the opening and pawed the sand.

Tartan reached his hand down to the great, bowed neck and rubbed it with a gloved hand. "Stop that," he cajoled the animal. "You wanted this – you hated being cooped up. Show me what it means to ride you."

Horses don't understand languages, his wife had told him. Horses understand emotions. You don't speak to them with your words, your words speak to them of your feelings.

He must have spoken loud and clear to Forgotten Son, who in one motion leapt for the open gate.

Tartan lurched back in the saddle and had to fight to right himself. The stallion pounded straight for the gate at a full-on gallop. Beyond it, he saw Bastard, the Duke's horse which had gone missing months ago, and Thunder Cloud, each with its rider waiting.

Forgotten Son called out for his brother and sister. Bastard answered. Thunder Cloud began to trot.

Someone had thought to close the steel gate between them. Forgotten Son didn't seem to care. Tartan Stowe had jumped once or twice, but jumping is an art form, and he'd never mastered it. An old breaking saddle was not the proper equipment to try this in, even had he known how.

"You have to prove yourself to him," he'd been told.

He leaned forward and took a short grip on the reins, one in each hand.

Hearing a scream behind him, Forgotten Son leapt for the top of the steel gate, reaching for the freedom outside of the palace walls. Bastard turned away from him and began to run, Thunder Cloud with him. Tartan's head felt the weightlessness of leaping on the back of a powerful horse, the combining of their energies as the animal took over, and his power launched them over the gate.

He heard as well as felt the hooves nick the upper steel rail. That alone could make a horse falter on the landing. Less than a second later the back hooves did the same. Now he was in real trouble. He fought to hold his body dead center over the horse's great neck. He tucked his elbows in as he'd seen other jumper so. In a space of time that seemed to crawl over long minutes but in fact could not have taken seconds, he waited for the horse to touch ground. If he'd lost his balance, he'd fall, and Tartan would have to push off or risk being crushed by the great stallion's weight.

The stallion hit the ground hard. He felt the beast stumble. Its legs were too far out behind it, the safe thing was to push off and crash to the ground, and pray that the horse didn't land after him.

"You have to prove yourself…"

No, he'd ride this out. Both survived, or both faltered.

The great stallion righted itself. Tartan felt a toe touch the earth. Bastard and Thunder Cloud were already a tenth of a daheer away from him and cantering – Forgotten Son did not want to be left behind.

He just knew that. Forgotten Son wanted finally to run free. This was the horse's gift to him – this is what he'd earned. This must be what the Emperor felt when he rode Blizzard.

He hadn't tamed the horse, he'd earned a place on the back of one of the Herd that Cannot be Tamed.

Hooves the size of a man's head drummed the hard-packed dirt outside of the Imperial stables. Dust and dirt clods flew in all directions. Tartan had to look down and watch for the horse's forward shoulder to find his lead, then leaned into it as he picked up the stallion's motion. He moved with Forgotten Son's as one animal and felt the power of a tremendous stallion.

As Forgotten Son closed on Thunder Cloud and Bastard, a lot of things that Tartan hadn't understood started making a lot of sense to him.

Chapter Twenty-One:

Whose Empire?

Once again, Tartan Stowe stood naked in a copper basin with his arms spread out, while his new personal maid, Kirren the Bounty Hunter, washed his body.

This time she had her work cut out for her. The Duke was bruised in more places than he'd realized. Blood had collected and matted in the hair around his knees and elbows, dirt had mingled with the sweat from his own body and his horse's even down into his boots. Torn skin at his shoulder blades had leaked blood down his back, and threads from his ruined shirt had to be picked out from the wound left behind. Kirren had worked his hair with wintergreen oil and rubbed his body first with a wash cloth, then with a rough brush to get down to the raw, pink skin.

Afterward she offered to 'service' him again, and this time he accepted. The woman showed a mastery of something that he hadn't even known was an art. When she finished she rubbed him down with a towel and he dressed himself while she left to fetch him a private meal.

The bed looked inviting, but he didn't dare lay down. He'd

sleep the day away and he had things that needed accomplishing. Instead he put on loose fitting pants with a draw string and a robe similar to the ones Wizards wore, then spent a little time looking out the window to the Heir's chambers to the people below.

Finally a knock sounded at the door. He bid the person enter, not turning – he planned to send Kirren back out once she dropped off the meal.

"You're Grace," a woman said, but it wasn't Kirren.

He turned to see Lee and Lupennen Mordetur, the latter closing the door behind them. He'd expected that Lee would be in close conference with J'her all day, taking back control of the capitol and the Empire.

Lupennen – he didn't know what to expect from that one.

"Highness," Tartan said, turning to face them, and indicating the divan by the window for them to sit on if they chose. "Highnesses," he corrected himself.

Lupennen stumped across the room and crawled up on to the divan, Lee sitting on its arm next to him. Tartan took one of the straight back chairs from the table on the other side of the room and placed it on the opposite side of the caw-fee table where he could face them. Tartan winced as he seated himself.

He anticipated that they would thank him for his service and dismiss him. He'd already been thinking about what needed to be done in Angador, now that he could finally return to it.

"Your mastery of the stallion was impressive," Lee informed him. "Worthy of my father himself."

"I have your half-brother to thank," Tartan said, lowering his head and acknowledging the praise.

"You listened," Lupennen informed him, the cat-like stare boring into Tartan. "Most people don't."

There wasn't a lot that Tartan could say to that and didn't try. Another knock at the door saw Kirren enter without invitation, a silver tray loaded with food on her shoulder and a bucket of ice with a wine bottle sticking out of it in her hand by her side.

An Angadorian Knight closed the door behind her.

"May I serve?" she asked, not at all surprised to find three in the room. Lee indicated the caw-fee table with an open hand.

Kirren sat the tray down and prepared six sammiches, each with the dressing that Tartan had come to love. She mixed beef with ham and lamb, lettuce and tomato on each of them, then topped them with a speckled cheese that Tartan hadn't seen before. He'd become used to Eldadorian goods and these were more and more rare these days.

She divided each of the sammiches in half and then poured three glasses of wine. She stood back from the table then, by the door, took her left hand in her right before her and waited patiently for them to finish.

"That will be all," Lee informed her. "Your services are no longer needed here."

"Yes, your Highness," Kirren responded, and then turned to leave.

"That is *all* of your services, Bounty Hunter," Lee pressed her, sitting with her back straight on the arm of the divan. "I don't expect to see you or any like you in the capitol again."

"Highness?" Kirren turned on her heel, her Uman eyes searching the Princess'.

Lee raised a hand glowing white with power. Tartan and Kirren flinched back from her instinctively. Lupennen kept up his usual stare, watching first Lee and then the Bounty Hunter.

As quickly as the light appeared, it died. Kirren took a step back and shook her head.

"There," Lee said. "Quick as done. There's a hex on you, Bounty Hunter – a powerful one. You'll die in three days if you're within thirty daheeri of me."

"What?" Kirren gasped. Even Tartan was surprised. The girl he knew when Lee had left the capitol had been just dabbling at the edges of her power. The one before her seemed as confident as the Empress.

"You heard me – there are no Bounty Hunters allowed in Galnesh Eldador," Lee informed her. "Now you'll be far away from here, or you'll be dead."

"The Emperor cannot strike out at the Guild," Kirren informed her.

"I am not the Emperor," Lee responded. "I would get moving if I were you – you don't have a lot of time."

Kirren opened her mouth up to argue, but then just shut it and turned on her heel. Lee seemed to dismiss her without another thought. This Princess had changed drastically since Tartan had last seen her, and he couldn't help wondering what she'd been through.

He'd planned on multiple uses for this Bounty Hunter contact – he didn't know where that stood now, however he couldn't help thinking that he'd just been handed an enemy.

Lee reached for a sammich, Lupennen after her. Tartan took one and a glass of wine.

"This food is safe," Lee said, then took a bite. Tartan hadn't considered otherwise but now thought that maybe he should have.

After she'd chewed a mouth full and taken a sip of wine, she turned to Tartan and she asked, "Were you aware that that maid was a Bounty Hunter?"

"I was, Highness," he answered her truthfully. A witch of her mother's caliber would know.

"You may be thinking that I have come back to retake the throne," she informed him, then took another bite and chewed, thinking of her words. Tartan did the same. He took another sip of wine, the flavor exploding in his mouth.

"In fact," she said, "I came to find two things that Nina of the Aschire sent here."

"A sword and shield?" Tartan asked her. This time *she* looked surprised.

Tartan pointed to them on a rack next to the room's one table.

Lee took another bite and put the sammich down. She stood and crossed the room, her hard-soled boots clattering against the stone floor. She stopped in front of the sword and shield, seemed to regard the lunging dog figure on the shield face, touched it and stood quiet. Watching her from behind, Tartan couldn't tell what she was doing. He took a bite of his sammich, noting that Lupennen had already eaten his and was reaching for a second.

He'd been no different when he was that age – either eating or hungry.

Lee finally pulled the sword and held it in front of her. She turned to face them, her eyes on the sword, holding it as one would if he or she were testing its balance.

"Have you been trained?" Tartan asked her.

"To use this?" she asked. She smiled. "I don't think *anyone* has been trained to use this."

"I wielded it against some Bounty Hunters," Tartan informed her.

She looked at him. "Not your friend?" she asked.

He shook his head. "No," he said. "My wife set upon me with several Bounty Hunters, her intent being to take my life."

Lee didn't seem much impressed by that news, either. "Where

is your wife now?" she asked, eyes still on the blade.

"Being readied for burial, if not buried," Tartan said.

She nodded again. "Wise move."

She replaced the sword and returned to her space on the divan, sitting on the arm next to Lupennen. She picked up her wine and her sammich, took a bite of one and a drink of the other. His father had never allowed him wine at so young an age, however he had no place to question a Princess of the Empire.

"As I was saying," she said, "I have not returned to take the throne. While my father is away from here, a strong mind is needed to run things, and I think that yours suits better than mine."

"Your will, of course, my Lady," Tartan said, lowering his head in deference to her. Lupennen kept chewing – he hadn't touched the wine. Tartan wondered that perhaps he should call for milk for all of them.

"However," he continued, "I think that the Eldadorian people, and certainly the Wolf Soldiers, will not follow a Stowe when a Mordetur is present to lead them."

"Two Mordeturs," she said.

"And yet, you want me," Tartan said.

She looked into his eyes, setting the sammich back down again.

"My brothers and I lack experience," she said. "We would have relied on Hectaro's council, however he's died. You've done exceptionally well here in my father's absence."

"Then your father's suit for peace..." Tartan said, looking from one Mordetur to the other.

Lee just smiled. "I think you knew better."

Tartan nodded. Sue for peace, attack Andoron while the rest of Fovea argues for a punishment that the Empire would never suffer. He'd come back for Conflu in the next season – finding the Fovean nations unready for him.

The war would go on, and someone would have to run things.

"I still don't believe that the people will accept it, my Lady," he said. "Perhaps Rennin from Steel City would be better – he was my father's most trusted Duke and has always been loyal to the Empire. If a Stowe sits the throne with a Mordetur available, people will think, 'Revolution,' and the scheming in the Earldoms and the Duchies will circumvent the war effort."

"This has been thought of," Lee said. "In fact, your actions of late have made it even easier for us to arrange this."

Tartan shook his head. Lee out-ranked him, as the Emperor would put it. He'd do what the family Mordetur needed of him, but he knew in his heart that Dukes like Ceberro would take this as an opportunity to raise intrigue and to pursue their own goals.

"Perhaps if I remained on as an advisor," he said, "while you sat in the actual throne."

"I have other things I need to do," she informed him. "My brother and I – Vulpe waits for us, and others as well. I will remain in the capitol as long as I can, however we cannot transition power back and forth, and one must lead the Empire in my father's name."

This was even worse, Tartan thought. He'd retain power with Lee here, and then it would look like he'd driven her away. Duchies and Earldoms looking for an excuse not to pay their taxes would take this as one – some of the larger ones could march.

She stood again and stepped around the table to the space right in front of him. He moved to stand, wincing at the effort, but she placed a soft hand on the side of his face and pushed him back down.

"Worry not, good Tartan," she said. "I see the concern in you – the fact that you would not leap on this as an opportunity to pursue your own interests speaks precisely of why it must be you who governs in my father's stead."

Tartan looked into her brown eyes. "My Lady," he said, finally, "I appreciate your praise – I bask in it. But there is no overlooking that I am, in fact, a Stowe. Your father succeeded mine, and in honesty, there are those who tremble at these times and who would see the Emperor out and the King returned. How can we transition power to me, and not make it look like revolution?"

She withdrew her hand and took his instead. She looked down, then back into his eyes and said, "It will be simple for the people to have you on the throne, simple for the Wolf Soldier guard to have you in command of Galnesh Eldador and caretaker of the Empire.

"Simple, that is," she said, as she leaned forward and kissed him on the forehead, "after I have you for my husband."

www.ingramcontent.com/pod-product-compliance
Lightning Source LLC
Chambersburg PA
CBHW071126130626

46556CB00011B/2580